Thrilling
Stories
of mystery and
adventure

Thrilling Stories

of mystery and adventure

Illustrated by Kay Wilson

Cover illustration by Ivan Lapper

Hamlyn

London · New York · Sydney · Toronto

Published 1982 by
The Hamlyn Publishing Group Limited
London · New York · Sydney · Toronto
Astronaut House, Feltham, Middlesex, England.

ISBN 0 600 36679 0

Printed in Yugoslavia

Contents

The Ultimate Assassin

Alan A Grant

THE SOLAR GLIDER COASTED IN LOW, silent and graceful as a hawk. Its red wings flashed in the late evening sun as it swooped between the two Sutors, the craggy promontories that guarded the entrance to the Cromarty Firth.

Beneath the glider, its pilot dangled from his carri-harness. His left hand brushed a control and the sun-powered machine arced in over the choppy water, to land perfectly on the 'styrene glidestrip that had replaced Old Cromarty pier.

To the few locals who watched as the pilot shrugged himself from his harness, he was just another glide-freak returning with the last of the sun's rays. One of any number of bronzed, fit young men who congregated each year at Scotland's premier glide resort. But if they'd looked closer they might have noticed there was something . . . different about this one. Perhaps it was in his eyes.

There was no joy there, no faraway dreamy look that characterised the other glide-freaks. Instead there was only emptiness – a sinister, icy emptiness.

Nikol had landed. He had come to kill.

+ + COMPUTEL
FROM: EUROPOL TO: KK4–GB
PERSONAL ATTENTION: RONALD X LEWIS, CAPT SOC
EASTPAKT AGENT 'NIKOL' BELIEVED IN GB SECTOR AS OF YESTERDAY. MISSION

ASSASSINATION. TARGET SPIROS
POPODOPOLOS, PRESIDENT, UNITED EUROPE.
GLAD THIS IS NOT MY BABY.
PIERRE + +

Captain Ronald Xavier Lewis of Special Operations Control stared at the computer printout. As leader of the action wing of British Counter-Intelligence, Nikol was indeed his baby. And one he could well do without.

'What do we know about this Nikol, Archie?' he asked.

Inspector Archie Marconi flipped a switch on the computer console and Nikol's record came up on the VDU. It was a long and bloody one, containing details of seventeen known political killings and suspected complicity in more than a dozen others.

'We know enough to tell us he's the Eastpakt countries' top operative. There's not a man in the world can touch him at his job – *killing*.'

Lewis sat back in his airchair and ran his fingers through his short sandy hair. His normally calm features were crumpled in a frown. 'We're going to need every man we've got on this one, Archie – and even then I'm not sure we can stop Nikol.'

Lewis leaned past Marconi's spare frame and punched a request into the computer. 'There's no point in us wasting time looking for him now. We don't know where he is. We don't even know what he looks like. Eastpakt gives him a new face for every mission.'

'So what do we do?' Archie asked. 'Cancel President Popodopolos' visit?'

'Fat chance,' Lewis laughed. 'There'll be five hundred thousand people in the Thames Superdome tomorrow to watch the Jetball Cup Final – and every one of them expects President Pop to be there handing out the medals! Are *you* going to explain to them why he's not there?'

Archie threw out his bony hands in mock horror. 'No fear! I'd rather face Nikol alone, armed with nothing but a thick stick!'

Details of the President's itinerary flashed up on the VDU. It was a whistle-stop visit. He would be in the country less than four hours, beaming in by matter transmitter from New Athens at 2.45 and departing as soon as the Jetball game was over.

'The transmitter station is absolutely secure,' Lewis said. 'The flight to the Superdome is by a secret route, under heavy guard all the way.' He stabbed the air with a forefinger. 'No, Archie, there's only one place Nikol can strike – the Superdome itself!'

'At least we'll get to see the game, Ron.'

'Don't count on it. Get a good night's sleep, Archie – I've a feeling we'll need it.'

Morning. Nikol scanned the bare room. He hadn't slept, but that would not affect his performance today.

There was a tap at the door. 'Breakfast, Mr MacPherson?' the landlady's voice called out.

'No' for me, lassie.' Nikol affected the gruff Scots accent he'd used when booking the room the night before. He'd travelled to London on the evening zoom from Inverness, just another jetball fan on his way to the big match.

The landlady shuffled off down the corridor. Nikol checked the time. 8.30. Three and a half hours to wait . . .

Outside the huge Thames Superdome, jetball fans were already beginning to queue. A thrill of barely suppressed excitement rippled through the air. Today's intercontinental cup final between Europe and South America promised to be a classic. The aerial agility and fiery tempers of the Latin Americans contrasted sharply with the Europeans' dour but aggressive attacking play. If both teams played up to even half their capabilities, it would be the game of the decade.

Inside the vast dome of the stadium, Ron Lewis issued his instructions to his men. The Superdome had already been thoroughly searched. Lewis was satisfied – Nikol was not there.

'I'll be with the president all the time. Archie here will be in charge of stadium security. We want two men with metal detectors on every gate. Nobody gets in – repeat, nobody! – until they've been checked with these detectors.

'Plainclothes men will mingle with the crowd in case Nikol gets through. Stay on the alert. Anyone makes a suspicious move, act first and ask your questions later. Anything to add to that, Archie?'

As the SOC agents gathered round Marconi, Lewis moved away. His slate-grey eyes squinted up at the vast sweep of the weather-proof dome enclosing the stadium. He prayed that dome would echo with cheers rather than screams today. But if Lewis had been a betting man, he wouldn't have put money on it.

Nikol left the boarding house at midday. He'd never been in London before, but he could have drawn a map of the city from memory. The garage, he knew, was only a short walk away.

At the garage Nikol ignored the reception kiosk and walked into the large hangar where all the coaches were lined up. He spotted the one he wanted with no trouble. It was garishly decorated in Euro-colours and the sides embla-zoned: EUROPE FOR THE CUP. It was on the near end of the first line. That suited his purpose.

'Can I help you, sir?' The pert little receptionist was standing behind him. He'd heard her approach.

Nikol's tone as he replied was smooth, cultured, with no trace of the rough Scots burr. 'Yes. I'd like to hire a coach. Is the manager available?'

'If you'll just wait here I'll get him for you, sir.'

Nikol watched as she walked across the garage floor and through a door marked 'Private'. Then he moved. His hand was a blur as he slipped a tiny heat-pellet from his belt and sent it flying into a waste cannister in the far corner.

The cannister ignited with a flash, and within seconds thick oily smoke was belching from it.

'Fire! Fire!' a mechanic shouted. Then men were running for extinguishers, beating at the fierce flames before they spread.

Nikol seized his chance, and padded quickly to the side of the coach. In one fluid motion he grasped the vehicle's underside and swung himself down into the inspection pit below.

'What can I do for you, matey?' An old mechanic looked round from a large black drum. His hand was smothered with grease. 'Come to 'elp me grease these 'ere axles, 'ave you?'

Nikol barely paused. His hand shot out and grasped the man's neck, his fingers searching for a pressure point. They found it, squeezed almost imperceptibly, and the mechanic's life snuffed out like a candle flame.

Nikol lifted the body as if it was weightless and crammed it into the drum, forcing it down into the grease. The lid lay nearby. Nikol replaced it on the drum. Effortlessly, his fingers forced rim and lid together, twisting them like toffee. It would take a blow-torch to unseal it.

'There's soot everywhere!' The voice came from the garage floor. 'Get that team coach out of here!'

Nikol saw feet run by, then the coach door wheezed open. He reached up, grabbed the axle and swung himself into the chassis, wedging his feet into a narrow gap.

His hands gripped a cross-spar above the axle. His fingers gouged dents in the metal as they locked on.

Twenty seconds later the luxury coach slid smoothly from the hangar. 'It's almost time anyway, Joe. Go straight to the hotel!' the manager's voice barked, and Nikol could picture the driver's wave as the coach picked up speed across the forecourt and eased itself into the city traffic.

'Now, Miss Barker,' the manager said as the vehicle disappeared from view, 'where's this chap you said came to hire a coach?'

Police had cordoned off the street outside the London Heights Hotel. At one o'clock the coach inched through the thousands of fans milling beyond the cordon, hoping to catch a glimpse of their jetball heroes. Along the way it had picked up an escort of ten police Delta motorcycles.

As the cavalcade came to a halt, the hotel's main doors were thrust open. The seventeen members of the European jetball team were ushered out, surrounded by an eager horde of pressmen and videographers.

Once more the coach doors wheezed open and the team entered, led by their captain, the gigantic French thruster, Alphonse Moute. Behind him, the tiny Swiss wing-thruster, Hans Konstanz, gave a cocky wave. It would be his job to take on the Peruvian hardman Jose Mecal. He was looking forward to flying rings round him. Last to board were the three British members of the squad – Wilkinson, Raj and O'Brien.

Manager Jurgen Jorgensen checked off the last name on his list. 'Okay, driver – take her away.'

The Delta sirens blared into sudden life, and up ahead police parted the crowd.

Motionless beneath the coach, well-hidden by its mud-skirts, Nikol still clung. He had been hanging there almost an hour, yet he felt no strain. He could hang there for days, if necessary. Of course, it would not be.

Every now and again he caught a glimpse of spinning wheels beside the coach. He ran their tread pattern quickly through his memory; they were Dupont X-way 33ABs, standard issue on police Delta machines.

Anyone with a sense of humour would have appreciated the irony of the situation. President Popodopolos was going to die – and the police were escorting his assassin to the kill-point!

Nikol did not laugh. He had no sense of humour.

By 1.45 the Thames Superdome was beginning to fill up. A continuous line of fans streamed through every entrance. Most were bedecked in the red, green and blue colours of the Euro-team, but here and there parties of orange-clad South Americans made up in noise what they lacked in numbers.

Archie Marconi stood high on the West Gate terrace, his eyes never still. Below him he could see his undercover men dotted among the jostling throng on the refreshment plaza. To his right, the West Entrances. The metal detector operators were having a field day – with cans, watches, metal-fibre underwear and heaven knew what else. So far, over two hundred offensive weapons had been confiscated and ninety-four arrests made. But there was no sign of Nikol.

The shrill whine of police sirens cut above the hubbub, then the main gates swung open and the Euro-team coach swept through. Marconi's men moved quickly to intercept anyone trying to slip inside in the coach's wake.

Marconi cursed under his breath. Rot Nikol! There was nothing he enjoyed more than a good game of jetball – but if the Eastpakt assassin didn't show soon, he doubted he would see a ball played. The game of the decade, too! He glanced at his watch. The game would start in little over an hour. Still plenty of time for Nikol to arrive . . .

The coach disgorged the team and their equipment at the

Players' Entrance.

'Take her up to the VIP Bays and park her, Joe,' Jorgensen's nasal Danish voice called.

Minutes later, the coach drew to a halt. Nikol waited till Joe's footsteps disappeared. Cat-like, he dropped to the ground. He paused, listened, then moved off down the narrow stairs.

He replayed the map of the Superdome in his memory. The Mid-Dome Maintenance Ducts were a short walk away along the West Terrace wall. It took him five minutes, stopping only once to avoid a tall fan waving a Euro-flag. His senses immediately identified the man as an SOC agent.

At the entrance to the maintenance access duct, Alf Redmond was repairing a worn cable which had shorted out an entire bank of dome lights. He snapped the final cable circuits back in place and smiled with satisfaction as the green GO light came on.

He was about to replace the cable cover when he heard the slight shuffle behind him. Alf turned – and the last thing he felt was a sharp, excruciating crack as Nikol's fingers tightened on his skull.

Nikol lifted the body in one hand. He began to climb the long, narrow spiral staircase that wound up inside the duct. From the jetball field below, the ducts looked like a network of narrow veins against the dome's clear plasteen surface. In fact, they were large enough to accommodate a man – and it was for the maintenance box at their hub, 200 metres above the playing surface, that the Eastpakt agent was heading.

At the GPO Matter Transmitter Arrival Station, Ron Lewis drummed his fingers impatiently. The President was fifteen seconds late. Didn't he realise that even such a short delay could knock a security schedule all to hell!

Popodopolos had been President since the European nations had banded together under one government eight years before, in 2041. Eight years, and not a scratch on him.

If an Eastpakt agent gets to him in my territory, SOC's failure would be a national disgrace. Lewis thought. His lips tightened. I intend to see it doesn't happen!

The red warning light flashed in the Trans-cube. Inside its plexiglass walls the President and his party began to rematerialise out of their dissembled molecules. The trip from New Athens had lasted only a fraction of a second.

As the President strolled out of the cube, Lewis introduced himself.

'Pleased to meet you, Captain Lewis.' The elderly President's swarthy face beamed at him. 'I'm sure you'll handle our security admirably.'

Lewis made general small talk until they were inside the two-deck hoverlimo that would whisk them to the Dome. Then he requested a private discussion with the President on the upper deck.

Lewis closed the top-deck door as the vehicle rose into the air from the GPO pad, a swarm of police hover-Deltas buzzing around it.

Lewis's face was grave. 'We have good reason to believe an attempt will be made on your life today.'

'Pah!' The President gave a dismissive wave. 'I know all about assassination attempts – nine have been made on me since I took office. But I am still here, Captain Lewis.' His dark features creased in a patronising smile. 'I'm sure I can rely on you to save me from the tenth.'

'This one may not be so easy, sir. It's Nikol.'

'Oh. Ah. I see. That's different then.'

'So you've heard about Nikol?' Lewis was not surprised.

'Yes – as Euro-President they do let me in on a few secrets! Let's see now – Nikol is an advanced model Mark-7

Kalashnikov Android. He looks like a human being, but has all the powers of a robot –'

'The world's most sophisticated killing machine – the ultimate assassin,' Lewis finished for him. 'We have similar robots ourselves – but none in Nikol's class.'

'So what do you propose to do, Captain Lewis?' Popodopolos' smile never wavered, but there was a nervous note in his voice.

'I'm afraid I'm going to have to insist on some rather *unusual* security precautions, Mr President . . .'

The Hoverlimo's flight to the Thames Superdrome was swift and uneventful. Only once did the Delta escort have to warn off a too-curious flyer.

A special covered landing pad had been erected at the Superdome. Popodopolos was hustled from it, invisible behind a phalanx of armed security troops, and hurried up the ramp leading to the central grandstand. There, he was quickly ushered into the VIP Viewbox.

As the crowd saw him, a mighty cheer rang out – more because it heralded the start of the game than any great joy at seeing their President.

Popodopolos waved through the three-inch-thick bullet-proof glass. 'So far so good, eh, Captain?'

Lewis nodded, then spoke into his radio: 'How does it look, Archie?'

'Nothing, Ron,' Marconi's voice crackled back. 'If he passed our boys, he must be a flaming magician!'

Lewis's eyes hooded as he stared out at the crowd. The team anthems had been played, and the teams were hovering in their mid-air positions, jittery, ready to begin.

Mr Wong, the Chinese referee, pressed his sonic bleeper, and big Alphonse Moute struck the hard leather ball a fierce blow with his prod. The game was under way!

Lewis had done everything he could, taken every pre-caution – and yet a grim suspicion nagged at his mind. Nikol was here . . . somewhere.

In the dome hub maintenance box, Nikol had unzipped his light jerkin, exposing his chest. Prising his fingers beneath the skin on one side, he pulled – and a section of his chest slid back. From the compartment inside he drew out four sections of dull grey metal.

He screwed them together quickly, his scanners automatically checking each part for correct alignment. Two seconds later the rifle was ready.

He crossed the floor, not even glancing at Alf Redmond's inert body. He extended one finger, drove it forward, piercing the steel plate of the box wall. He moved his fingers to the side, slicing through the steel like a knife through butter.

When he'd finished he had made a perfect hole, half a metre square, in the wall of the box which faced the central grandstand.

Nikol poked his rifle through the hole and squinted down the short barrel. There were no sights along it. Nikol's scanners would automatically make the adjustments required.

He corrected his aim by a few millimetres. One clean shot in the forehead, that's all it would need.

On the field, the action was fast and furious. Already, the Peruvian hardman had nearly crippled tiny Hans Konstanz. A fist fight was now developing between the opposing defensive lines.

But Lewis paid scant attention to the game. His mind was racing. By now he was sure that – if Nikol was indeed here – the attack would come *after* the game, when the President left

Nikol extended one finger and drove it forward, piercing the steel plate of the box wall.

the protection of his box to present the winners' medals. That would be the maximum danger point.

The President reached over and tapped Lewis on the shoulder. 'I say, Captain – young Onassis is having rather a good game, isn't he? Don't you ag---AAAAAGH!'

It happened so fast no-one could have prevented it. One moment the President was smiling at Lewis, the next a blinding bolt of white-hot energy had burned through the bulletproof glass and exploded against the old man's head!

The President's body hit the floor.

'My God! He's dead!' an aide yelled.

Lewis's keen eyes frantically raked the roof of the dome. There! 'Archie! The maintenance box!' he screamed into his radio.

In the maintenance box, Nikol snapped the laser rifle back into his chest compartment. He must leave no evidence to link Eastpakt to this killing.

Nikol's ultra-sensitive audio receptors picked up the sound of many feet pounding up the duct stairwells. He had known from the beginning there would be no escape. The President was a target worth taking risks for. Eastpakt could build another Nikol. There would never be another Popodopolos.

Nikol's fist came back and punched at the box wall. Once – twice – and on the third blow metal rivets gave and a whole panel went spinning down towards the playing surface far below.

There was a hammering on the door. A voice Nikol identified as Inspector Archibald Marconi's boomed: 'He's in there! Blast that ruddy door open!'

Several shots ripped into the lock and the door flew open. Nikol leapt.

In the bowl below, Hans Konstanz twisted around Jose Mecal at ten metres and drew back his prod to thrust the ball into the path of the oncoming Moute. But Moute was staring upwards.

'Mon dieu! Look!'

Halfway down, Nikol detonated the charges concealed at five strategic points on his robotic body. They burst into fierce phosphorescent flame.

He hit the ground a blazing wreck. The force of impact scattered hot metal and globules of burning plasti-skin as far as the lower tier of the grandstand. Nikol's mission was complete.

High above, Archie Marconi gazed open-mouthed from the rent in the maintenance box wall. It was a full five seconds before he could gather his wits and speak into his radio:

'Guess we won't find any evidence in that mess, chief. The President – is he . . .?'

'Dead?' In the VIP viewbox Ron Lewis looked down at the form crumpled at his feet. 'Nikol thought so, thank god.'

Already realisation had dawned on the medicos who'd swarmed to the fallen president's side. Where the laser beam had burned a hole in the president's head, bare wires and twisted circuits were visible.

'Hey! This isn't President Popodopolos! It's a *robot*!'

Lewis turned to one of Popodopolos' dumbfounded aides. 'Your President is still in the hoverlimo, concealed on the upper deck. Go tell him the coast is clear.'

Lewis smiled grimly as the man went off. He had been almost certain from the start that Nikol would succeed. It had taken his technicians all night to adapt one of the SOC robots sufficiently to pass as President Popodopolos.

On the field, Lewis's own men were moving in to clear up the smouldering debris. The players stood by, impatient now to restart the game.

Up in the maintenance box, Archie Marconi heard the news with an idea forming in his head. His men had carted away Alf Redmond's body, but Archie lingered, looking down on the pitch through Nikol's escape hole.

Best view in the dome, he thought.

He picked up his radio. 'Everything under control up here, Ron,' he reported. 'Just a few odds and ends to clear up. Might take me a while . . .'

Archie lay flat on the floor and poked his head through the hole. It was going to be a great game.

Search for the Missing Millionaire

John Radford

IT TURNED OUT that the little guy with the specs wasn't from the hire purchase company coming to repossess the MG. When you're a struggling private detective you have to think about things like that.

I hadn't had a case in a fortnight, and was feeling pretty grouchy, wondering where all the free-spending clients you see on TV were living now. Obviously it wasn't in North Yorkshire. Then the small person walked in my office, if you can call a leaky attic over a launderette an office.

'Mr Jimmy Gordon?' he asked. I grunted. 'My name is Trubshawe. I'm private secretary to Mr Egon Carlssen. You are familiar with the name?' I was. Everybody had heard of Carlssen. He was one of those millionaire recluses.

'I've heard of him,' I said, trying not to sound over-keen. He didn't waste words.

'Mr Carlssen has disappeared.'

I sat bolt upright. 'Disappeared?'

'Quite so. I returned to Farne Abbey last evening from London, and he was not there. He prefers not to go out, as you may have heard. He has a fear of travelling. In cars, particularly. I inquired of the staff as to his whereabouts, but they knew nothing.' He stopped and peered at me over his glasses. He was obviously waiting for me to say something.

'And you want me to find him?'

Trubshawe pulled an envelope from his inside pocket and passed it over. I opened it and two wads of notes fell out. 'As quickly as possible, please.'

I was choking a bit at the sight of all that money. 'Have you been to the police?'

He looked shocked. 'Certainly not! You must understand, Mr Gordon, that if news of this matter got about, it could have the most disastrous consequences for Mr Carlssen's business interests. The stock-market could . . . well . . .'

I nodded. He didn't have to draw me a picture. But there was still something that wasn't quite right.

'Why me, Mr Trubshawe? You could afford one of the big national agencies.'

'Indeed, Mr Gordon, and I don't doubt that they would have assured me of their confidence on this matter, but a large agency employs a large number of people. The fewer who know about this, the better it will be. You alone will be the one.'

'You mean,' I said, 'that if the story gets out, you'll know where to come looking for the blabbermouth, right?'

'Exactly, Mr Gordon. Do you accept the case?'

I looked at the huge wad that was lying on the desk, smelling sweetly of real food – I'd been living on beans on toast for three days – and two months back payments on the MG. I took a deep breath. 'I'll take the case.'

'You'll probably want to start at Farne Abbey,' he said. 'There's a couple, Mr and Mrs Garfield, the only staff Mr Carlssen keeps. They live in the gatehouse cottage. They will give you every assistance.'

'Won't you be there?' I asked.

'I must attend a meeting in Zurich for two days. If I do not, then questions will be asked. You understand?'

I understood.

Apart from grabbing a quick meal of real steak and real chips with my new-found wealth, the first place I went to was the local newspaper offices. The editor, Jack Billings, had given me a hand with a case or two in the past. I had to be careful what I said: that man has a nose for a story that would make a bloodhound look as if it had a cold in the head.

'What do you know about Egon Carlssen?' I asked him, casually. He looked at me suspiciously.

'Why?'

'Just asking,' I hedged.

'Just asking?' Obviously he didn't believe me.

'Jack,' I said, 'if I told you what I'm doing, all the favours you've ever done me wouldn't get me another case after this one. You know me: if there's anything in it you'll be the first to know.' He thought for a minute, then shrugged and walked over to a filing cabinet by the wall and sorted through it.

'Carlssen,' he said, at last, opening a file. 'Egon Gustav Carlssen. Head of the Carlssen Group: shipping, oil, rubber, coffee, and pharmaceuticals. He bought Farne Abbey, that's some kind of crumbling pile on the Northumbrian coast, in June 1978. Probably one of the ten richest men in the world, he lives like a recluse. There are no known pictures of him. All his business is conducted through a secretary.' He closed the file. 'That's all I've got. What's he done, put in a bid for the moon? He owns everything else.' I grinned.

'See you later, Jack!' I said as I left the office.

Farne Abbey was just about the most desolate place I'd ever seen. Perched on a cliff-top overlooking the sea, it was the only building for miles around. I parked outside the rusting iron gates and the high perimeter wall, and pulled on an ancient bell-pull. There was a cottage just inside, and a moment later a gnarled son of the soil came out and asked me who I was. I told him.

'Oh, yes, sir.' He unlocked the gates and let me in. 'Mr

Trubshawe said you'd be coming. I suppose you'll want to look at the house? My wife's up there. She does the cleaning, I do the gardening, you see.' I tried grilling him a bit as we walked up to the gloomy old place, but it was a waste of time. He'd been hired by Trubshawe, got his wages from Trubshawe, and had never seen Carlssen all the time he'd worked there. Neither, he said, had his wife. Great!

'Surely somebody must see him,' I insisted. 'The doctor, maybe? And who does the cooking?'

'My wife cooks a meal once a day, in the evening,' said Garfield, 'and, as for the doctor, well, Mr Trubshawe *is* a doctor.' I was surprised. Trubshawe hadn't told me that.

I spent the next hour looking round the house. It was just as gloomy and depressing inside as out. Half the rooms were unused, full of dust, and smelling of damp. Of the others, there were two bedrooms, a room kitted out as an office, with telephones and a teleprinter, and a sitting room full of fancy antique furniture. I went down to the kitchen. Mrs Garfield was there, cleaning up. She was a cheery old soul; had a face as long as a coffin lid. As I went in she was lugging a heavy-looking dustbin out into the yard. I gave her a hand. Well, I've always been a bit of a gent. Whatever was in it smelled awful.

'Slops,' she said, seeing my nose wrinkle. 'Pig man from the next village calls for them once a week. Never seen such a waste of food, I haven't! It's criminal!'

'Small appetites?' I inquired. 'Carlssen and Trubshawe?'

She nodded in disgust. 'Beats me why they have a full dinner o'nights. Must be as thin as a rake, that Mr Carlssen, what he eats!'

Fascinating. It was getting late, so I drove to the nearest village and put up for the night at the pub.

I couldn't sleep that night. It was hot, and the bed was like a model of the Yorkshire dales. Anyway, I was trying to straighten out my thoughts. Nothing seemed to have any significance. I'd seen the high-walled estate. Carlssen must be over sixty. He couldn't have climbed the walls. And the gate made more noise than the Liverpool Philharmonic tuning up. It would have woken the Garfields, for sure. And what about the getaway? He hated cars, and anyway Trubshawe had the only one. A helicopter? Impossible to cover up the noise of a helicopter.

I wandered over to the window and looked out. The moon was full, and the sea sparkled as it rose and fell in the distance. I caught sight of something – a light, bobbing up and down. As my eyes got accustomed to the gloom I saw it was a luxury yacht, one of those floating gin-palaces favoured by the rich, the sort of thing Carlssen might own. Then it clicked. What's quiet, fast, can travel by night? A boat. Once Carlssen was out of the grounds, what could be simpler than to take a boat and skip? It fitted all right, but it led to another question: who was driving the boat, and why?

I got up early and drove over to the Abbey, parked the heap somewhere inconspicuous, and took a walk along the beach under the cliff-face. The tide was on its way out, and the sand was clean and clear. After a hundred yards or so, I came to one of those miniature streams that often seem to be flowing down beaches. While I was looking for a place to cross I spotted something else, floating in the water. It was a used matchstick. I followed the stream back to the rock and found more. The stream seemed to be coming from beneath a rocky outcrop at the base of the cliff, and I got down and peered under it. It was obviously a hollow that collected water at high tide, and let it flow out gradually at low tide. There was nothing unusual in that. But matchsticks? From an underground rock-pool? The water seemed to be pretty deep under the rock. Deep enough for a man to scramble under, perhaps?

I wandered over to the window and looked out.

I took my clothes off and slid into the water. It was icy.

Ten yards in, the rocky ceiling came down to the surface. I held my breath and clawed my way along under the water until my hand came out in air. I bobbed up. There was almost no light, but, as I got used to the gloom, I could pick out some features. I was in an underground cavern, and there was a shelf of rock above me. I pulled myself up and bumped into something wobbly. It was a table, and, as I groped about my hand brushed against something familiar: matches. I struck one. There was a hurricane lantern on the table, and I lit it.

The cavern was long and narrow, stretching back into the darkness. By the table was a low camp-bed, with signs that it had been used recently. There were remains of food, and a copy of Saturday's newspaper. Somebody had spent some time here, on Saturday. Long enough to eat, and maybe to sleep, and I thought I knew whom: Carlssen, waiting for the boat.

I picked up the lantern and walked back along the passage. It went up steeply, with steps here and there, and finished up in a high cave with a steep flight of steps leading up to a big wooden door. I didn't have to have a map to figure out where I was: under Farne Abbey.

Now I knew how Carlssen had got out, and probably how he had got away, but it didn't help me towards working out where he'd gone. And there was another thing, I thought, as I walked back to the sea end of the passage. Trubshawe must know about the passage. But he hadn't told me about it. I ducked into the icy water again, and came up in the sunshine.

Back at the village pub, there was a message waiting for me: Jack Billings had phoned, and asked me to ring back. I did.

'How did you know I was here?' I asked.

'I phoned Farne Abbey. I guessed you were working on

something over there. They told me where you were staying. I take it you're working on something for Carlssen?'

I hedged again.

'All right, I won't ask, but I thought you'd be interested in a news item that's just come in.'

'I might.' Not half!

'The Carlssen Group's in trouble. The Food and Drugs Administration in America have just banned Sorbanol. It's one of Carlssen Pharmaceutical's products.'

'A drug?' I asked.

'Yes – a protein substitute. Turns out it has some constituent that builds up in the body and causes brain-damage. They've sold container-loads of the stuff.'

I thought for a moment. So Carlssen had been peddling unsafe drugs. Now I knew why he'd gone, as well as how.

'There's more,' Jack went on. 'Carlssen stock has been changing hands on the stock market over the past few weeks. It looks as if Carlssen is getting out.'

That gave me more to think about. Trubshawe had been worried sick about the stock-market position. But he must have known that Carlssen was selling – he was the chief leg-man. He hadn't told me that. There were getting to be a lot of things that Trubshawe hadn't told me.

'Thanks, Jack,' I said.

'Anything to tell me, O great detective?' he asked.

'Not till everything's cleared up!' I said.

'And you collect your fee!' he said as he hung up. I wasn't so sure. If Trubshawe had been in on Carlssen's escape, as he must have been, and if he found out that I'd found out, I reckoned I'd be as likely to collect a one-way ticket to somewhere I'd rather not be. These boys don't play with monopoly money. And they play for keeps.

The one thing that plagued me was this. If the whole thing had been carefully stage-managed by Trubshawe, why had he called me in to find his boss? There was only one possible answer. He picked me for the job because I was a small, local unsuccessful inquiry agent. A nobody who could be relied on to muck up the trail in case the police got interested later on. He picked me because he thought I was so dumb I'd find nothing. I seethed a bit, but my brain was going into overdrive. One or two bits of information I'd received were forming themselves into a pattern I hadn't suspected.

I spent the afternoon working hard. Trubshawe was due back the following day, and I had to be ready. I went to the library, and then the post office, where I spent a small fortune on telephone calls. Then I went and bought a big plastic bag and a crowbar. My final visit was to the police station.

Back at Farne Abbey, Garfield told me that Trubshawe had phoned to say he'd be back at ten the following morning, and that he'd asked how I was getting on. I left a report I'd typed out at the pub, telling Trubshawe I'd been able to find out nothing at all, and told Garfield I was going home.

I drove away, then dumped the car out of sight. I had to get back into that underwater cavern. If I was right, the boys in blue would be picking Carlssen up the following day, and if I was wrong – well, beans on toast is nice and filling, and I'd never had any money anyway.

With my clothes safely in the plastic bag, I swam into the cavern, dried off, and dressed again. I laid the crowbar beside the camp-bed and lay down to get some rest. I was going to need it.

By nine-thirty the following morning, I was climbing the wooden staircase under Farne Abbey with the lantern in one hand and the crowbar in the other. The door was old and it gave easily. I found myself in a wine-cellar, with more steps leading up to the ground floor.

The wine-cellar door was concealed in the panelling of the

hall – that's how I'd missed it on my first visit. I closed it quietly, and went up to the office. All I had to do now was wait. I hid behind a row of filing-cabinets.

I didn't have to wait for long. I heard a car pull up outside, and within a few minutes Trubshawe came into the room, holding what I recognised as the report I'd left with Garfield. He sat down and read it. He smiled.

'Excellent . . .' he murmured as he dropped it on to the desk. I looked at my watch: it was now or never. If I didn't find out the truth I was going to look pretty silly when the fuzz showed up. I stepped out into the room.

I don't know quite what I expected Trubshawe to do, but in the event he didn't even flinch. He looked up, not at all surprised to see me.

'Ah, Mr Gordon,' he said, taking off his glasses. 'How kind of you to call. You've saved me the trouble of sending your fee by post.'

'That's all right, Mr Trubshawe,' I said, trying to out-cool him. My heart was going like a steam-hammer. 'Or maybe I should call you by your real name, Mr Carlssen!'

Even that didn't shake him. He smiled.

'I see I was mistaken in taking you for a dummy,' he said pleasantly. 'However, it's no matter, since you won't be telling anyone. Mr Garfield, who is by no means the country idiot he seems, is downstairs – ah – suitably armed. Mr Carlssen's personal effects will be found floating in the cave. It will seem that he tried to get away, and was battered to death on the rocks. His body – your body, Mr Gordon – will be unrecognisable, I assure you. I had hoped that my carefully planted items in the subterranean passage would lead you to believe that Carlssen had escaped without trace, but since you didn't, well, we shall have to arrange this little – ah – accident, to dispose of Carlssen. Then the good Mr Trubshawe will be in the clear – the innocent victim of his unscrupulous employer. And I must thank you for your report . . .' He tapped the envelope on the desk. 'That will be a great help towards convincing the police that I did everything in my power to find the missing millionaire. But we are wasting time . . .'

He rang a bell, and Garfield appeared in the doorway waving a shotgun. 'If you would come this way?' The country gunslinger prodded me in the ribs with his weapon and I went back down to the cellar. I wasn't too worried. I reasoned that they wouldn't want to shoot me. Drownings aren't usually accompanied by a bellyfull of buckshot. I planned to wait until we reached the cave, then take a dive into the water and get away. But Carlssen had thought of that. He tied a rope round my waist and kept a tight grip on it. So much for that idea.

When we reached the cave, Carlssen looked at his watch. 'Another twenty minutes before high tide,' he said, quietly. 'We shall have to wait.'

I shut my eyes. I'd made a terrible mistake. I hadn't checked the tide-tables. Outside the cave there wouldn't be a cohort of coppers waiting with baited handcuffs, just a few million gallons of cold, salty water. If I didn't move now, there was a fair chance I'd never move again. I jerked on the rope, causing Carlssen to lose his balance. Garfield jumped forward, and I ducked under the barrel of his gun and butted him in the stomach, sending him sprawling. The gun went off, bringing down a miniature landslide from the roof. But Carlssen was getting up. He'd dropped the rope. He was coming for me. If I was going to get away, it was going to be within the next three-quarters of a second. I dived into the water. Of course, I'd forgotten that, this far back, it was only a couple of feet deep.

When I woke I thought I'd died and gone somewhere not

nice. I was surrounded by black-clad figures, and there was a lot of shouting going on. As my vision cleared, the figures resolved themselves into the shape of police frogmen, and the shouting was a couple of them laying Garfield and Carlssen by the heels. I was safe. I flaked out again.

Jack came to see me in hospital. He was grinning from shoulder to shoulder over the big story he'd sent in to one of the national dailies.

'I'll buy you a drink,' he said enthusiastically, 'when you're glued back together again.' I groaned. 'How did you figure it out?' he went on. I tried to smile an easy smile, but my face hurt. My back hurt, too. In fact I hurt in places where I didn't even know I had places.

'It all came together when you told me about the case against Carlssen Pharmaceuticals,' I croaked. 'Trubshawe must have known about it, but he didn't tell me. I found out there were quite a few things Trubshawe hadn't bothered to tell me. Then Mrs Garfield was going on about all the food that was wasted up at the house, when she cooked for two. Then there was Carlssen. Nobody had seen him for years, except Trubshawe. And why did he bury himself in a dump like Farne Abbey? I got an idea: Carlssen didn't exist, or maybe Trubshawe had bumped him off, possibly years ago, and taken over the empire. That led me to another question: who was Trubshawe? Garfield told me he was a doctor, so I checked the medical directory down at the library. I couldn't find him there. I rang the British Medical Association in London, and the Royal College of Surgeons, and about a hundred other places. They'd never heard of him. I looked him up in every reference book I could find. Until he appeared as number two in the Carlssen organisation, eight years ago, he didn't exist. So it wasn't Carlssen who'd mysteriously disappeared, it was Trubshawe who'd mysteriously appeared from nowhere.'

'You're a genius, Jimmy,' Jack said, as the nurse came to tell him that visiting time was over. 'You'll go far.'

'Yeah!' I thought, as he went out. 'I shan't even get paid for this case!' Then I brightened up a bit. I'd still got a bit of the money Trubshawe had given me. It would pay off the backlog of hire purchase I owed on the MG, and maybe buy me one more really good dinner before I went back to beans on toast.

I fell asleep and dreamed about steak and chips and a bottle of really good Burgundy. It was great.

The Sleeper

Alan A Grant

Daily Herald, October 4th, 1981.
RUSSIAN PILOT DEFECTS!
Revolutionary new plane in British hands
A top-secret Soviet Uganoff-14 jet-fighter last night made a shock landing at RAF Mistleigh, a small training unit on the east coast of Yorkshire. Its pilot – whose name has not yet been revealed – has requested political asylum. The plane is believed to be fitted with the latest Soviet Laser Attack System, a subject of much speculation in Western military circles. It is being held under guard at Mistleigh pending a decision on its future by the Ministry of Defence. The Soviet Embassy in London issued the following statement: 'This aircraft is the property of the USSR. We demand its immediate return. Failure to comply could cause serious damage to future Soviet–British relations.' (For full story see Pages 2 and 3.)

KGB Headquarters, October 4th, 4.30 am.

MAJOR IVAN ILLYAVITCH stared at the information which had come in for a full five minutes before turning to his aide.

'The British will give us the plane back – in time,' he scowled, 'but not before they have had a very close look at it. We cannot afford that. It is our duty to prevent it happening.'

'I know, sir,' the aide agreed. 'I have already done some checking. It appears we have an operative working inside the base at Mistleigh.'

'We have?' The major was surprised.

'Yes, sir – a 'sleeper'. He has been inactive since the end of the Second World War. But he could easily become active again.'

The aide handed Illyavitch a thin file. For a minute the major studied it, then lifted his phone and spoke sharply into it: 'Get me our embassy in London. The red line – scramble Code 7.'

Group Captain Bob Smith watched the flight of BA Hawk trainer planes touch down on the landing strip at Mistleigh, and made a mental note to have a word with young Harrison. The boy would make a good pilot one day – if he could learn to control that youthful enthusiasm. Why, he'd almost had the tail off that Hawk during the simulated dogfight that had just taken place!

The phone was ringing as Smith pushed open the door of his office. It would be his wife Mary, calling to remind him about his dental appointment.

He picked up the receiver. 'Group Captain here –'

But instead of his wife, he was greeted by a man's nasal voice. 'Sleeping beauty, it is time to wake.'

Then the line went dead.

All the colour drained from Bob Smith's face. His hand shook as he replaced the receiver. 'No,' he muttered. 'Not now, not after all these years . . .'

Perhaps it was a hoax, or a mistake. But no, he dismissed the thought at once. They were the code words all right – the code words that had remained buried in his memory all these years, unused.

He slumped in his chair and cradled his head in his hands. Suddenly, it was all clear to him. This had something to do with the plane, the Uganoff-14 strike fighter, the sleek Soviet craft that lay under guard in Hangar 3.

The phone rang again and the Group Captain picked it up

in a trembling hand. But this time it *was* his wife.

'Have you remembered your dental appointment, Bob?'

'I'll have to cancel it, dear,' he said numbly. 'Something . . . urgent has come up.'

Five minutes later Bob Smith drove his car out through the base gates and turned left on to the narrow country lane that connected with the main road. He stopped at the first public telephone kiosk he passed, and dialled a number – a number that had been imprinted in his mind.

The voice that answered said only 'Yes?'

'Kuryakin,' Smith replied simply.

The man had obviously been waiting for the call. 'You will drive along the A171. You will take the Egton turn-off, and stop at the third lay-by. Is that understood?'

Smith's tremulous voice repeated 'Understood'.

He got back into his car and began to drive, his mind a turmoil of seething emotions. He was 57 years old, near retirement. He had hoped – no, believed – that he would be allowed to retire in peace. Now he knew that was not so. Still, perhaps he could talk to them, reason with them. Surely they'd listen.

He should have known better!

A dark green Austin Maxi was parked in the lay-by when Smith's car drew up. Its bonnet was raised, and a man in a tweed jacket appeared to be tinkering with the engine. Smith approached him cautiously, unsure.

'Good morning, Kuryakin,' the man greeted him, looking up. 'Pretend that you are assisting me. We can never tell who might be watching.'

The Group Captain leaned forward, as if he was peering at the engine. 'Listen – whatever you want from me, I'm not interested.'

The thickset man didn't even glance at him. 'It is of no importance whether you are interested or not, Kuryakin.

You will do what you are told to do. I am sure there is no need to remind you what will happen if you do not.'

Bob Smith needed no reminding. He knew the KGB only too well. His first dealings with them had been in Stalingrad, in 1945. Then, he had not been Bob Smith, but Nikita Kuryakin, a 21-year-old pilot officer with the Soviet Air Force. Two security officers had called him to KGB headquarters, where he was informed of a fantastic plan.

'A young British pilot died this morning in hospital here,' he was told. 'You bear an astonishing resemblance to him: age, physical build, eye colour. With a few minor alterations, you could *be* him.'

'In fact,' the other went on, 'you *are* going to be him.'

'But why, sir?' the nervous young Kuryakin had asked.

'You know what a "sleeper" is, Kuryakin?'

'No, sir.'

'A sleeper,' the first official told him, 'is an agent planted in an enemy country under a false identity. He takes no active part in espionage work. Instead, he plays out his new role as if he *is* the person he is replacing. Like any normal ambitious young man, he builds a good career, is promoted, achieves power . . .'

The KGB man stared hard at Kuryakin for a moment. 'Then, when he is in a position to be of use to us, he is activated.'

From that moment on, Nikita Kuryakin's life was not his own. He underwent intensive training at a special KGB school: he learned to speak English with a strong Huddersfield accent, just as the real Robert Smith had done. He learned every detail of Smith's life, every minor event, every personal foible.

And when his training was over, Nikita Kuryakin *was* Bob Smith.

The real Smith's only relatives had died in a German air-raid in 1941; there was no-one who would be able to expose Kuryakin as an imposter. The real Smith was buried in an unmarked grave in Stalingrad, and it was Kuryakin who returned to England in his place . . .

The ploy had worked like a charm. No-one even suspected the fraud. Kuryakin played his part perfectly – he married an English girl, had a family. And he had risen slowly through the ranks of the RAF. As the years passed he even began to *feel* English. The Soviet Union was like another world to him, an alien world.

But the ploy had worked *too* well. Kuryakin had come to love his new life, come to love this country that he had been sent to undermine. So much so that in 1975 he had taken the decision to forsake any notion of ever working for his motherland again. They had not called on him for thirty years; surely they never would.

It was then that he took a definite step to ensure that his KGB overlords would be even less likely to use him. He'd been offered an important desk job at the Ministry of Defence; to take it would have given him access to highly classified information on Britain's defences. Even though the job would have meant promotion and a large salary increase, Smith had turned it down. Instead, using connections he had made, he arranged for himself to be transferred to the Mistleigh base, a Primary Training Unit of absolutely no interest to the Soviets.

At least, that was the case until the defecting pilot had turned up like a bad rouble in his Uganoff-14 . . .

'Do you hear me, Kuryakin?' Smith was brought back to the present with a jolt by the Russian's harsh voice. 'I said – you have a nice wife, two fine daughters, an easy life . . . It would not be so easy if they found out you are a KGB agent!'

There was nothing Smith could say to that. He knew that if his true identity was revealed, it would totally destroy the life he had spent thirty-five years building. It would mean jail for him, shame and ruin for his family.

Bob Smith took a deep breath. 'What do you want me to do?' he asked as evenly as he could.

'Oh, just a little job, Kuryakin.' The Russian lifted a small device from where it was concealed behind the carburettor and surreptitiously handed it over. It was a gleaming steel cylinder five centimetres in diameter and eight centimetres high. On its flat top was a dial.

'What is it?' Smith demanded.

'It's a bomb, Kuryakin – a small but very powerful bomb. To set it, you need only twist this dial so that the arrow points to the red mark on the cylinder. After that, you have five minutes to get clear.'

Smith was horrified. 'And you – you want me to plant it on the Uganoff?'

'Excellent, Kuryakin! Still as sharp as your dossier says,' the Russian said sarcastically. 'Yes, we want you to plant it on the plane. The Ministry of Defence scientists will be arriving tonight to study it. The plane *must* be destroyed before they get to Mistleigh.'

The Russian slammed the car bonnet shut and said, 'There, that just about does it.'

He got into the car and started the engine, winding down the window to utter one last threat. 'I am sure you will cooperate, comrade. Just think of your wife and children . . .'

Then the Maxi roared away.

The small steel cylinder seemed to burn the flesh of Smith's hand, and he thrust it in his pocket. He hardly noticed the road as he drove back to his country house near the airbase. All he could think of was the bomb in his pocket – and what would happen if he did not use it. He had been given an odious choice: to betray the country he had come to love . . . or to ruin his own family.

His wife Mary met him with a peck on the cheek. Their two daughters were already seated at the table. Cynthia, the elder by two years, worked in a shop in a nearby town; she was telling her sister Dorothy of a strange customer she'd served that morning.

'He was a sort of fat man in a tweed jacket with some kind of foreign accent,' she was saying – and the colour drained from her father's face as she went on: 'He said the strangest thing – "You have a nice job here. It would be a pity if it had to end soon." I asked him what the heck he meant, but he just smiled horribly and told me to ask my father. Then he walked out. Really weird, it was . . .'

'A fat man in a tweed jacket, did you say?' Smith's wife came in with a tureen of soup. 'What a coincidence! When I was coming out of Tesco's a man just like that helped me load my shopping into the Mini. For some reason he kept calling me Mrs Kuryakin.' Mary Smith looked keenly at her husband. 'What's the matter, Bob?'

'N-nothing,' he replied dully, getting to his feet again. 'I'm just not hungry. I think I'll drive back to the base . . .'

'Bob–?' his wife began, but he was already through the door.

He felt as if a clammy hand was squeezing his heart as he drove off. The KGB were making sure that he got the message, damn them!

By the time he reached the base, his mind was made up. There was nothing else for it – he'd have to go along with them. He parked the car in his reserved bay and walked slowly towards Hangar 3. Two armed RAF guards saluted as he reached the entrance.

'Afternoon, sir.'

'I'm just going to take a look at our prize,' Smith told them. 'Probably won't get a chance once the boffins arrive.'

'Look out for booby traps, sir,' the guard joked.

Then Smith was past them and inside the large hangar. The plane was a real beauty. Though not half as versatile as the RAF's own Harrier jump-jets, the murderous-looking laser cannon slung under each wing set it in a different class where strike power was concerned.

Smith scrambled up on the wing and leaned into the cockpit, as if inspecting it. One hand strayed to his pocket, felt for the tiny bomb that nestled there. It felt as if it weighed a ton as he took it out, glancing round to make sure he was unobserved. His trembling fingers made to twist the dial to the set position. And then he stopped.

It was no good. He couldn't do it.

He thought of Britain, this country that he had come to call his own. He thought of how different it was from the land of his birth! Here a man was free to do as he wished, free to raise his family without fear of sudden arrest, free to think his own thoughts.

If he did not set the bomb, his family could be destroyed. And yet . . . yet . . . Could he ever look his family in the face again if he went through with this terrible act of treachery?

For the first time since the phone call that morning, Bob Smith felt a sense of relief. A small smile played about his lips as he returned the bomb to his jacket pocket. No – Nikita Kuryakin was dead now . . . and Group Captain Bob Smith was no traitor.

His step was almost light as he left the hangar.

'Nice looking machine,' he remarked to the guards. 'The boffins are going to have a field day with it.'

Minutes later he was back in his car and heading off-base. He drove for half an hour, then parked on an isolated stretch of moorland.

He trudged across the thick heather until he was well away from the lonely road. There was no hesitation this time. Taking the device from his pocket, he twisted the dial and

Smith scrambled up on the wing and leaned into the cockpit, as if inspecting it.

placed the bomb in a shallow dip.

Hurriedly he loped back across the moor to his car and stood there, waiting. Five minutes to the second after it had been set, the bomb exploded with astonishing violence. The blast wave caught him, thrust him back against the car. It would have completely demolished the plane, the hangar – and probably the guards, too, Smith thought.

As the last wisps of smoke drifted away from the large crater, Bob Smith slid into the driving seat and switched on the ignition.

An hour later Group Captain Bob Smith drew up outside Police Headquarters in the city of York. He walked steadily up the steps, not looking to left or right, and made straight for the reception desk.

'Good afternoon, sir,' the desk sergeant smiled. 'What can we do for you?'

'I'd like to see someone from Special Branch. I've come to turn myself in.'

Prairie Mouse and the Mountain Lion

Alan A Grant

EVER SINCE HE COULD REMEMBER, Prairie Mouse had hated his name.

Prairie Mouse was not his birth-name, of course; that was Full-Head-of-Hair, as it was the Blackfoot Indian custom to call newborn children after some circumstance surrounding their birth. Prairie Mouse was what the other boys of the tribe called him, because he was small and skinny and not very strong. The cruel nickname had stuck. Now everyone in his tribe – the Blood branch of the Blackfeet – called him nothing else, even though he had proved his courage countless times in the dangerous games played by the Blackfoot boys.

Prairie Mouse was twelve years old when he decided to win himself a new name. He explained his plan to his best friend, Hooknose.

'Tonight when the tribe is sleeping, I am going into the hills to kill a mountain lion and bring it back. Then no-one will call me Prairie Mouse again!'

Hooknose was impressed. 'It is a brave plan – but a dangerous one,' he applauded. 'I had better come with you. I could do with an adventure. And besides, there had better be someone to tell your father if you are killed!'

Prairie Mouse's father was a renowned warrior, Twelve Killer, who had won his name after a fierce battle with the tribe's ancient enemies, the Crows, when he had brought back twelve scalps. This was a man's name, given only after a Blackfoot brave had been on the warpath. Until he himself

45

was a man, Prairie Mouse would settle for a new nickname: Lion Hunter would suit him well.

That night Prairie Mouse waited until his father went to sit with the tribe's elders round the campfire. Then, making an excuse to his mother, Clear Water, he left the teepee. Outside, hidden in the bole of a hollow tree, he had left his bow and quiver of arrows. Hooknose was already waiting there for him, his own bow slung over his shoulder and a rawhide food-bag tied at his waist.

It was a sultry summer's night and both boys wore only breech-cloths and antelope-hide moccasins. Slinking in the shadows to avoid the camp sentries, they crept away from the sprawl of teepees and began to make their way across the wide Montana plain. They travelled at a steady lope, heading towards the towering outline of the Rocky Mountains, not ten kilometres away.

It was 1832 and the White Man was still a rare and unusual sight this far west of the Missouri. The country was wild, rugged, and teeming with animal life; the great buffalo herds still roamed in their millions, and in the Rockies, mountain lions and bears still held sway.

It was not long before Prairie Mouse and Hooknose reached the foothills. Ten kilometres was nothing to a Blackfoot Indian, who would think little of covering huge distances in a day. The two boys were not even breathing heavily as they made their way silently up the rugged, wooded slope.

In a gully three hundred metres up they paused, listening intently to the night sounds. From the south came the eerie howl of a timber wolf; it was answered by another, more distant.

Then Prairie Mouse's keen ears heard the sound he was after – the spine-tingling screech of a mountain lion.

'It is above us,' he whispered. 'Not far – maybe two buffalo arrows' distance.'

The Indians measured distance by the longest length at which their tribe had shot a buffalo; in this case, two buffalo arrows equalled about seven hundred metres.

'Let us see if we can draw him closer.' Prairie Mouse threw back his head and uttered a roar indistinguishable from that which they had just heard, a skill he had learned from his uncle, One-arm. He let the cry fade abruptly, waited a second, repeated it.

He was rewarded by an answering roar.

'He thinks another is invading his territory,' Prairie Mouse hissed to Hooknose. 'He will be here soon to sort him out.'

The two boys crouched low behind a large boulder, and Prairie Mouse notched an arrow into his bowstring. Hook-nose made to do the same, but Prairie Mouse signalled 'no'. This lion was *his*!

Minutes later there was a low growl from the shadowy trees ahead. It came again, closer –

And then they saw it, motionless on a low branch not forty paces away. It was a big one. Moonlight tinged its tawny pelt almost white, and its mouth was open in a warning snarl.

Prairie Mouse rose from his crouch; carefully, deliberately, he aimed the arrow, drawing back the bowstring as far as his young arm would pull it. The mountain lion tilted its head from side to side, puzzled. It had expected to find another of its own kind. Then it came to a sudden decision. Its legs tensed like coiled springs. Its fierce eyes flashed.

It leapt, flying through the air – just as Prairie Mouse's arrow sped from his bow. The lion heard the arrow's *swishhh* and twisted in mid-air to avoid it. It screeched with pain as the sharp flint tip pierced its ear, ripping the tender flesh.

It hit the ground not twenty paces from the boys. But the sudden pain had shown it that these were not defenceless victims, and before Prairie Mouse could loose his second shot, it had turned on its heels and bolted for the shelter of the dark trees.

Immediately the boys were on their feet and after it, the thrill of the chase overcoming all sense of fear or caution. But the beast was gone. When next they heard its cry, it was a good five arrow-lengths away – and still running.

'You've lost that one, Prairie Mouse,' Hooknose said disappointedly. But his friend was not listening; he was bending in the clearing where they stood, examining the ground.

'Look, Hooknose – hoofmarks. Many horses have been this way, and recently.'

'You are right.' Hooknose nodded. 'But our tribe have not been here for several days. Who can they belong to?'

It was Prairie Mouse who found the answer. A long flint arrowhead with sharp barbs that denoted only one tribe –

'Crows! Our hated enemies!'

'But what would *they* do here? Unless—' Hooknose began, and Prairie Mouse finished for him:

'They have come to attack our tribe – to sneak up from behind when we least suspect them!' The boy made an instant decision. 'Hooknose – you must return to the camp now and give warning. I will follow the trail and see if I can determine their strength. Go now!'

There was no need for further talk. Hooknose went off at a run back down the mountain slope, while Prairie Mouse trotted silently forward. He had been keen to win that new name – but now all that was forgotten. The safety of the tribe must come first!

He heard their horses first, up ahead. Soon, the beasts were visible in the moonlight, enclosed in a hastily erected wooden corral made of branches strung between tree-trunks. The

48

'*Look, Hooknose – hoofmarks. Many horses have been this way,
and recently.*'

young Blackfoot stood up slowly, casually, allowing the horses to get a good look at him so they would not be frightened by his presence. Then he was creeping slowly by them, making no sudden movement, until he could see the Crow encampment.

Their night fire was small; above it on poles were stretched several buffalo skins, so the rising smoke would not glow and give them away. There were about sixty of them, their faces and bodies streaked with war-paint. They were seated round the fire, and though he knew little of the Crow language, Prairie Mouse could tell from the aggressive gestures that they were discussing the impending attack. He must get closer.

His heart pounding like a tom-tom, the boy dropped flat on his stomach and wormed his way closer to the fire. At last he was just outside the circle cast by its glow, pressed close to the hard ground behind a large stone. A few paces to his rear, the horses stood quietly.

One of the Crow braves was on his feet, a big man wearing a full war-bonnet – a sign that he had killed at least five enemy in battle. By the double tomahawk scar that ran across his chest, Prairie Mouse recognised him as none other than Mad Wolf, a renowned Crow warrior.

Prairie Mouse knew enough of Indian signs to interpret Mad Wolf's meaning. At dawn the Crows would attack, and Blackfoot blood would stain the earth!

Prairie Mouse's first instinct was to get back to the tribe with what he had learned. But the wargames he had played with the other Blackfoot boys had prepared him for a moment such as this. Deliberately, he calmed his nerves and surveyed the Crow warriors. He was in the perfect position to spy on the enemy; he must make use of it.

Altogether he counted fifty-nine Crow; of these, twenty were armed with the White Man's fire-sticks. That could bring down a buffalo easily at six arrows' distance; a formidable weapon. His own tribe possessed but a dozen.

As well as Mad Wolf there were other Crow warriors he recognised: there was Smoke Stealer, and Two Bear Hands, so-called because it was said that he had once strangled a bear. Prairie Mouse did not believe it; the Crows were known boasters.

There was also Ekitrensh, the medicine man, and the two giant brothers He-who-Laughs and Strange Skunk, sons of a minor chief. Prairie Mouse noticed that one brave had his arm strapped to his side – a trail injury that would weaken him in battle.

Prairie Mouse's eyes narrowed. The Crow band was strong, very strong. They could inflict heavy losses with a sneak attack. A good thing he'd sent Hooknose back with a warning!

But now Prairie Mouse must get out of here himself . . .

He inched his way backwards with great caution, silent as a flea. The glow of the fire receded, then he was creeping back under a bar of the corral. But his luck could not hold for ever.

One of the horses, a skittish pinto he had noticed and avoided earlier, gave a sharp whinny. Prairie Mouse froze where he stopped. He heard a voice at the fire rap an order, and two braves moved to investigate. He was caught – dead! Unless—

Prairie Mouse's lungs filled with air and his mouth opened in a startling roar – the same screech he'd used earlier to attract the mountain lion. The horses went wild!

Rearing up and kicking out, they wheeled round in panic. The white pinto ran straight at him and Prairie Mouse dived, rolled out of its path. It charged past him, then crashed through the flimsy fence. The others crowded each other in a mad attempt to follow it, their eyes rolling and foam spitting from their mouths.

In the rearing maelstrom of horseflesh Prairie Mouse dodged a wild-eyed mare and seized his chance. As a midnight-black stallion careered by, he leapt. His fingers locked in its mane and he swung himself up, his legs scrambling for purchase on its back. It bucked once, then recognised the smell of human flesh and calmed enough for Prairie Mouse to steer it through the broken corral.

Behind him the entire Crow band was on its feet and shouting. He recognised their word for 'lion' and knew that no-one would suspect a spy. The Crow braves were running round, frantically trying to stop their stampeding mounts. A group had cornered several horses inside the corral and were calming them with difficulty. A few were already on horseback, twisting through the trees, pursuing the run-aways. They needed their steeds for the morning's attack, and they needed them fresh, in good condition. Many would be hurt in the mad scramble; the braves had to bring them under control as quickly as they could.

Prairie Mouse kept low against his horse's side, kicking its rump with his heels, spurring it on. He twisted its neck sharply as the shape of a large pine loomed before him. The horse swerved, galloped round it, nearly scraping the boy from its side. Then they were moving at speed down a narrow gulley, loose rocks and scree cascading alongside them.

Behind him the sounds of pursuit were fading, and Prairie Mouse felt it safe to bring his mount under control. He patted it firmly on the neck, whispered soothing words in its ear.

At last it came to a stop in a small moonlit clearing, and Prairie Mouse took his bearings. He had come too far to the north. The Blackfoot camp lay many buffalo arrows back, past the Crows. His quickest – and safest – way home was to cut directly through the foothills to the prairie, then turn south.

He let his mount drink briefly at a trickling mountain

stream, then steered it down the wooded slope at a walk. No sense risking an accident now, when the worst danger was well past.

When he reached the prairie a sense of wild elation pounded in his veins. He restrained the urge to utter a wild whoop, and instead dug his heels into the horse's flanks.

They galloped across the flat earth at a fast pace. The horse was steady on his feet and full of running now that its fright was gone. Prairie Mouse was glad he had chosen this one; it was a good horse, and he knew he would be allowed to keep it. His first spoil of war!

Prairie Mouse did not slacken speed all the way back. At last the Blackfoot camp could be seen in the moonlight, quiet, seemingly asleep – though he knew that was but a ruse, for his tribe would be alerted now, and ready.

As he passed a high butte he waved and at last gave vent to his feelings. Throwing back his head, he cupped his hand to his mouth and let out a shriek of triumph.

Atop the butte the Blackfoot lookout recognised the boy and signalled the all-clear sign back to the camp.

Prairie Mouse raced into camp still whooping, and shadowy figures rose from their places of concealment and came to greet him. His father was among them, fire-stick in his hand.

Prairie Mouse reined in his horse and dismounted before it had even stopped. Hardly had his feet touched the ground than he was blurting out his story to the chief and the assembled braves.

'They had many fire-sticks – twenty of them! And Mad Wolf was there, and Ekitrensh . . .'

The tribe listened in silence until he had finished. Then the chief asked him a few searching questions. Prairie Mouse was happy that he could provide all the information required.

The chief grasped his shoulder firmly. His eyes pierced the

boy. 'You have done well, son of Twelve Killer. You could have returned with Hooknose; that would have brought you honour enough. But you stayed to spy and learn more; that was the deed of a man. What is it the other boys call you—?'

Prairie Mouse looked at the ground and forced out his cruel nickname: 'Prairie Mouse.'

The chief looked at the boy's father, a slight smile playing across his chiselled features. 'I think this son of yours has done enough to deserve better than that, eh, Twelve Killer?'

Twelve Killer nodded, and the chief went on: 'He has behaved like a man tonight – it is time he had a man's name. Have you any suggestions?'

Prairie Mouse's father gave a mock scowl. 'How about He-who-sneaks-out-when-he-should-be-in-bed?'

There was a murmur of laughter and Prairie Mouse flushed. The chief held up his hand for silence. 'I think you can overlook your son's misbehaviour for once, Twelve Killer. No, I have something more appropriate in mind.'

He put both hands on the boy's shoulders and said solemnly: 'It was the roar of a lion that saved you tonight and brought you back to us. And yet you are such a small man . . . the name of 'Lion' is too big for you yet to wear . . .'

He paused, and raised his voice so that all could hear. 'Let your first man's name be *Mouse-who-Roars*. I have spoken. Let it be so!'

Mouse-who-Roars' heart swelled with pride till he thought it would burst. Wait till Hooknose and the others heard about this! Never again could they laugh when they called him by his nickname; Prairie Mouse was gone for ever.

It was his father's sharp voice which jolted him back to reality. 'Well, Mouse-who-Roars,' he was saying, 'it is time you were leaving us. We must prepare for battle.'

'But, Father –' the boy began to protest. 'I have the right to stay and fight!'

'You may be a man – but a very small one! Until you have grown as big as your head, your place is with the squaws and children!'

Mouse-who-Roars argued no further. A Blackfoot boy did not contradict his father when he spoke in that tone.

Disappointed, but with his head held high, he strode towards the protected hollow where the women and children would wait out the impending fight.

News of his new name had already spread, and many of the boys cleared a space beside them, bidding him sit there. But Mouse-who-Roars walked over to Hooknose.

'I should have stayed with you,' Hooknose said bitterly. 'Well, never mind – I am very happy for you.'

Snake Tongue – a boy older by a whole summer than Mouse-who-Roars – tried to conceal his envy, and made a biting remark: 'If you've got a man's name, why aren't you out waiting to join in the battle with the men?'

Mouse-who-Roars   just smiled and looked scornfully down his nose. 'Hah,' he crowed, 'they're saving me in case there's *real* trouble!'

The Tip-Off

M S Goodall

THE CORNER OF EAST 37TH and Springdale is one lousy place to wait even at the best of times. At five o'clock in the morning, wedged between an over-full trash can and a crate of empty milk bottles, it's more like a form of self-inflicted torture.

There's a wind blowing too. An icy blast that skims across San Francisco Bay and wraps itself around the waterfront with the unexpected venom of a cold shower. For the fiftieth time I look up and down the street. Nothing stirs. Nothing moves. Real dead part of town, this. Just block after block of decaying brownstone buildings. A maze of investment company offices, insurance brokers and cheap real estate joints.

And of course banks. That's what I'm doing now. Watching a bank. Or maybe not so much watching as waiting for something to happen. That's the worst of being a Private Investigator. You spend more time watching and waiting than you do living. A kind of motionless heap in a vacuum watching the world drift by, that's what I feel like sometimes. Ed Bannon, Private Eye. Mr Nobody!

I curse silently and try to win a fraction more space from that stinking trash can. Five-thirty. What the heck's gone wrong? The action should have happened over an hour ago. It's the silence – the big fat empty nothingness that worries me. Maybe I've got the times wrong. Maybe . . .

Next moment I'm on my feet and high-tailing it out of that

alley like I've got wings on my heels. Six or seven blocks away, the crackle of gunfire is stabbing at my ears like a drum-roll. The deep thump of sawn-off shotguns, mixed with the even deeper thump of .45 Magnums. It's the mob, all right. The mob I was supposed to nail an hour ago in that alley. Only somewhere along the line I've loused it up. Yes sir, I've loused it up good.

I'm halfway down West 59th Street before I realise they're operating somewhere near my office. And that makes it worse. Ten times worse. The big heist happening right on my doorstep and I'm caught napping like a flat-footed alley cat.

They're piling into a car when I get there. Four of them. Big, granite-headed hoods with black jackets and faces squashed behind nylon stocking masks. Like specimens from outer space, only twice as deadly.

The driver's in second gear with his foot on the boards, when I jump for the back bumper. Grabbing the boot-lid of a Buick is about as safe as holding on to a slab of ice. But somehow I make it. Two squashed faces in the back jerk round. My .22 Beretta smashes into the back window and bounces off. Armoured glass, I'm really messing things up. A black-gloved hand comes snaking out of the side window. Too late I see the fist is holding a spanner the size of a shovel.

'Sucker.' The hood spits the word at me like a blob of lead, then he's smashing that tool across my knuckles. I slide off like a rag doll and hit the sidewalk at high speed. Red lights explode in my head like Cape Kennedy firing signals. Then I'm sinking into a black, oily pit and wondering how the heck I'm going to explain to the cops. Wondering why in the name of Holy Toledo I ever took this job on in the first place. I must have been mad . . . mad . . . mad . . . mad.

It all began forty-eight hours before. I'm sitting in the twelve-by-nine pine-lined box I call my office, when Easton walks in.

The driver's in second gear with his foot on the boards, when I jump for the back bumper.

Sergeant Joe Easton, City Homicide Squad. He's fifty-five. Tall, tough, and with a face like badly-rolled hardcore. Me, I don't like the guy. Never have done.

'Morning, Bannon.' His voice sounds like a handful of pebbles being scraped across a cheese grater. 'I want to talk to you . . .'

'Sorry, I'm busy.'

'We need help, Bannon. Your help.'

'Well now, that's a new angle.' I lean back and shoot him one of my mirthless grins. I'm suspicious, but playing it cool. 'Since when have the cops stooped low enough to hire a Private Eye?'

He stares at me like I'm something that's just crawled out of a sewer, and sits down hard in the only other chair I possess. 'Ever heard of Giles Ramsden?' he asks.

'The big-time rackets boss? Sure, who hasn't?'

'Well, to cut it short, we think he's the brain behind the latest flood of bank jobs. Five in the last two months.'

'Smooth, well-planned, and murderously efficient,' I say smugly. 'Those guys must have you worried. But the question is still the same – why come to me?'

Easton leans forward and dents my blotter with a fist the size of a water melon. 'Because we've had a tip-off,' he grates slowly. 'A whisper that the next heist is planned for the nineteenth. Only trouble is, we don't know where or at what time.'

'Some tip-off,' I sneer. 'It's about as good as shooting craps without any dice.'

'I know that, Bannon, which is why I've come to you. That stool-pigeon must have been scared. So scared he would only give us a date. We can't find him in the time available but you can. It shouldn't be too difficult with the kind of underworld contacts you've got.'

'The nineteenth is only two days from now. That isn't very

long to find anybody in this jungle,' I reply softly. 'Especially a scared informer.'

'Maybe not, but he's our only lead. He must be someone close to the Ramsden mob, so start there. Cover every hoodlum and strong-arm merchant in his organisation and you'll come up with something.'

'You hope.'

Easton stands up and fills the doorway. 'Okay, wise guy, but don't let me down. Four weeks from now I retire – and I want this bunch nailed before I hand in my badge, savvy?'

'Sure.' I lean back, stick my size nines on the desk and flash him another of my mirthless smiles. On a day like this, my mirthless smiles are pretty good. 'Don't worry, Sergeant. One last feather in your cap, then you can go and spend the evening of your life raising chickens. I won't let you down.'

Half an hour later, with the .22 Beretta sitting snugly in its leather under my left armpit, I'm gum-shoeing it downstairs. The building is quiet now, the offices dead and empty. Only Bert McLusky, night guard for the Stateways Investment Corporation, is still on duty. He sees me coming and flicks a finger at his cap. 'Hi, Mr Bannon, you look worried.' His lined old face is as cheerful as ever.

'I'm always worried when I have work to do, Bert. It's like a disease.'

He laughs and opens the main door with a rattle of keys. 'I guess it's time you got a nice steady job, Ed,' he says. 'Then you'd be happy all the time, like me.'

'Maybe you've got something there, old-timer. I'll have a word with my favourite analyst! See you.'

Outside, it's dark. I begin to walk, heading away from the flashing neon signs towards the darker mantle of the waterfront world. The pool rooms, the cheap bars, the clip joints – those are the places I'll start looking. Somewhere in the dirty web of the underworld, I'll find my man. I shrug my shoulders and quicken my step. Maybe, with a lot of luck and a lot of dough changing hands among the right people, it won't take long. Five, six hours I can be back in bed. Asleep. Happy.

But man, am I wrong! So wrong it isn't true. By dawn I've covered the whole waterfront with the proverbial fine-toothed comb. And nothing. Not a single whisper. Not a solitary lead. I stagger back to my pad with nothing more than two shoes full of blisters and a head that feels like it's filled with lead balls.

I just don't get it. There's something about this case that doesn't click any more. But what? I stick my aching head under the cold tap and hold it there. If only I could think. Work out what's keeping this stoolie so deep underground.

The 'phone rings with a suddenness that makes me shudder. I grab a towel and answer it, ready to blow Easton's head off with a verbal shotgun if it happens to be him. I'm thinking wrong again. It isn't him.

'Bannon? Ed Bannon?' It's a chick's voice with a tinkle of bells buried in the middle of it.

'Yup. Who's this?'

'Honey Marshall. The word is you want information.'

'Right first time, sweetheart.' I sit down and reach for a pen. Things are looking up. Honey Marshall. She's a girl I've met a couple of times down the lower end of clubland. Blonde, kind of sweet in her own way. Maybe good connections once, but too many nights crammed into too short a time, have left their mark. But she isn't even on the fringes of the Ramsden mob, which is something else that doesn't make sense.

'Okay, Honey, shoot. You know what I'm after?'

'Sure, but I can't talk on the 'phone. Meet me in an hour in the top room of the Club Rainbow. And come alone.'

She slams the 'phone down and leaves me staring at the

wall like some kind of mixed-up schoolkid. Why the cloak-and-dagger angle? Somebody, somewhere, is mighty scared. I dial a number, chew my lip and wait. Maybe Easton can provide some of the answers.

'Hello, police headquarters? Give me Homicide.'

The desk clerk works fast. 'Easton speaking . . .'

'Easton, this is Bannon. Listen, I've got a lead . . . dame called Honey Marshall. Any of your guys know whether she's been tied in with the Ramsden mob recently?'

'Could be, but it's doubtful. Why, what's the drift?'

'She knows something. Asked me to meet her at the Club Rainbow in an hour.'

'Then be there, Bannon. And keep me informed.'

I hang up and start towelling. Quick shave, change and a bite to eat make me feel about fifty per cent better. Forty five minutes later, I'm ready to meet Honey.

The Club Rainbow is two blocks from the waterfront. Dirty, small and cheap. Through the main bar and up the stairs and I'm on a small landing. The door of Honey's room is staring me in the face. Only it doesn't feel right. Suddenly I smell trouble. Big trouble. I pat my .22 Beretta, adjust my shoulder holster and knock quietly. No answer.

I try the door knob. It opens. Honey is sitting in a chair on the far side of the room, facing the door. She's kind of smiling, and for one crazy second I think she's going to burst into song. Then I see the blood. I'm across that floor in a flash and easing her on to a sofa. It won't do any good, though, I know that at a glance. There's a bullet hole in her back, and I judge she's only got about a minute left to live.

I bend down, mouth close to her ear. 'Who, Honey? Who did it?'

Her eyelids flicker, then open. I was wrong about that minute. She's got maybe thirty seconds, no more. 'Come on, Honey, talk!' My voice is harsh with urgency.

'Tip-off . . . East . . . 37th . . .'

My judgement of life and death is pretty good. When I bend down again, she's stopped breathing. She's dead.

I ease my shape out of the room and beat it. The cops can deal with her later. Right now I've got some thinking to do. Two words, that's all. 'East . . . 37th'. Not much to go on, but it might be enough.

Twenty minutes later I'm back in my office, feet up, thinking cap rammed on tight. One thing's sure. Whoever killed Honey must have been keeping pretty close tabs on her. Which means the odds on me living to a ripe old age are shortening fast. 'East – 37th'. I grab my 'Frisco directory and thumb through. East 37th intersects with Springdale. And bang on the corner is a bank. Head office of the National Consolidated. My peanut brain rings ten thousand bells and screams 'jackpot'. This must be the tip-off. The scene of the next bank heist. The job planned for the nineteenth. Tomorrow morning.

I dial police headquarters and ask for Easton. There isn't much time. Things are happening fast. Too fast.

'Easton speaking . . .' The cheese-grater voice rasps down the line.

'Bannon here, Sarge. Listen, I think I've got it. Somebody rubbed out Honey, but she managed to mumble something just before she died. As far as I can make out, the job is planned for the National Consolidated on East 37th.'

'What about the time?'

'Sorry, no dice. You'll have to keep your men out of the area until the balloon goes up . . . don't want to scare them off. I'll cover the intersection from dawn and signal you when the time comes.'

'Okay, Bannon, I'll fix it. Good luck.'

Good luck, he'd said. Oh, man, do I feel a goof-ball now. I've loused this up, all right, loused it up good. Slowly, the red lights stop flashing in my head and the street stops going round. The Buick is well clear, and only my half-pulped knuckles tell me the whole thing isn't a dream.

I open my eyes and look up. Easton is standing over me, dabbing water on the tennis ball that's suddenly sprouted on my forehead.

'What did they hit?' I ask painfully.

'Stateways Investment Corporation,' he replies quietly. 'Got away with a cool million in negotiable bonds.'

'*Stateways?*' Next moment I'm on my feet, reeling against the wall. The Stateways Investment Corporation. Just two floors below my office. All at once I'm feeling sick. 'The guard – Bert McLusky. Is he all right?'

'Sure,' nods Easton. 'They clobbered him pretty hard, but he'll pull through.' His face goes tight and ugly, and I feel sick again.

'Okay, okay, you don't have to tell me,' I mumble into a blood-stained handkerchief. 'Your Chief wants to see me, right?'

The Sergeant nods again. 'And how. You're one lousy Private Investigator as far as he's concerned, Bannon. You boobed and he wants to know why.'

Half an hour later I'm trying to explain. Captain Rossi listens but I can tell by his eyes that all he wants to do is use my face as a doormat. I decide to make one last final plea.

'Captain, I'm sorry. Sure, Honey must have been talking through her hat, but at least Easton's men were in the general area. You must have had road blocks up so fast that Buick didn't stand a chance.'

'Oh, sure, we nailed the Buick, all right, Bannon – and four men. Only they didn't have the stolen money on them. They said they were just four innocent travellers going home from an all-night party. They had no police records, nothing, and

64

without hard evidence we couldn't even hold them for speeding.'

'That loot must be *somewhere*.' My voice creeps up into the falsetto range. The Captain leers at me like a maniac. 'Brilliant,' he says. 'Now perhaps you'll look in your crystal ball and tell me where.'

'Look, Captain, I'm only trying to—'

'Out, Bannon! Just get out and stay out!'

Feeling like a man on his last walk to the electric chair, I beat it fast. Boy, what a mess. Slipping up on a case is bad enough, but when it ruins your reputation with the cops, it's downright serious. Moodily, I stand across the street and look back at the police building. Nothing about this assignment has made sense at all. Not one single—

Suddenly I'm staring. Staring like a dummy at the stonework above the police station entrance. That's when it clicks. That's when the whole lousy business becomes so clear I feel like kicking myself down the street. Man, what a dope I've been. What a dim, google-eyed sucker.

I take off like a greyhound back to my office. Nothing looks touched, but I know now that something has been, somewhere. Without bothering to look I phone Captain Rossi. He very nearly slams down the receiver, but my natural charm wins the day. I just had to convince the captain that it was worth visiting my office tonight.

'Tonight?' he asks. 'You want me to come to your office tonight?'

'You got it, Captain. Believe me, it's important, so trust me. One other thing – make sure you come alone. And don't tell a soul.'

'Okay, but if this is another goof on your part, Bannon, I'll—'

'No goof, Captain. This time your favourite Private Eye is right on the ball.'

By eight that evening, the two of us are crammed in the coffin that passes as my office washroom. The lights are out. It's dark. Quiet. Rossi starts to get restless at approximately eight forty-five. 'I don't know what the heck you're up to, pal, but—'

'Ssssh, listen.'

He does just that, then tenses. Someone is walking up the stairs. Slowly, furtively. A black shadow pastes itself against the glass on my door. A rustling noise, then the shadow is inside, moving quickly across to the floorboards under my desk.

We make our move. I get there first, the taste of revenge sweet on my tongue. The shadow rises, blue steel glinting in his hand. I swing a straight, hard bunch of fives and hear his head snap back with a crack. The shadow moans, then lies still. The lights click on and the shadow becomes a man. I bend down.

'Good evening, Sergeant Easton,' I say right into his badly-rolled hardcore face. And I flash him another of my famous mirthless smiles.

An hour later, it's all over. Three burly cops are leading Easton away, and Captain Rossi is busily counting the loot recovered from the hole under my office floorboards. 'I still don't get it, Bannon,' he says, looking slightly ill. 'Easton has been in the force all his life. Why turn crooked now?'

'Easy,' I reply, clearing a space on the desk for my size nines. 'He was retiring next month. Retiring on a pension that would hardly keep him in feed for the chickens he wanted to raise. He felt the force had cheated him, Captain – that life owed him something. Thirty years of hard work with precious little to show for it can affect even the best of men.'

'He had a good run while it lasted.'

'Too good. I had a hunch from the start that there was something fishy about this job. That tip-off he told me about.

It didn't exist. He sent me out on a wild goose chase after an imaginary stool-pigeon only so he could get me out of the way on the morning of the robbery. It worked, too. While I was flogging my guts out chasing shadows, he and his hired hoods were robbing Stateways and stashing the loot up here.'

'But where did Honey Marshall fit in?' Rossi is staring at me with eyes that shine with something very close to admiration.

'She was Easton's one weak link. Now I'm no gambler, but I'll lay odds that Honey stumbled on the truth by mistake. When Easton realised she might blow the whole deal, he had to get rid of her.'

'Murder too, uh? That's bad.' Rossi stops counting money and hoists one fat hip on to the end of my desk. He jabs a finger at me. 'Just one more thing,' he says. 'What put you on to it? When you left my office this morning you had no more idea who was behind these raids than I had.'

'That's because all along I figured Honey's dying words had been "East . . . 37th", meaning the street. What she was trying to say was "Easton . . . 37th". The name of the cop and the police *precinct number*! You know, I'm real glad you have it in letters a foot high above your station entrance, Captain. "San Francisco Police Department", it says. "37th Precinct". Yes, sir, I'm real glad.'

Captain Rossi strikes a match on one of my size nines and tosses me a big fat cigar. 'I'm glad too, Bannon,' he says quietly.

'Great, remind me to send you the bill.' And just for kicks, I flash him a mirthless smile!

A Kind of Freedom

Angus Allan

LEX TARRANT CROSSED HIS LEGS, folded his arms, and curled his lip with studied insolence. The faded denim of his prison fatigues struck a grating discord in the governor's plush office, and the governor himself shifted uncomfortably as he exchanged a glance with the anonymous, grey-suited man from the State Department.

'Let's get this straight,' said Tarrant, with the confident air of one who had nothing left to lose. A vicious armed robber, with a double killing behind him, he was in the sixth year of a life sentence imposed by a United States Federal Court. 'You want *me* to go behind the Iron Curtain. You want *me* to rescue this – uh – Professor Denby from . . .' he snapped his fingers together . . . 'what did you call it . . .?'

'Czarnow,' said the man from the State Department. 'One of the tightest security fortresses in Europe. They kidnapped Denby, and that's where they've got him.'

Tarrant got up and impertinently helped himself to a glass of water from the carafe on the governor's desk. He chuckled, but there was no humour in the glittering eyes set deeply in his lean, raw-boned face. 'And all because I resemble the commandant. Gorshin? No, Gorsky. Major Gorsky.'

'Resemble him? You're his double, Tarrant. *And* you speak the language. What's more, you have a reputation for iron nerve, and if you agree to this mission, you're gonna need it.'

'Well, mister, I'll tell you,' said Tarrant. He was well aware of this grey man's need, and took a perverse pleasure in keeping him on tenterhooks. 'I'll do it. On one condition. A free pardon when I succeed.'

The prison governor snorted with impatience. 'Hang it, Tarrant, you know that's out of the question. There can be no reversing the decision of a Federal Court.'

'Then the deal's off.' Tarrant drained his glass and strode to the door.

'Wait.' The man from the State Department hadn't raised his voice, but there was authority there. 'My people can fix anything. You'll get your pardon. Not when you succeed, but *if* you succeed. You'd better realise you've got less than a fifty-fifty chance of pulling it off, Tarrant.'

'Spare me the lecture,' sneered the convict. 'I'll take those odds.'

Twenty minutes later, Lex Tarrant, clad in the civilian clothes he hadn't worn for six long years, left the jail in the back of a discreet black sedan, lounging on the leather upholstery alongside the man in grey . . .

The crash course had taken just five days. Tarrant had undergone intensive instruction in the layout of Czarnow Castle. He had absorbed every detail of Major Gorsky's character, his very mannerisms. He had learned the names of the commandant's aides, and how to recognise them. He had trained hard to hone a fine edge on his already superb standard of fitness. And he had, to his immense personal satisfaction, managed to fray the nerves of everybody he came across in the secret establishment deep in the Arizona desert.

Now, standing at the steps of a coach in the northbound express, due at any moment to pull out of Vienna's Central Station, he took his leave of the man in grey for the last time. He had refused to take the man's offered hand. Had flung the casual gesture of good luck back in his face. 'Mister,' said

Tarrant, 'you and your kind make me sick in the stomach, see? A bunch of mealy-mouthed schemers with fat bank balances and all the perks you can screw. Chee! And they call *me* a criminal!'

'Insult me as much as you like,' said the State Department representative. 'Just bring Denby out, okay?'

Vaguely irritated that his sneers had failed to ruffle his man, Tarrant boarded, and the long train, double-headed by a pair of powerful diesels, drew away on the long journey up through Europe.

Tarrant's clothes were genuinely made in the Eastern Bloc. His papers, expertly forged, declared him to be Zoltan Maraczek, civil engineer. His passport would have fooled the keenest-eyed investigator of the KGB itself. And so it was no surprise that he passed through frontier after frontier un-challenged and unquestioned. He was relaxed. At ease. His own mother had come from central Europe. He had never been here before – but curiously, it felt like home. For the first time, a thought entered his mind. One that made him laugh aloud, and drew enquiring glances from those who shared his compartment. But he gave them no hint that he was considering a glorious double cross. 'Suppose,' he said to himself, 'that I turned myself in to the authorities. Told them the whole plot. I could give them exact details of that place in Arizona. Blow the whistle on that smug, self-satisfied jerk in the grey suit and all his set-up. Yeah! There'd be no risk at all, and I'd be sitting pretty for the rest of my life, with a nice flat in Moscow and a neat holiday home somewhere on the Black Sea.'

Then, perversely, he put the idea behind him. He'd been given a challenge, and it'd be far, far sweeter to prove to those cool cats from the secret service that he, Lex Tarrant, had what it takes to spit in the eye of fate. Less than a fifty-fifty chance? He'd show 'em!

Tarrant left the train at Pozcen, a small town in a rural area not thirty kilometres from Czarnow Castle. With a rare obedience to orders, he buried his papers in a thick wood beyond the outskirts, and exchanged his sober suit for a close-fitting overall in a matt black material that had done duty, carefully folded and zipped, as an apparent toilet bag. A pair of leather gloves became a balaclava-type hood and a mask that covered his lower face. From his attaché case he selected and kept two objects that looked like fat, ball-point pens, and something that appeared to be a pocket calculator. Then he unscrewed the top of an after-shave bottle and poured its contents on the attaché case itself, with its legitimate cargo of engineering papers and plans. The chemical – for indeed that was what the bottle contained – reduced the lot to fizzling fragments within seconds.

Tarrant had done his homework well. He covered the thirty kilometres in five hours, and there were still thirty minutes before break of dawn as he sank to the ground on the edge of a copse and took his first look at his target.

Czarnow Castle had been originally built in the Middle Ages. Over the years it had been added to, adapted, embellished. It stood in the centre of a flat plain, once marshland, but long drained and refilled. It stood stark against a wan, moonlit sky, its turrets and battlements architecturally desecrated at intervals by squat, concrete watchtowers, raised on ugly lattices of steel. Tarrant knew that each tower contained heavy machine guns serviced by four-man teams. And dual arc-lights, pointing both inwards and outwards, were mounted there. The outer ones were not illuminated. Even in the Eastern Bloc, Tarrant had been told, energy conservation was a prime political factor. And besides – Czarnow was designed to keep its prisoners *in*. Even the most imaginative of administrators – and imagination was seldom the strongpoint of such people – would have scoffed at the idea of someone actually wanting to break *into* such a grim, ghastly place. Many were the legends concerning Czarnow; its torture chambers, its dungeons, the unspeakable cruelty that reigned there. The people of the country were said to use its dread name to frighten disobedient children, and some of the elders would even refuse to call it by name, averting their eyes whenever their work took them within sight of the place.

Lex Tarrant, his costume blending perfectly with the shadows, worked his way up the flank of a drainage ditch to within ten metres of the towering walls. He could actually hear the soft voices of the guards in the nearest tower. 'Stupid, pathetic fools.' He felt he wanted to speak the words aloud. There was no doubt in his mind that he, Lex, was infinitely superior to these goons. A wave of furious contempt for all authority welled up in him. These men in their steel helmets, these jacks-in-office were just the same as the mindless morons (as he considered them) who manned the watchtowers on the prison he had so recently left. With supreme confidence, he wormed his way across open ground to the foot of a towering escarpment and tugged out the pocket calculator. It would have solved many an equation, but that was not its prime function. At the pressing of a predetermined sequence of buttons, it shot an incredibly slender length of poly-synthetic cord upwards – a cord tipped with a tiny grapnel that hooked over the battlements. Tarrant tugged to make certain it was secure. Then – for the filament had breaking strain of more than two hundred pounds – he swarmed up it, his rubber soled shoes making no sound.

At the top, he sank into the shadows and pressed another sequence that retracted, silently, the line. To his left, the tower above the main gate. To his right, another. And below him, the open courtyard, bathed in the stark light of the inward-facing arcs.

A shadow among shadows, Tarrant crawled to where he had been told there would be a ventilator grille. He was not disappointed. One of the tools he had brought with him, one of those innocent-looking ball-point pens, was in fact an ultrasonic drill, which made short work of the mountings. Gently, he slid the grille aside, dropped within, and replaced it after him. His feet were braced against the sides of a vertical shaft now, and slowly, he inched his way downwards. The shaft, he knew, terminated in the office of Major Maran Gorsky, Czarnow's brutal commandant . . .

Maran Gorsky was nothing if not fastidious. He had returned to his office after a rather gruelling session in dungeon number ten. There, he had personally supervised the long session of interrogation of a so-called 'enemy of the State'. The fellow had broken and confessed. Eventually. But it had been – a tiresome event. He looked at himself petulantly in the mirror, poked out a pink tongue, licked his finger, and popped a wayward strand of hair back into place.

He sat down, leafing through a dossier that came to hand from a pile in his in-tray. Denby. Yes, that American scientist. He was proving more than a nuisance. All the well-tried techniques of brain-washing, all the threats and cajolement, all the cooping-up in pitch-dark cells for days on end, had failed. The man had spirit. Well, he, Gorsky, would break that spirit in the end. Perhaps multiple injections of Scopolamine . . .? Gorsky was not aware that he was speaking aloud.

An appalling clatter from behind him made him spring to his feet, with such alarm that he overturned his chair and caught his elbow sickeningly on the edge of the radio-link at his side. His jaw dropped and his eyes widened in amazed disbelief. A lithe figure had dropped to the carpet from the ventilator shaft high on the rear wall . . . and as the figure

73

ripped off the black mask, his foot stilling the diminishing metallic ringing of the fallen grille, Gorsky found himself looking – into his own eyes!

'You're a real cosy fellow,' said Lex Tarrant in Gorsky's own tongue. 'Scopolamine, eh? You'd inject a human being with that stuff?' For a brief instant, Tarrant remembered how he himself had callously shot down the two policemen who had interrupted the robbery that had been his last, but then the image was gone, for Gorsky, a strangled cry bubbling in his throat, had lunged for the alarm button set into the radio console. 'Oh no you don't!' Tarrant covered the distance between them in two paces, and his flat-held hand came round like a scythe, to take the commandant right beneath the jawline and send the man cartwheeling across his desk in a wild snowstorm of books and papers.

Tarrant didn't even bother to check whether his blow had killed Gorsky. He didn't care. With steel-nerved calm, he stripped the man from his uniform and put it on. Then, with almost astonishing lack of nerves, his victim bundled into a cupboard, he opened the door of the room. The door – padded and soundproofed – that led to the sanctum of Lieutenant Karnovicz, the Castle adjutant.

'Ah, Karnovicz,' said Tarrant, his accent faultless. 'Would you be so kind as to have Professor Denby brought up to me? I have some – ah – special questions to ask him. I would not like to be disturbed.'

Karnovicz grinned. 'At once, Commandant. Do you need anything – special?'

'No. Not at all,' said Tarrant. 'I've been thinking – I shall use the *old-fashioned* methods.'

Professor Denby, beyond middle-age, made even older by his experiences at the hands of his captors, was hauled from the dungeon where he had been kept. But neither his body nor his spirit had been broken, and he gave vent to a furious

A lithe figure had dropped to the carpet from the ventilator shaft high on the rear wall . . .

burst of defiance as Karnovicz and a couple of guards propelled him into the commandant's room.

Tarrant waited until the connecting door had been closed. He locked it. Then, reverting to the English language, he identified himself. And showed Denby the unconscious figure of Gorsky, crammed into the cupboard. Tarrant drew Denby's attention to the fact that the major was hardly as immaculate as he normally liked to be.

It took Denby more than ten minutes to grasp the situation. The shock to the man was more, even, than Tarrant had expected. Worse, when it finally got through to the scientist that he was within one ace of rescue, his emotions broke loose, and he actually fell prone on the carpet and hugged Tarrant's legs.

There could have been no greater impact. Tarrant, tough as he was, stared down in horror at Denby's tears. To hear about the frightful stresses of political interrogation had been one thing. To witness their effect was another.

'Look – we – we've got to get out of here.' Tarrant had time to recognise emotion in his own voice. Emotion that he had long thought impossible. This white-haired old man was treating him as if he were a god . . .

'Professor! You've *got* to calm down! I can't get you clear if you don't co-operate!' But Denby was beyond reason.

Tarrant took a deep breath. He actually closed his eyes as he bunched his fist and swung it, to catch the scientist on the side of the jaw . . .

The guards on the main gate of Czarnow Castle saluted, dutifully, as Major Gorsky drove his staff car past them. They were not paid to wonder why he had the American professor slumped beside him in the passenger seat. They were not paid, either, to wonder why Major Gorsky looked so white. They didn't know he was really an American convict, name of Lex Tarrant, who had staked his all – and won.

The road led eastwards. But only for a couple of kilometres. Then it turned north, and finally, west. His car, his uniform, gave Tarrant the passage of the frontiers, and his impeccable command of the language made escape almost absurdly easy.

Until the final stage.

He had not killed Gorsky, and Gorsky, released by an inquisitive and over-eager Karnovicz, had made the wires hum between Czarnow and the last divide of east and west! The guards at Pfornitzheim opened up on the approaching car without preamble, and machine-gun bullets fragmented the windscreen and struck sparks from the heavy plating of the bonnet!

Denby had recovered – to accept his own death?

'Hang on, professor! The frontier's only one kilometre away!' Tarrant spun the wheel and the vehicle careered from the highway to go bouncing and leaping over the ruts of a farmer's field. The powerful headlights picked up the strands of a first barrier, but the heavy car smashed through it as though it had been made of fusewire. Now mortar-bombs were bursting around them, and Tarrant guessed that in this, a no-man's-land, there would be mines . . .

He was wrong. This section was patrolled by armoured cars, and the hammering of heavy cannon, that churned the ground around them, took his eyes to the dark green leviathan that pounded down towards them. 'They've got us cold, professor! Can you drive . . .?'

Denby, his mouth dry, nodded. Briefly, Lex Tarrant stopped. He scrambled out of the car, and was aware that Denby had taken the wheel. Then Tarrant ran towards the armoured car, yelling in his mother's native tongue . . .

It was enough. Enough to throw the crew of the challenger into momentary indecision. Would an escaping imposter run towards them, like this . . .?

They recovered their wits, though. In time to put a burst of fire into the gesticulating figure before them, but *not* in time to prevent Denby crashing his way to liberty.

Tarrant sank to the earth. There was pain – intolerable pain – in his chest. He saw his own blood, staining Gorsky's jacket. He couldn't speak, but he could think. Mistily, his eyes registered the carved rubber of the armoured car's offside wheel, that came to a skidding halt not a metre from his head.

Before he died, he had a brief vision of a man in a grey suit, looking down at him. The man seemed to be saying: 'Well done, Tarrant. You made it for Denby. Whatever you did in the past, you've wiped your slate clean. You've won a kind of freedom . . .'

Tarrant's last words, unintelligible to the soldiers who climbed down to look at him, were typical. He said: 'Go to hell . . .'

Scarecrows Can't Move

J M H Lloyd-Williams

'DON'T BE DAFT, scarecrows can't move!'

James Carter was eleven years old . . . and he knew a thing or two about life! His younger sister, Jennifer, was not so sure.

'Wurzel Gummidge can move . . . I've seen him on television!' She thought for a second. 'Maybe this scarecrow can move as well!'

They looked at the battered figure in front of them. As scarecrows go, it was not really a very good one. It did not even have a face, just an old sack filled with straw. A weather-beaten hat was perched on top of the sack. A faded blue blazer, which one day must have been someone's pride and joy, was draped around the scarecrow's body. More straw gaped out of the front of the blazer and out of the sleeves.

Two thick pieces of wood were its 'legs'. They were rammed into the earth quite firmly. James tugged at one of them.

'If this old thing does move, it would have to be really strong to get its legs out of the ground!' The thick clay soil in the ploughed field was heavy after recent rain.

Jennifer sighed. Sometimes boys didn't know what they were talking about. 'Facts are facts,' she said. 'We play in this field regularly and three times in the past week we've found the scarecrow in a different position. Facing a different way!'

'It must be the farmer who moves it – so the birds don't get used to it being in one position!' James was already trotting away. It was tea time and mysteries could wait. Food was more important when you were hungry!

They went back to the field the following day. The scarecrow had not moved. James grinned. 'It's realised we know it can move . . . and now it's frightened! It'll probably never move again,' he said, kicking a lump of earth in his sister's direction.

'Don't you be so certain. I'm sure we haven't seen or heard the last of this!' And Jennifer was right!

James and Jennifer were watching the midday television news, two days later, when they saw something which would plunge them into an incredible adventure – and deadly danger! Suddenly, on the screen, they glimpsed a view of the field where they spent so much of their time. There was the familiar brown earth. The trees. The hedgerows. And the scarecrow! But the camera only dwelt on the scarecrow for a few seconds, for when it panned down to the ground, the reason for all the interest was apparent. A man's body lay there. Still and lifeless!

A television reporter was speaking. 'The mystery man's corpse was found here, alongside the scarecrow. He had been shot once, through the heart. The reason for the killing is puzzling local residents. Robbery was not the motive, for he had over one hundred pounds in his wallet. There's no sign of the murder weapon.'

The two children looked at each other, wide-eyed. 'I . . . I knew there was a mystery surrounding that scarecrow,' said Jennifer.

They didn't say another word. Together, they dashed out of the house, into the street and headed for open country.

Five minutes later, they were in the familiar ploughed field. The scarecrow still stood there, but the area alongside it was surrounded by white tape, indicating where the body had been found.

Jennifer shuddered. 'Ugh! It's horrible to think a dead man was lying there!'

'He's gone now,' said James. 'Don't be so childish.'

They cautiously moved forward, not quite knowing what to expect. Then Jennifer saw something!

'Look! The scarecrow's moved again!'

Sure enough, the scarecrow was now re-positioned a few metres from where it had been the last time they saw it and it was now facing a different direction.

For a few moments, they stood and looked at the scarecrow, their minds racing.

'Scarecrows can't move!' James said eventually. 'It doesn't make sense.'

They were just about to investigate further when suddenly a hand clamped tight on each of their shoulders! Jennifer screamed. Could this be the murderer? Were they going to be the next victims?

It was with the utmost relief that they looked round and saw the familiar, blue uniform of a policeman. ''ello, 'ello, 'ello! What's all this then?'

The children explained why they had come to the field, but they didn't mention the moving scarecrow.

'You're lucky,' the policeman said sternly. 'We have finished searching the field for clues. You would have been in trouble if you had disturbed anything before we had finished our checks!'

'Is it all right if we stay around here for a while?' asked James.

'Sure it is,' said the policeman walking away. 'Just don't get up to any mischief.'

When they were alone, James and Jennifer discussed the situation. They were convinced the moving scarecrow was closely linked with the murder. 'But what do we do?'

James thought for a moment. 'What we do is keep watch.

When the scarecrow moves again, we will be here to see it move! Luckily it's the school holidays, so we have plenty of spare time. I'll stay here all day and you can keep me supplied with food and drink.'

Jennifer snorted. 'Greedy guts!' she said.

Sticking to their plan, the two children kept watch from the cover of nearby bushes. It was a long, boring watch, with hardly anything happening. The only movement they saw was the occasional rabbit or field mouse.

On the third day, when they were thoroughly bored, James decided that they would need one further supply of food to last them until dusk. Jennifer raced away, little realising that the next time she saw her brother would be under very different circumstances!

James sat in the summer sunshine, listening to the birds singing. Everything seemed very peaceful. But suddenly he heard the sound of a car engine and was soon aware of someone walking along on the edge of the field. The man was dressed in a shabby raincoat, with a trilby hat pulled down over his eyes. James had never seen such a suspicious character!

Hardly daring to breathe, James crouched down in the undergrowth as the man came nearer. The young boy almost gasped aloud as he saw the stranger walk right up to the scarecrow and put his hand into one of the pockets of the old blazer. He pulled something from the pocket and gave a grunt of satisfaction.

Then he moved the scarecrow back to its original position! This done, the man started back across the field to where he had left his car. James knew he had to act fast and as quietly as he could, he raced along a dip on the other side of the hedge which separated him from the man.

He had to get to the car before the man did!

He made it just in time and threw himself in front of the

back seat and desperately tried to keep as small as possible.

The man came back into the car, started the engine and they were soon speeding through the countryside. They travelled at high speed for several minutes and then the vehicle pulled into the yard of a farmhouse. The man got out, and as he walked away from the car, James raised his head and peered through the window. He saw the man enter an old barn and close the door behind him.

Furtively, James crept out of the car and tip-toed towards the barn. From inside, he heard the sound of voices.

'So you got the microfilm?'

'Sure I did . . . it was in the usual place. There were no problems at all. The law was nowhere to be seen.'

With a sharp intake of breath, James realised he had discovered the secret of the moving scarecrow. It was being used to hide microfilm! When there was something to collect, the scarecrow was moved as a signal!

In his eagerness to hear every word that was said, James leant against the door of the barn. Unfortunately, the ancient lock chose that moment to give way and the door swung open, causing the boy to stumble inside.

The two men, who had been talking, looked up. One was the man James had followed. The other one was thick set, with close-cropped, ginger hair and a small beard. It was the bearded man who recovered first. 'We're being spied on! Grab him!'

They plunged towards James, but he was too fast for them. He ducked under their outstretched arms, raced across the floor of the barn and climbed a ladder which led to a hay-loft. No Olympic sprinter could have moved as fast!

Once at the top of the ladder, he looked around anxiously, trying to find a hiding place or way of escape. There were some old packing cases on one side of the loft and the rest of the floor was covered by heaps of straw.

He heard the sound of his pursuers climbing the ladder below him! James dashed across the loft, picked up one of the packing cases and hurled it through the gap in the floor on to the ladder. He heard one of the men cry out as he was hit by the case, causing him to lose his balance and fall on to his companion. Both men crashed to the ground and for a moment there was silence.

James knew this was his chance to escape. He climbed on to two of the remaining packing cases and stood on top of them. He was now right under the roof of the barn and he pushed frantically against the old tiles in a desperate attempt to break through. For a few vital seconds, it seemed as if the tiles would not give way. Then, as he heard the men starting to climb the ladder again, his hands burst through into the fresh air. It took only another few seconds to pull his body through the hole he had made and climb on to the roof.

Cautiously, he made his way round the edge of the roof, trying to find a place where he could climb down. But more danger threatened!

Some of the old tiles on the edge of the roof gave way beneath his weight and he crashed over the edge, his fingers clutching at the remaining tiles as he fought for a grip. Just in time, he managed to grab hold of a piece of guttering and he found himself hanging precariously above the long drop to the ground below.

The ginger-haired man poked his head through the hole in the roof and spotted James.

'There he is . . . we've got him!'

James, however, was not so sure! He started to move along the guttering. He looked below, trying to find a place where he could climb down, or a place where he could make a soft landing. As he reached the edge of the building, he saw the ideal thing. Bales of hay were stacked against the side of the barn.

The man was on the roof, climbing towards James. It was now or never!

85

The man was on the roof, climbing towards James. It was now or never! The boy swung his legs and propelled himself in the direction of the bales of hay. His body plunged towards the earth for what seemed an eternity. Then, with a thud, he landed on the hay. For a moment, the breath was knocked from his body, but he knew there was little time to lose, as the second man would, by this time, be coming down the ladder, ready to chase after him again.

James jumped down from the hay and raced across the yard. He glanced behind him. There was no sign of his pursuers. He reached the gate that led out of the farmyard and into the road, swung it open and for a wonderful moment he thought he was free. But his hopes were dashed!

He ran straight into the imposing figure of a man, who was about to come through the gate himself. The newcomer was a huge man, bald and fat. Sweat was pouring down his forehead, which he was in the act of mopping, with a large, white handkerchief, when James crashed into him.

The man may have been fat, but he was strong. A vice-like grip clamped round James' neck and he knew there was no escape, although he made a few kicks at the man's shins, just for good measure.

James was carried by the scruff of the neck back towards the barn, his feet clear of the ground. The other two men were waiting.

'Look what I've found,' said the fat man, throwing James to the ground in front of the others.

'That interfering kid has been spying on us,' said one of them. 'What shall we do with him?'

The fat man thought for a moment.

'If he presents any danger to our organisation, he must be eliminated, just as that detective was! Dispose of him immediately! Take him outside into the nearest field and do what you have to do!'

The bearded man grabbed James and hauled him off the ground.

'Come with me, you brat. You will do no more snooping!'

James was dragged out into the open, across the farmyard, through a gate and into a field. His captor carried a menacing revolver in one hand, which he kept pressed against the boy's head.

A thousand thoughts flashed through James' mind. The man was going to shoot him! He didn't want to die. He would never see his parents or sister again. His school-friends. His whole world was going to vanish when the man pulled the trigger. He wished he had never seen that the scarecrow had moved!

By this time, they were in the middle of the field. The man pushed James hard in the back, so he staggered a few metres away from him. Then he raised his gun and aimed it straight at the boy. This really seemed to be the end.

Suddenly, there was an enormous bellow. James and the man looked towards the direction from which the terrifying sound had come. Standing looking at them from the other side of the field was the most enormous bull, snorting and pawing at the ground! It was about to charge! For a split second, the man hesitated. Then, when the bull started to charge, he forgot all about James and started a mad dash for safety. James realised he had to do the same thing himself and within a few moments, he and the man were running side by side towards the safety of a fence, which surrounded the field. But the animal was gaining on them!

All at once, just as he reached the fence, the man pitched forward, tripping over a mound of earth. James kept running, now oblivious to everything except the need to get to the safety of the fence.

Suddenly, there was a piercing scream. James looked back. The man was flying through the air after being tossed by the bull. He cleared the fence and crashed down in the neighbouring field with a tremendous splash! James vaulted over the wooden gate in the fence, almost as if it wasn't there. He was safe! As he moved forward, he saw the gunman staggering out of an evil smelling duck pond! The man seemed barely conscious, but he still had hold of the gun in his hand. The boy was about to race away, when the villain was suddenly aware of him. Shaking slightly, the man raised the gun and pointed it at James.

'You . . . you're not going to get away, kid. I'll still do what I've set out to do!'

James braced himself for the shot, but it never came. For just as the man was about to squeeze the trigger, he collapsed, unconscious at the edge of the pond.

For the first time for quite a while, James could stop and get his breath. Could all these amazing things have been happening to him? It all seemed like a nightmare.

'James, are you all right?'

It was his sister! Jennifer was running up to him, her face anxious.

'I saw what that man was going to do, so I let out the bull into the field. It was all I could think of,' she said.

James was not the type to show much affection, but for once he put his arms round his sister and hugged her.

'You saved my life,' he said.

'Think nothing of it,' Jennifer replied, as they both became aware of a rumbling noise. Jennifer gave a little scream. 'Don't say the bull's broken loose!'

James grinned. 'That wasn't the bull, it was my stomach. I'm starving!'

But there was no time to eat! Anxiously, they made their way back to the farm, using all the cover they could find. The fat man and his companion were standing talking in the farmyard.

'Something must have gone wrong,' said the fat man. 'There hasn't been the sound of a shot. You'd better go and see what's happened.'

The other man drew a revolver. 'Don't worry, boss, I'll deal with that interfering kid once and for all!'

The man strode across the farmyard and walked towards the field. But he stopped suddenly when he saw the bull waiting for him on the other side of the fence. He quickly decided there was no way he was going to go that way! As he turned, he was amazed to see James sitting on the grass in front of him.

'Hello!' said James.

'You stupid kid!' sneered the villain, aiming his gun at the boy. 'I don't know what game you think you are playing, but it's a deadly one!'

Once again, it seemed that James was doomed. There was a sudden sound above the gunman's head and he looked up, startled, his hat falling off. A moment later, he wished he hadn't looked up. A wasp's nest descended on to him, crashed on his head and broke open. The angry insects buzzed viciously around his face and he screamed in terror. Above, in the safety of the tree, Jennifer looked pleased with herself.

'Our ambush worked a treat!'

Dropping his gun, the man could think of only one thing – getting rid of the buzzing, swarming pests. Somehow, he had to get away from them. He raced away down a path, but tripped over an old tree root and crashed against the tree, knocking himself out.

Jennifer climbed down.

'And now there's only one,' she grinned. 'Let's go and deal with him.'

They crept back towards the barn. The fat man was sitting inside, checking pieces of microfilm that had been removed from the scarecrow. He gave a grunt of satisfaction. 'This stuff is worth a fortune!' he said to himself.

Jennifer and James decided to make new plans. They were almost enjoying their battle against the crooks. Five minutes went by and then the door of the barn burst open and James ran inside. The fat man looked up, startled. James sped up the steps of the ladder and the fat man followed, breathlessly. Once in the loft, the boy ran round the back of the packing cases with the man close behind him. Then he ran down the ladder again and jumped the last few steps to the ground. A plank of wood was lodged against a window and he scurried along it and jumped out of the open window. Unarmed, the fat man had no choice but to follow, the plank bending precariously under his weight. With a great deal of difficulty, he jumped. Too late, he realised it was a trap!

Beneath the window, was a large barrel of water. He splashed into it, water cascading everywhere as his huge frame rammed into the barrel. For a while, he struggled desperately to free himself, but slowly the truth dawned on him. He was stuck!

Cursing and spluttering, he became aware of the two children watching him, happy smiles on their faces.

'He doesn't look so dangerous now,' said Jennifer. 'He looks more like a circus clown! Let's go and get the police.'

'One thing you never told me,' said James, 'How did you manage to find me?'

'Easy,' said Jennifer. 'I followed the fat man. He went to check the scarecrow and came straight here afterwards.'

Twenty minutes later, James and Jennifer were guiding a protesting policeman to the scene.

'Microfilm? Men with guns? I don't believe it!'

The local policeman had heard children's stories before and was very sceptical, but when he saw the wet, defeated figure trapped in the water barrel, he knew there was at least some truth in their story.

'There are two other crooks unconscious nearby,' said James, pointing towards the field. 'I hope you've got enough handcuffs!'

A week went by. The criminals had been taken away and dealt with. James and Jennifer and their parents received an invitation to visit the local police station. When they got there, they met two smart, plain-clothes detectives, who announced they were from MI5.

'You children certainly put paid to that spy network,' said one of them. 'An employee at a nearby, top-secret research establishment had been stealing microfilm and placing it on the scarecrow, awaiting collection by his accomplices.'

James beamed with delight. 'I guess that makes us heroes,' he said.

Jennifer frowned. 'You might be a hero, but I'm a heroine!'

'I wish I could say that you were,' said the policeman, 'but unfortunately, you children ruined everything. We knew all about the spy network and were deliberately feeding them with false information so that the foreign power they work for would not know how far our experimental work had developed. If only you had kept away from that scarecrow, we could have carried on with our plans!'

'B-but the man who was killed . . .' stammered Jennifer. 'You can't let them go around killing people!'

'The man who died was one of our men,' said the policeman. 'Those rats would have paid for their crime eventually!'

The other policeman interrupted. 'Don't be too hard on them! These children have been in terrible danger. They had tremendous initiative to overcome those thugs. Their whole adventure could have had a tragic ending.'

James and Jennifer walked away from the police station and headed for home, with their parents. On the way, they walked past the familiar field with the scarecrow standing silhouetted against the sky-line. Jennifer looked at it and gasped.

'The scarecrow . . . it's moved!'

'Don't be daft,' said James. 'Scarecrows can't move.'

The Vegas Caper

M S Goodall

ZACK PETERS HAD DECIDED that he didn't really like Las Vegas. He didn't like the endless neon lights which tumbled in a mad confusion of colours towards the edge of the Nevada desert, and he disliked the fact that the city never slept. It made the whole set-up into a mad, crazy kind of dream. A man-made boom town in the middle of nowhere.

But Zack had to eat, and as a footloose teenager at present on a motor-cycling tour across America, he certainly wasn't going to turn down the offer of a week's work at one of the leading show-palaces in town. For the next seven days, he was to be assistant and general dogsbody to the 'Amazing Mr Grace', entertainer and magician extraordinary who was starring at the 'Blue Parrot', a casino-cum-cabaret joint in the heart of Vegas.

'Crazy name,' thought Zack as he turned away from the window of his boss's rented apartment. 'I've never seen a grey parrot, let alone a blue one.' Draining a bottle of coke, he glanced at his watch. It was eleven o'clock in the morning, which left him with plenty of time to get Mr Grace's props and equipment ready for the grand opening that night.

At eleven-fifteen there was a knock on the front door. Zack opened it and saw a cheeky-faced delivery boy standing on the porch. 'Express package for the Amazing Mr Grace,' said the lad cheerfully. 'Sign here, please.'

Even as Zack scribbled his name, the famous magician came out of an adjoining room and walked into the hall. Mr

Grace was a tall, well-groomed man in his mid-forties. With his smooth black hair, piercing eyes and long, sensitive fingers, he looked every inch the compelling man of mystery.

'Open that for me, Zack, will you?' he said. 'I need a cup of coffee.'

'Right.' Swiftly, Zack cut the string and unwrapped the paper. Inside was a cardboard box containing a small, cuddly toy bird. Its blue, furry head nodded gently up and down, the pointed beak almost tapping its fat, squat little feet. As Zack lifted it out, he saw a white card tucked into one of the toy's feet. 'To The Amazing Mr Grace,' he read aloud. 'Welcome to Las Vegas. Please accept this as a lucky mascot for your week's engagement. The Manager, "Blue Parrot" nightclub.'

Zack shook his head in wonder. 'These publicity guys think of everything, don't they? It's one of these ornaments for the back window ledge of a car. They used to make nodding dogs, now they make nodding parrots! Have a look, boss.'

Zack held the toy up and Mr Grace suddenly went glassy-eyed. 'Atchooo!' He reeled back against a table, nose twitching violently. 'AAAA-TISHOOO!' The magician sneezed again and groped feebly for a large white handkerchief.

'What's up?' asked Zack in amazement.

'D-Don't come any closer with that – atchoo – thing! The sight of anything furry always – aaachooo – brings on my hay-fever.'

Hurriedly, Zack retreated. 'I'd no idea, Mr Grace. What shall I do with it? Throw it away?'

The magician blew his nose hard and dabbed at his streaming eyes. 'No, that might upset the management,' he said hoarsely. 'At a distance of ten paces I'm okay, so stick it on the mantelpiece in the lounge. I'll remember to keep my distance and avoid any future sneezing fits.'

94

Zack did as he was told. The lounge was a large room running the whole length of the house. After placing the toy parrot on the mantelpiece, he turned to find the Amazing Mr Grace seated by a table at the far end of the room, deeply engrossed in rehearsing some card tricks for the evening's performance. 'I'll leave you to it, boss,' said Zack quietly. 'I want to clean your car before I start getting the rest of your props together.'

'Fine,' said the magician. 'See you later.'

Zack withdrew to the car outside which was parked by the kerb, and got busy with hose and sponge. Inside, Mr Grace whistled softly to himself as he concentrated on his sleight of hand. He was lost in a world of his own. The world of the master magician.

Then, quite suddenly, it happened. As if motivated by the touch of an unseen hand, the parrot's head swivelled to the right. Whirr . . . click! The beady glass eyes blinked in unison then focused once again on Mr Grace's distant face. Whirr . . . click! Whirr . . . click! Time and again those beady eyes opened and shut. And not once did they waver from the magician's features. As Mr Grace worked, that nodding head followed his every move and watched every change of expression on his dark, handsome face.

Meanwhile, high on a desert track overlooking the apartment block, two men sat in a parked car and glanced quickly at each other. One held a pair of binoculars in his hands, while the other toyed nervously with a square black box from which an aerial protruded. The man with the binoculars was tall, slim and dark, about Mr Grace's age. The other was in his fifties, bearded, and with a swarthy complexion. Both were grim-faced men, with eyes as cold as a winter's dawn. Stonily they watched as Mr Grace finished his work-out, put his cards away, rose, stretched himself, and then strolled into an adjoining bathroom to have a shower.

'Okay, he's gone.' The younger man's voice was taut with excitement as he peered through his binoculars. 'You can bring it back now.'

Swiftly, the man with the black box pressed a button. There was a faint humming noise, and on the mantelpiece in Mr Grace's lounge, the toy parrot stretched its fabric wings and began to stir! Next moment a hidden rocket motor in the parrot's back burst into life with the faint hiss of exhaust gases. Slowly, steadily, the bird rose off the wooden surround, banked gently on its outstretched wings and flew sedately out of a half-open window.

Outside, Zack Peters had finished hosing the car down and was about to switch the water off. In the sudden silence he heard what sounded like the droning flight of a bumble bee, and looked up. His eyes popped and his jaw dropped. The furry blue parrot was gaining height and purring smoothly over a wall towards open country beyond.

Zack blinked hard and looked again. He definitely wasn't seeing things. The toy bird was airborne under power and heading for the desert. Just for a second, he hesitated. If he dashed indoors to get the Amazing Mr Grace, the parrot would have vanished before they got outside again. Besides . . . a flying woollen toy? Who would believe him?

'I don't know what the heck is going on,' thought Zack grimly, 'but I smell trouble. I'm going to straddle my speed-iron and keep that parrot in sight.'

It took Zack less than fifteen seconds to grab his visored crash helmet and kick his motor-cycle into life. The bike was a big Harley Davidson, sleek, fast, and tuned to perfection. Body held low against the sudden surge of power, Zack skidded round a corner, roared over a patch of waste ground and turned right on to a rutted desert track.

It was just then, that he saw the two men in the parked car, less than three hundred metres away at the top of the hill. The parrot was whirring in through the driver's window, being deftly caught by the cold-eyed man with the beard. As the car moved off, Zack hit full throttle and roared in pursuit. The younger man in the passenger seat glanced back and yelled in surprise: 'We've been spotted! Somebody's chasin' us.'

'We're in too deep for this thing to blow up in our faces now, Lacey.' The driver's voice was little more than a snarl. 'You know what to do, so get on with it.'

Sweating, the man called Lacey fumbled in the back seat. A kilometre further on, the car skidded to a halt round a sharp bend, and as Zack swept round after it, he saw the danger just a second too late. Lacey was out of the car, kneeling on the sand, a high-powered rifle held rigidly against his shoulder. Even as Zack tried to jink left, he felt a colossal impact on his temple. It was like running into a brick wall. There was an explosion of lights, sudden, violent pain . . . then blackness. Out of control, Zack plummeted over some rocks, nose-dived into a ravine and lay still.

On the desert ridge above, the two men looked down in relief. 'Nice shot, Lacey. He's a goner.'

'Yeah, so let's get outta here. Time's running short and we still have a lot to do.'

Darkness fell, and in the lonely ravine, Zack Peters stirred at last. He'd been lucky – perhaps even luckier than he'd ever been before. The single bullet had caught him a glancing blow, and the heavy crash helmet had absorbed most of the impact. With his head clearing, Zack sat up and checked his Harley. The petrol tank was badly dented and his front wheel slightly buckled, but at least the bike could be ridden. Perhaps it was too late now, but he had to try and locate those men in the car. Solve the mystery of the flying blue parrot once and for all.

Out of control, Zack plummeted over some rocks and nose-dived into a ravine.

Scrambling back up the slope, Zack swung into his saddle and moved on up the track. He kept his engine revs low and began to follow the deep tyre marks in the sand. Half an hour later, the trail led to a lonely ranch-house deep in the desert. Of the car, there was no sign, and the house itself wore a black, deserted look.

But it had been used recently, of that there was no doubt. Finding an open window, Zack let himself into a darkened lounge. Pinned to one wall of the lounge were photographs of the Amazing Mr Grace. Dozens of them. Profiles, quarter-face, half-face, full-face. Each one revealing the magician's features in stark, perfect detail.

'So that nodding blue parrot was a remote-control *camera*,' thought Zack grimly. 'The men must have developed the film and made these prints while I was out cold in the ravine. But why go to all that trouble to take secret photographs of Mr Grace? What's behind it all? And where have those two hoods gone to now?'

Puzzled and worried, Zack roared off back to Mr Grace's apartment. The magician wasn't there. Glancing at his watch, Zack realised that the entertainer would have already left for his first performance at the 'Blue Parrot'. If the answer to the mystery was to be found anywhere, it was to be found there. Hurrying outside, Zack rode through the centre of Las Vegas and parked his smoking machine at the rear of the nightclub.

Everything seemed to be in order when Zack walked inside. The Amazing Mr Grace was standing in the wings, waiting to go on. He was wearing full evening dress with a long black cape swirling from his shoulders. His hair was slicked back as usual, but his eyes seemed strangely restive, cold and nervous. 'Sorry I'm late, boss,' said Zack softly, 'Are you okay?'

'Yes, of course I'm okay. Just first-night nerves, that's all.

I'll be fine once I'm on stage.'

The manager of the 'Blue Parrot' suddenly appeared – a tall, drawling man in a white tuxedo and stetson hat. 'Great tuh meet yuh, pal,' he boomed, flashing two gold teeth and pumping Mr Grace's hand like a slot-machine handle. 'Ah heah yo' the tops when it comes tuh the trade of the tricks. An' tonight, boy, yo'll plumb *hafta* be good.'

'What's so special about tonight?' asked Mr Grace nervously.

'The joint is packed as usual,' said the manager, rubbing his hands. 'But we got a whole lotta VIPs in as well. An' top dog among 'em is Mr Hiram P. Mulloy. *The* Hiram P. Mulloy. Guess yuh've heard of him, uh?'

'Sure,' said the magician casually. 'He's a big wheel in the FBI, isn't he?'

'The *biggest* wheel in the FBI,' said the manager greasily. 'He's on vacation right heah in Vegas, so be a smash tonight, boy. His kinda custom we sure can use again.'

'I shall perform as I always do,' said Mr Grace suavely. 'With a touch of pure magic.'

To a roll of drums, the magician took his opening bow. The stage was an unusual one. Not raised, but sunken; flanked and backed by velvet curtains and facing a series of terraced steps on which were placed rows of tables. As the manager had said, the club was packed.

Mr Grace's act went well. He had half an hour on stage alone, before the grand finale when he would invite a female member of the audience to take part in a spectacular levitation illusion. Zack watched from the wings, eyes scanning the audience, every sense ready and waiting for an unknown danger that so far had failed to materialise. Then he gasped. Out on the stage, the Amazing Mr Grace was bowing low to applause from the audience. He had just finished drawing a live white rabbit out of a top hat, and stood with the animal clutched to his chest, idly stroking the creature's soft fur.

Zack felt his muscles tense. 'Is it possible?' he breathed. 'Is it really possible?' Then it all came back, every single incident, and he knew that it was. The drums rolled again, and it was time for the grand finale. A long trestle table was placed on the stage, and leading a young woman from the audience, Mr Grace made her lie down face upwards, then covered her with a white sheet. A long, gleaming magic wand flashed into his hand as he turned to face the eager spectators.

'Ladies and gentlemen,' said Mr Grace steadily. 'I must now ask for complete silence. I intend to raise this young lady – *levitate* her – off the table and into the air. I shall do this by willpower alone, by a feat of mind over matter. Gravity, ladies and gentlemen, will be defied before your very eyes.'

No one said a word. No one even coughed. This illusion was one of Mr Grace's best, and he knew how to grip an audience. But this time, Zack knew, it would be different. He had no idea exactly what was going to happen, but he had to be ready at all costs.

The lights dimmed, and suddenly the stage was lit only by a glimmering pink glow from the footlights. Almost imperiously, the Amazing Mr Grace raised his magic wand and moved it slowly – horizontally – through the air, its gleaming black tip pointed at a table near the back of the club.

That was when Zack Peters made his move. The end of the cane was hollow. It wasn't a magic wand but a cunningly-constructed weapon. A gun with a silencer screwed to the end of the barrel. Zack was on the stage in two bounds. Even as the Amazing Mr Grace moved sideways, Zack closed with him. His right hand became a fist which swept up and down – straight into the middle of the magician's face. Mr Grace yelled just once, then crashed backwards on to the floor, wand skidding away towards the wings. Zack knelt, his hands groping at the base of Mr Grace's neck. Even as the lights came on and the audience went mad, he knew he'd been right.

'Just as I thought,' he said aloud. '*A mask!*' He pulled hard, and instantly, eerily, Mr Grace's face began to crumble. Another tug and a wad of pliable plastic slipped to the floor . . . revealing the flushed, angry features of the man called Lacey!

'Very neat,' said Zack grimly. 'But now it's time you answered a few questions, my friend. Who are you? What have you done with the *real* Mr Grace . . . and what's behind this little charade?'

Lacey's mouth was slack, his eyes glazed. He was beaten and he knew it. 'My name is Luke Lacey. I was an out of work magician and actor in New York until a guy called Carelli hired me for this impersonation job. He's a big noise in the East Coast crime syndicate, an' he wanted Hiram Mulloy outta the way. Dead. With the FBI chief off their backs, the hoods could have relaxed for a spell. Mulloy was sitting in the third row. Carelli figured that—'

'Sure, I can guess what he figured,' said Zack angrily. 'With you in disguise and firing from a darkened stage, no one would have known *where* the shot came from.'

'The toy parrot came from Carelli too,' Lacey went on. 'After I got the pictures of Mr Grace, the rest was easy. I built the new face this afternoon, then clobbered the poor sucker in his apartment before he left for the show.'

'Okay, pal, just one more thing.' Zack's voice rose sharply. 'Where are Carelli and Mr Grace now? I want the answer and I want it fast.'

With Lacey safely deposited in the arms of the FBI chief, Zack rammed on his crash helmet and rode like a maniac through the Las Vegas traffic towards Lexington and Maine. He spotted the house almost immediately and swept smoothly into action. Carelli was sitting in the dimly-lit lounge when Zack burst crazily through the door. On the other side of the room lay the Amazing Mr Grace, bound and gagged.

Carelli moved fast for the gun which lay on the coffee table beside him, but Zack Peters moved even faster. Swinging a gloved fist, he connected just below his opponent's left ear and sent him flying soundlessly to the carpet.

Smiling slightly, Zack bent down beside the glassy-eyed Mr Grace. 'All right?' he asked, as he untied the magician's bonds.

'More than a little bewildered,' said Mr Grace. 'First I saw a character who could have been my twin brother, then he hit me – hard. Would you mind telling me what's going on, Zack? How you found me?'

Zack smiled again. 'It's a long story, Mr Grace, but somebody tried to take your place tonight. The only thing wrong with his impersonation was when he drew a white rabbit out of a hat and stood there *stroking* it. The guy didn't even sneeze. In fact he didn't even show signs of a hay-feverish nose-twitch. And after a certain episode with a toy parrot this morning, that didn't make sense at all. If you get my drift.'

'Would you please,' said Mr Grace weakly . . . 'clarify all that?'

'All in good time, boss,' said Zack cheerfully. 'I'll tell you more on the way back to the nightclub. Among other things, you have a levitation act to finish. The first one went slightly wrong, and you wouldn't want to harm your reputation, would you? Anyway, as you guys have a habit of saying . . . *the show must go on!*'

The Amazing Mr Grace allowed himself to be led to the door without saying a word. Under the circumstances, there was nothing he could say!

Tonight, the Wire

Alan A Grant

JANUARY, 1981. The squat black shape of a State Security car sat amid the thick snow that carpeted the small backstreet in Sopron, Hungary.

Inside, two bored-looking plainclothes security officers waited, one idly popping mints into his mouth, the other buried in the pages of an official magazine. Occasionally, they would look across at the lighted third-floor window of the tenement building opposite.

'Our Doctor Mazny is spending a long time with his mother today,' one remarked.

'That one always has plenty to say,' the other replied, not looking up from his magazine. As far as the two men were concerned, their surveillance of Doctor Mazny and his family was just routine. It had been going on for the last three years, and would continue until the good doctor said enough to get himself arrested. To them, today was just like any other.

Across the road in the third-floor apartment, Doctor Josef Mazny parted the curtains and stared out at the parked car. State Security had dogged his every move since his name had first been linked with the anti-government dissident movement.

'It will be good to see the last of those two – and others like them,' he said with feeling. 'In our new life we shall be free to say what we want, to do what we want, without fear of arrest and torture by people like that.'

Turning to his two sons, he asked them: 'Are you ready? Remember, when we leave this house there will be no turning back.'

Anton – at fourteen, three years older than his brother Jan – coughed nervously. 'We are ready, Father.'

Grandmother Mazny came in from the apartment's spartan kitchen, with a large cardboard box in her gnarled hands. 'I finished these last night,' she said. 'They fit like gloves, don't you worry.'

She pulled three gleaming white snow-suits from the box, their fabric stiff with the padding the old woman had torn from her own mattress. 'They will keep you warm,' she went on. 'It is bitter cold in the forest now.'

Doctor Mazny took the suits and crammed them into a kitbag. 'You will not change your mind, Mother? There is still time for you to come with us.'

'Hah!' the old woman laughed. 'I am eighty-four years old, Josef! How would I get across the wire?'

Josef Mazny's face was serious. 'When we have gone, the State Security Police will make trouble for you.'

'Pah!' his mother cackled. 'What can they do to an old woman? Nothing! No, I do not fear them, Josef – I fear only for your future, and that of my grandsons if they remain in this country. Look at what happened to your dear wife—'

Mazny's wife Hana had died three months earlier – a heart attack. Mazny knew it had been brought on by the strain of continuous intensive surveillance. Now, without her, there was no longer any reason to stay in Hungary. He loved his homeland deeply, and had he no other responsibilities he would have remained to carry on his campaign against the cruel regime that stifled the nation. But he had two sons, and they deserved a proper future.

So the decision had been taken. This night, Joseph Mazny and his sons would cross the wire into Austria – and freedom!

The old woman fought back her tears as she said: 'Come – kiss me one last time.' The two children hugged their grandmother in a tearful farewell.

Mazny himself was already heaving the kitbag on his back. 'It is time, my sons,' he announced. He clasped his mother to him. 'You have Jorge Honig's address in Vienna? Write to us there. Perhaps one day we will be able to get you out, too.'

'Yes, yes, I will keep hoping, Josef,' the old lady said. But in her heart of hearts she knew they would never meet again.

It was not until the door had closed behind them that she allowed her tears to flow . . .

Josef Mazny led his sons quickly down the stairs to the ground floor, out of the tenement's rear door into the courtyard, then out through the building opposite.

The car was waiting, the keys in the ignition. It belonged to a friend whose name had not yet been linked to the dissident movement. He would not report it 'missing' until the next day; by then, the Maznys would be safe.

To the doctor's relief, the engine fired first time. A minute later he was heading for the backstreets which would take them on to the main Sopron–Vienna road. He glanced at his sons in the back seat; they were struggling not to show it, but their hearts were heavy with grief.

'Come, cheer up – we will see Granny again,' he lied. 'Jan, why don't you sing us that song you learned in school?'

The frail blond child cleared his throat and began to sing, faltering at first, then more steadily as his older brother joined in. It was a nonsense song, about a cart with only three wheels, but it served its purpose – it took their minds off the grim reality of their situation.

It was over fifty kilometres to the Austro–Hungarian border. Mazny drove carefully, not wishing to draw any unwelcome attention.

Two kilometres before they reached the border check-point, Mazny pulled off the road on to a narrow forestry track and killed the engine. He pulled the snow-suits from his pack.

'Put them on now, boys. From here we must go on foot.' The doctor looked up at the grey, leaden sky. An hour till dusk, he estimated. By then they must be through the woods and in position.

Their white suits blended with the heavy fall of snow that blanketed the trail leading to the forest. Almost immediately, young Jan sank up to his chest in a snowdrift. As his father pulled him out, the boy's lips trembled.

'I – I don't like this, Dad,' he whimpered. 'I'm frightened. Can't – can't we go home?'

It was Anton who answered him. The fourteen-year-old's understanding of the situation was better than his brother's. He had read of freedom and heard many stories from his father's friends; to him a new life in the West was something worth fighting for. Perhaps even dying for.

'There's no going back now, Jan,' he said firmly. 'Hey, come on – stop whining. Father needs all the help we can give him.'

Josef swept Jan up into his arms and trudged on through the thick snow. Soon, they were beneath the canopy of the forest, where only a light covering of snow had penetrated the trees' thick foliage. The going was easier now, and soon they were approaching the border.

'Quiet now,' Mazny hissed, motioning his sons to conceal themselves near the edge of the trees.

Beyond was a cleared corridor a hundred metres wide. Two parallel fences ran along the corridor, four metres high and topped with a vicious tangle of barbed wire. The snow lay thick in the twenty-metre gap between the fences. Far to the right in the gathering gloom Mazny could just make out the dim shape of a wooden observation tower. He knew there would be guards there, and dogs, but it was a chance they would have to take. There were observation posts all along the entire length of the border; they could not be avoided.

The doctor took out his torch and flashed it once. From across the wire, on the Austrian side, came a brief answering flash. Jorge Honig was there, waiting. Himself an escaped Czech, Honig had devoted his life to helping the others make the break for freedom. Mazny knew his plump wife would have hot goulash waiting when they reached Vienna – *if* they reached Vienna!

Mazny handed the kitbag to Anton after extracting a pair of heavy-duty wire-cutters. 'I go first,' he whispered. 'As soon as the wire is cut, you follow – Jan first, then you, Anton. Keep low. When the searchlight passes, lie absolutely still.'

It was pitch dark now, and Mazny blessed the thick clouds that blotted out the moon. As quickly as he could, he wormed his way forward towards the fence.

Suddenly, a roving searchlight illuminated the corridor between the fences, and Mazny froze, his white suit blending perfectly with his surroundings. Then the light was moving on.

Mazny wielded the heavy cutters, snipping a strand of wire at the edge of the snow-line. Gradually, he cut his way downwards, making sure that the parted wires would remain hidden by the snowdrift.

Twice more the searchlight swept by him, but his camouflage was adequate. He was not seen. At last the gap was big enough, and he wriggled through and lay flat.

Behind him his sons were already moving, Anton pushing Jan from the rear. Mazny was glad of his older son's maturity; he was taking this well, without giving way to the fear that undoubtedly welled up inside him. Mazny could rely on him to keep Jan in order.

They slithered through the wire to join their father, then

The doctor took out his torch and flashed it once.

all three were inching across the corridor. Off his own bat, Anton had picked up a fallen branch and was using it to fluff up the snow behind them so no trail would show.

Then Mazny was at the second fence, his cutters already busy.

'I'm cold, Father,' Jan whined, his teeth chattering.

'Hush,' came Anton's voice. 'It won't be long now.'

Out of the darkness the searchlight stabbed. They flattened against the snow, and the bright beam moved on. It stopped – and Mazny's heart pounded as it backtracked towards them, hovering over them.

A guttural voice from the tower called out, and next moment a volley of shots burst over their heads. Jan screamed and Mazny leapt to his feet, rapping out: 'Quickly! We have only one chance now. Anton – you first!'

He stood with his back to the fence, his hands clasped in front of him. Anton placed his foot in his father's hands. Next second he was soaring upwards through the air, reaching out to grasp the top strand of barbed wire.

The sharp prongs dug into his flesh, and Anton flinched. But somehow the boy kept going, pulling himself up as more shots cracked by, close to his face. Then he was atop the wire, reaching down for Jan's hands as his father hoisted the younger boy up. Jan was howling with terror, but Anton had him, hauling him up, lifting him over the top of the wire, dropping him into a deep drift on the other side.

Bullets whipped around them, and there was an edge of panic in Anton's voice as he called: 'I'm stuck, Father! I'm stuck!'

A bullet ripped into Josef Mazny's leg and the doctor sprawled in the snow, blood gushing from the wound. He knew the bone was broken.

Clutching the wire, he heaved himself desperately to his one good foot. From the direction of the tower there came a baying – and then, through the snow, leaping like dolphins over the drifts, came the sinister black shapes of two Doberman guard dogs.

His every nerve jangling with agony, his fingers numb, Mazny hauled himself hand over hand up the fence. Then he was just below Anton, his fingers grabbing at the material of the boy's snow-suit, ripping at it.

'Jump, Anton!' he croaked. 'For pity's sake *jump!*'

The boy obeyed, launching himself from the wire, leaving a large strip of white material clinging to the barbs. He hit the ground beside his terrified brother and was on his feet at once.

'Come on, Father!' he yelled. 'Come on, come on, come on!'

But the dogs were there, leaping for the doctor. Cruel jaws closed round his blood-smeared ankle and he screamed with the pain. Then the guard's rifles found their target – and before his sons' horrified eyes, their father died.

He fell back and hit the ground in a lifeless heap, the dogs still ripping at him.

Jan stood as if paralysed, a look of total shock on his face. His father couldn't be dead . . . he couldn't be!

Anton suppressed the urge to break down there and then, and clutched at his brother's arm, pulling him roughly away from the wire.

'Run, Jan – run!' he shouted, and the two of them were stumbling towards the woods where Honig's torch was now a steady beam. Bullets spattered the snow around them, and suddenly Anton gasped as one tore through the fleshy part of his upper arm. He staggered, almost fell – then Honig was crashing through the woods towards them. The man's strong arm was around him, lifting him almost bodily as if he weighed nothing.

Jan was already in the woods, sheltered from the vicious barrage by the close-packed pine trees. Honig ran past him, urging him on. 'Keep moving!' he shouted.

The two boys knew little of the rest of their journey to Honig's waiting car. He bundled them into the back. Jan was howling uncontrollably, but Honig ignored him, turning to Anton, inspecting his wound.

'It's deep but clean,' he told the pain-wracked boy. 'It will wait till we get to Vienna.'

Honig slipped into the front seat, gunned the engine and the car moved off. As they sped along the Vienna road, Jan's cries gradually subsided as he drifted off into a fitful sleep.

Anton had not uttered a word since Honig had reached him. He sat staring straight ahead, his face whiter than his blood-stained snow-suit. When at last the boy found his voice, it was cracked with emotion.

'Why, Herr Honig? Why did Father have to die?'

'Sometimes we must pay a high price for freedom, Anton,' the man replied evenly. 'You may think it *too* high a price, but take comfort from this . . .'

Honig turned to look deep into the boy's eyes. 'Your father thought enough of freedom to give his life so that you and your brother will never know tyranny again.'

Anton swallowed hard, slipped his good arm round his sleeping brother. Herr Honig was right. He could imagine the same words coming from his father's lips.

But that did not stop the tears of grief from streaming down his face.

Operation Doom

John Wagner

PHILIPPE NOEL COULD TELL the two men were Gestapo as soon as they stepped from their Mercedes. Their long black leather coats and hats pulled down to shade the eyes were a dead giveaway.

They strode briskly into the Pension Noel, the small hotel run by Philippe's parents, and rapped authoritatively on the reception desk where Philippe's father stood.

'Your two best rooms, Noel!' one of them barked. His face was scarred and battered like a boxer's. Philippe could make out the tell-tale bulge of a pistol beneath his coat.

'I'm very sorry, monsieur.' Philippe's father spread his hands in an expressive Gallic gesture. 'All my rooms are taken.'

'I'm not asking you, I'm telling you!' The man's tone was imperious. He was used to being obeyed.

The other Gestapo man, a tall, thin type with a hooked beak of a nose, was looking round, locating the door to the dining room. 'We will eat now. Bring food and wine. Have the rooms vacated by the time we've finished.'

The men didn't wait to hear Philippe's father's reply. They were already walking through into the small dining room. Monsieur Noel beckoned to Philippe. 'Run and tell your mother to prepare some food, son.'

'But, Father, you can't let those thugs push you around!'

Philippe's father cut him short. 'Don't be foolish, lad. You do not disobey men like those.' He cast a furtive glance in the direction of the dining room and lowered his voice. 'Soon the Allies will be here and we will be rid of the Germans forever. Until then, we have no choice.'

It was late August 1944, and the long-awaited Allied offensive against Hitler's hordes was well under way. Only a day earlier General De Gaulle had entered Paris in triumph. Already the German forces in southern France were retreating northwards, pursued by the American General Patch's troops. The *maquis* – the French resistance fighters – were becoming bolder every day, striking at the fleeing Axis troops wherever and whenever they could.

Philippe served the two Gestapo men the food his mother had prepared, and one of the few bottles of good wine that remained in the Noel cellar.

He watched as they ate. Wendelman and Staube, their names were. Staube, the one whose face looked like it had been in a hundred street fights, shovelled food into his mouth as if he hadn't eaten for weeks, though his protuberant stomach was ample evidence to the contrary.

The other, Wendelman, only picked at his plate. He turned and gave Philippe a searching look.

'You look like a bright young lad.' His thin mouth twisted in a false smile. 'How'd you like to earn a thousand francs?'

It was a fantastic sum for any thirteen-year-old boy to be offered. Philippe gulped. 'I'd love to, sir.'

Wendelman looked sly. 'The cursed *maquis* have been harassing the strategic withdrawal of our glorious army – we know for a fact one such group operates from *this* town, Vouziers.'

The German secret policeman reached inside his coat and brought out a bulging wad of notes, spreading them out on the table before Philippe's wide-eyed stare. 'Just give me a name, boy – one name – and all this is yours. No one else need ever hear of it.'

The German secret policeman reached inside his coat and brought out a bulging wad of notes.

Philippe stiffened. 'I – I don't know any Resistance men.'

'The boy's lying,' Staube accused, without lifting his face from his plate. 'What say we beat the truth out of him?'

'P-please, sir,' Philippe stuttered, 'I don't know anything!'

For a moment Wendelman's gimlet eyes pierced the boy, then he waved dismissively. 'Go on, boy – off with you. The Gestapo do not waste time with children.'

'Unless it is necessary,' Philippe heard Staube mutter through a mouthful of food, as he quickly left the room.

After dumping their belongings in their rooms, the Gestapo men left the hotel.

When they returned late in the afternoon, they had another man with them. Philippe recognised him as Gaston Le Clerc, a local butcher who, it was rumoured, was an active member of the Vouziers *maquis*. His face was bruised and three teeth were missing.

They marched him upstairs. On the top step Staube turned and shouted,back to Philippe's father: 'Make sure we are not disturbed!'

Five minutes later the first scream rang through the hotel. It was followed by another, and another. Curious and frightened guests gathered at the foot of the stairs.

'Blasted Gestapo!' old M Filbert spat through clenched teeth. 'They're nothing better than animals!'

'Please—' Philippe's father shooed them away. 'Don't make a scene – they could turn on any one of us next.'

The screams continued almost unabated for half an hour. Then Staube's head appeared over the stairway bannister.

'Noel! Send up bread and cheese and two bottles of that good wine – immediately!' he ordered.

Philippe carried the tray upstairs and knocked nervously on the room door. It swung open at once and Staube snatched the tray.

Beyond him, Philippe's startled eyes took in the bloody scene. Gaston Le Clerc was strapped to a chair, his face a mask of blood. Wendelman was leaning over him, a short cosh in his hand. As Staube slammed the door shut, Wendelman's arm was drawing back to deliver another blow.

Philippe felt sick as he walked downstairs. Behind him the screams had started anew.

'They – they're killing him, Father!' Philippe was almost in tears. 'Can't you stop them?'

'I told you before, Philippe – there is nothing we can do except keep out of it.'

It seemed like an eternity before the screams finally died away. Philippe kept his eyes averted as he heard heavy footsteps descending the stairs.

Wendelman was dangling his room key in his hand. 'I will keep this, Noel. See that no one enters that room in our absence. Where is your telephone? I have an urgent call to make.'

Wendelman spoke briefly into the receiver, then the two men left the hotel and roared off at speed in their Mercedes.

Philippe could think of only one thing – Gaston Le Clerc's smashed face. He knew better than to approach his father again, so he waited until his attention was diverted, then he opened the cabinet that held the pass keys to every room. Taking one out, he went quickly to the kitchen where he filled a jug with water and picked up a clean towel from the hamper.

Warily, he made his way upstairs and turned the key in the lock of the Gestapo man's door.

The first sight of Gaston almost caused him to faint, but he bit his lip and crossed to the injured man's side. He seemed unconscious, but as Philippe wet the towel and pressed it to his face, Le Clerc opened one badly-swollen eye.

'No, boy,' he croaked, 'never mind me. I . . . I am a dead

man in any case.' His head lolled and a thin trickle of blood ran from his ear. 'I talked . . . told them everything. You – you must warn the others.'

'Who?' Philippe questioned. 'What do you mean, Monsieur Le Clerc?'

'Tonight – Operation Doom. The *maquis* are waiting to blow up . . . supply train ten kilometres north . . . on the bridge near Attigny.' The stricken butcher's voice faded, then: 'You must warn them – it is a trap! The train will stop before. . . . it reaches bridge. German troops will pour out . . . kill them all. You must warn them . . .'

Le Clerc's head nodded forward as he lost consciousness. For a moment Philippe stood there uncertain, then he rushed from the room, hurriedly locking the door behind him.

He knew it was pointless to tell his father – he would only forbid Philippe to get involved. Instead, he rushed to the shed behind the hotel and wheeled out his bicycle.

Moments later, he was furiously pedalling the heavy machine north along the Attigny road.

It was dark now and the curfew was in force. Any citizen caught out on the streets would be liable to be shot.

But Philippe had not given a moment's thought to his own personal danger: he kept seeing a picture of Gaston Le Clerc's smashed face. Somehow he had to stop the same thing happening to the brave Resistance men.

Up ahead there came the growl of a large vehicle. A moment later the glow of shuttered headlights pierced the night.

Philippe ran his bicycle off the road and into a ditch, and lay there barely daring to breathe, until the German patrol had rumbled by. Then he picked himself up, leapt into the saddle and was off again.

A kilometre from the bridge at Attigny, where the railway track ran close to the road, Philippe dismounted and concealed the bicycle in the undergrowth. Then he was on the railway itself, running along as fast as his tired legs would take him.

Soon, up ahead, the bridge began to take shape in the moonlight. But behind him, very faint, Philippe could hear a train whistle. It was coming!

Philippe forced his aching body to one final effort. The bridge was looming larger, only a hundred metres away. Then he was beside it, gathering his breath in his burning lungs.

'It's a trap! It's a trap!' he rasped. There was no reply – and the vibration of the rails told him the train was fast approaching.

'This is Philippe Noel!' he shouted desperately, his voice rising almost to a scream. 'Gaston sent me to warn you! The Gestapo know about Operation Doom!'

It was all he got out before rough hands clamped over his mouth. He didn't struggle as he was dragged into the brush that lined the railway embankment. Then he heard a gruff voice which he recognised as Monsieur Godot, a farmer from west of Vouziers.

'It's young Noel, all right,' Godot was saying. 'What's all this about, young man?'

Philippe gasped out his story as quickly as he could. 'The Gestapo have arranged for troops to be on the train,' he finished. 'It will stop before it gets to the bridge. You'll all be killed!'

Godot made his decision instantly. 'The boy wouldn't lie to us. Let's get moving!' He turned to one of the shadowy shapes around him. 'Albert – blow the bridge!'

'But, Pierre, if the train will not go on it—'

Godot silenced his objection. 'The bridge is still of vital importance to the Nazi retreat. Blow it, I said!'

Mere seconds later, as the charges the *maquis* had planted

on the pillars of the bridge were detonated, the night erupted.

Philippe watched as the iron and concrete structure seemed to rise in the air with an ear-splitting roar, then folded in on itself and fell tumbling into the swirling waters of the River Aisne below.

Debris rained around them as Philippe and a small group of Resistance fighters scrambled up the steep slope leading away from the railway.

'Look there!' one of the men shouted, pointing downwards. They turned to see the blunt-nosed engine of the supply train sweep into view round a bend in the track. It was decelerating rapidly, sparks flying from its wheels as the brakes locked on.

Before the final echoes of the night's destruction had died away, the train had come to rest. The doors on its carriages were suddenly thrust open and well-armed troops poured out. They began to swarm up the slope after the *maquis*.

Staube and Wendelman appeared from one of the carriages behind the troops.

'After them!' Staube shouted. 'I want every last one of those swine eliminated!'

On top of the ridge, Philippe grabbed Godot's arm and pointed back down at the distinctive figures of the Gestapo men.

'It's them, Monsieur,' the boy exclaimed. 'The ones who tortured Gaston!'

Godot's face was grim. 'Is that so?' He licked his finger and touched it against the front sight of his rifle barrel. He took aim, then loosed off two rapid shots. Staube and Wendelman fell almost together as the bullets found their mark.

'They will torture no more,' Godot said. And then they were running again as a hail of German shots cleaved the air around them. Philippe stumbled, almost fell, but Godot's powerful arm was there, supporting him.

'You must keep running, Philippe,' the Resistance leader urged. 'Be strong!'

'I – I'm all right,' the boy gasped, though he craved for rest. 'I can outrun Germans any day.'

'That's the spirit! Come – we will lead them a merry chase. My men know these hills like their own back yards.'

Then they were rushing along the narrow sheep trail that wound upwards towards a small copse. Behind them the sounds of pursuit were receding, the German torch beams little more than pinpricks of light.

Godot shouted to his men: 'We're losing them! Slow down!' The Resistance leader saw Philippe's startled face and smiled broadly, moonlight flashing off his stained teeth. 'What's the use of having Germans chase us if we can't kill a few?' he laughed.

The *maquis* men reached the copse at a slow trot and turned, waiting. Godot fired three quick shots and called at the top of his voice:

'Here we are, you pig-dogs! Come and get us!'

As the first straggling line of pursuers came into range, a dozen *maquis* guns spoke as one. For years these men had lived under the Nazi yoke – now their guns would redress some of the balance.

The sudden fusillade threw the Germans into confusion. Many lay dead, others dying. The rest threw themselves to the ground, firing anywhere and everywhere in their panic. Then from amid their ranks a machine gun opened up, spattering the wood, ripping chunks from the trees.

'We move again,' Godot called. Then the Frenchmen were melting through the trees, doubling back towards the river on the other side of the hill.

Godot laughed as he ran, and Philippe found himself wondering at such a man, who could face danger and death with such careless bravado.

Godot was in the lead as they reached the foot of the slope and the narrow wooden footbridge used by herdsmen to move their animals across the deep gorge of the Aisne. They pounded over it in single file and at the far side Godot halted them.

'Albert – the spare charge. Fix it to the bridge,' he ordered.

The man called Albert bent quickly to his task, his practised fingers securing a small explosive charge to the underside of the wooden slatted bridge. Then the *maquis* were diving for the shelter of the rocks as the first German torch came into view.

The Germans halted at the far side of the bridge, uncertain what to do, until an officer came up panting and cursing.

'What are you waiting for, you sluggards? Get after them – they must have crossed here!'

The long stream of Germans had almost reached the other side when Albert depressed the plunger of his detonator box, and the flimsy bridge shattered like matchwood. Then the *maquis* guns opened up again, and the shocked Germans on the opposite bank began to fall.

They kept up the fire for less than a minute, then Godot was motioning them away, along the trail winding off through the undergrowth.

It was fully half an hour before the *maquis* men came to a halt in a leafy glade far from the scene of the firefight. The men were laughing, patting each other on the back, retelling their own parts of the night's business.

Philippe did not join in. He lay flat on his back in the grass, totally exhausted.

Godot knelt and put a small flask to the boy's lips. The stinging taste of brandy brought life back to Philippe's face, and he sat up spluttering.

'We have much to thank you for,' Godot told him sincerely. 'If not for your warning we would all be dead.'

Philippe felt a glow of pride as Godot went on. 'Our names will be known to the Germans now, so we dare not return to Vouziers. Do you know the old path that runs south of the railway line?'

Philippe nodded. 'Good,' Godot said. 'One of the men will escort you there. You can make your own way home. You will be back well before curfew ends.'

Philippe's bicycle was still hidden near the railway line, but the boy knew he could return for it the next day.

'What about you, Monsieur Godot?' Philippe asked. 'What will you do?'

The *maquis* leader smiled. 'What we have been doing for years – carrying on the fight. The Allied advance will soon push the Nazis from our land. Until then we will remain in these hills, doing what we can to hinder the enemy's retreat.'

Philippe got back to the Pension Noel shortly before dawn and slipped in through the back door. His whole body ached and he could barely keep his eyes from closing, but there was one thing that he must still attend to.

He took the pass keys from the cabinet and stumbled up the stairs, once more unlocking the door of the Gestapo man's room.

Gaston was not there. The chair to which he had been tied was lying in pieces and the window was wide open.

'So there you are!' Monsieur Noel stood framed in the doorway.

'Gaston – where is he?' Philippe blurted.

'Gone,' his father replied. 'You were right, Philippe – I could not leave him here to die. So I set him free and made it look as if he escaped. Let's hope it's good enough to fool those Gestapo thugs.'

'Don't worry, Father,' Philippe told him. 'Staube and Wendelman will not be coming back.'

A Voice from Beyond

Angus Allan

IN THE EARLY HOURS OF THE MORNING, the car had passed on to the Severn Bridge practically unnoticed. The darkness was made almost impenetrable by the thin mist that hung like a shroud from the cables above, and the two men who climbed from the vehicle as it stopped did so with unhurried confidence. Neither spoke as, from the boot, they hauled the drugged, inert body of Ronan Kellaway, Second Secretary of a certain Department H in the Foreign Office.

Callously, the men heaved their victim to the parapet and pushed him into space. Far, far below, the impact snapped Ronan Kellaway like a plastic doll, but by that time, his ice-cold assassins were already back in their car and driving on their way . . .

'There is,' said Commander James G Rice, the man in charge of one of the most highly-trained sections of what is loosely known as 'Civil Intelligence', 'something about Kellaway's death I don't like.' He entwined his fingers and looked evenly at the pair who faced him across his desk. Vince Samson and Jeff Hegarty were his best agents. At the peak of physical condition. Experts at their clandestine craft. Steel-tough and capable of much, much more than a passing glance might have suggested. Samson eased his long limbs in his chair and shrugged. 'Seems clear-cut enough to me, sir,' he said. 'He committed suicide. The confession tape he left makes it as clear as daylight. He'd been selling secrets to the enemy, and he couldn't live with his guilt any more.'

Hegarty, alert and wiry, a redhead with intense eyes, leaned forward. 'And the lab *has* cleared the tape, sir. Analysis shows that the voice on it *is* Kellaway's, without a shadow of doubt.'

Commander Rice nodded slowly. 'His car was found abandoned on the far side of the bridge,' he said. 'And apart from a suspiciously neat set of Kellaway's prints on the steering wheel, it was clean throughout. Let's assume he drove from London. There would have been blurred prints of his all over the place. And listen – why would he have gone across the bridge, and then walked back? Yes, gentlemen, I know that the behaviour of a man who has decided to kill himself would not be rational, but 'n this case, it bothers me, and I have no intention of closing the file on him just yet.'

Dismissed from their boss's presence, Samson and Hegarty sighed wearily. 'Kellaway was a pal of the old man's,' said Samson. 'That's why he wants us to do some digging.'

'Sure. A right old waste of time, Vince. Kellaway was known to be fond of gambling. He probably got into debt at some time, had an approach from the other side, and turned double agent to get himself out of bother.'

Vince Samson nodded. It was a familiar enough pattern. 'And yet,' he said thoughtfully, 'there was no kind of motive revealed in his confession tape. You'd have thought he'd have – bared his soul, so to speak. Even left some names of his contacts as a kind of atonement . . .'

The passes they carried took Samson and Hegarty to the dead man's office without question. In the annexe, Kellaway's assistant, Jeremy Kane – already making his preparations to step into his late boss's shoes – was clearly prepared to be helpful. A thin, almost bird-like young man, fastidious in his dress as he was in his precise movements, Kane struck both agents as being somehow *too* helpful. They had expected the usual sort of cool reserve that normally accompanies meetings between men of different government departments.

'Feel free to examine anything you want,' beamed Kane. 'If you need me, just call. My time is yours, gentlemen.'

Samson and Hegarty turned over Kellaway's office with a fine-tooth comb. They found that he had been in the habit of making notes – not on paper, but on tape cassettes.

A meticulous character, Hegarty painstakingly examined every one of more than fifty such tapes, kept in one of the filing cabinets. He beckoned Samson over, and held up four particular cassettes. 'Every other one has been wound back to the start,' he said. 'But not these.'

'So?'

'So nothing. Or maybe, so everything. We'll take 'em away with us, but not a word to that Jeremy Kane feller.'

'Come off it, Jeff,' scoffed Samson. 'If there's anything fishy about Kane, he'll spot they're missing as soon as we're gone.'

Hegarty grinned. 'There's a whole stack of unused tapes in the bottom drawer of the desk. I'll take four out, copy the labelling of these ones onto 'em, and drop the blanks in the filing cabinet. Okay?'

Ten minutes later, they took a friendly and apparently grateful farewell of Jeremy Kane, and told him they wouldn't be bothering him any more. The talents of Samson and Hegarty included the ability to lie with real conviction.

Another twenty minutes passed, and, after swift contact with Commander Rice from a public phone box, to learn Jeremy Kane's home address, they were standing in the man's bachelor flat in Kensington. There had been no trouble at all in picking the lock of his front door.

'Now then,' chuckled Hegarty. 'This is going to take a long time, but if the guv'nor's people see to it that Kane's kept nice and busy, there'll be no chance of him coming home unexpectedly, and catching us in the act.'

'We might still be wasting our time, Jeff,' said Samson.

His colleague winked. 'I think Commander Rice's hunch must have been catching, Vince. Don't ask me why, but I think we might be on to something . . .'

Commander James G Rice had set wheels of his own in motion. Kellaway's body, which had of course been re-covered from the Severn, was undergoing the most minute forensic scrutiny by the pathologists of his department, and basement computers were running detailed checks on the tapes that Hegarty had sent in from Kellaway's office, breaking them down word by word. At a quarter past four in the afternoon, Rice's red telephone buzzed, and he picked up the receiver. 'Yes, Samson,' said the Commander.

'Kane's flat's almost as clean as a whistle, sir. Almost.'

'Well? Hang it, man, don't give me riddles.'

'Sorry, sir. We found nothing except a business card, which had fallen down the back of one of his bedside drawers. It's for a firm called "Topnote Sound Studios Limited". Out in Hackney.'

'Interesting,' said Rice. 'Anything else?'

'Not here, sir,' said Samson. 'But Jeff – I mean, Hegarty, sir – remembered something from one of those report files you're always making us read. In our – uh – spare time, sir.'

'Your hinted sarcasm is not lost on me,' said the Com-mander, drily. 'Go on.'

'Well, there was a report on a new drug the other side are using. Glycotane. It's administered as a spray, and causes paralysis of the motor system. It oxidises to leave no trace.'

'Just a moment . . .' Commander Rice laid down the red phone and thumbed the button on his desk intercom. He was instantly in touch with the pathology department. 'Professor Walters? Would – er – Glycotane be in any way consistent with Kellaway's death?'

There was a long pause. Scientists do not readily jump to conclusions. Then – 'I don't see why not, Commander. If Kellaway *had* been drugged that way, he could have been thrown over the bridge. But that is only conjecture. We have certainly found no other indications of drugging – puncture-marks, for example.'

'Thank you, Professor.' The Commander picked up the red phone again. 'Samson? Thank Hegarty for his attention to detail, will you? It may be that he's right. You will now, of course, be paying a visit to the Topnote Sound Studios Limited, I suppose . . .'

'We will, sir. Be in touch later.'

Samson and Hegarty left Kane's flat in perfect order. They had even returned the business card to the spot where they had found it. Nobody in the world could ever have known that the place had been searched from top to bottom.

It was a long journey to Hackney in the growing rush-hour. Clear across London by tube and bus – for these were real agents, and not the fast-car merchants so beloved of television serials. The last part of their trek was on foot, and they passed the Topnote premises on the other side of the run-down backstreet where it was situated. It was more of a shop, really, with the name Joe Jarman over the door, and a window crammed full of new and secondhand sound equip-ment. The legend 'Topnote Sound Studios Ltd' seemed to have been added almost as an afterthought, and by someone whose skills certainly fell short of signwriting.

'Crummy dump,' said Hegarty, laconically. 'And closed.'

'What of it?' shrugged Samson. 'I'd be surprised if Joe Jarman didn't live in the flat above, and after all, we *are* the managers of a pop group who need a demo tape made.'

'So we are,' grinned Hegarty. 'Uh – what do we call the group, Vince?'

'How about – "Secret Service"?'

It took a fair few minutes of knocking and ringing to coax Joe Jarman down to open up. A discouragingly big man, somewhere in his thirties, he was anything but friendly. A ragged beard framed his jaw, and there was a good deal of muscle under the stained sweatshirt he wore tucked into a pair of old jeans. Also, he was bare-foot, and Samson's keen eyes took in the ridges of hard skin that hinted at more than a passing knowledge of karate.

'Come back tomorrow,' snapped Jarman. 'I don't give up my spare time for anything. Not even *good* business.'

'Now, now,' said Samson, evenly. 'Are you suggesting that our group isn't a winner? Just because you haven't heard of it yet, friend . . .'

'Spare me the sales talk. I've heard it all before. You've got a bunch of kids who think they're in line for the big time. Beat it, I said. And when you do come back, bring 'em with you. I'd want to hear the sound *they* make, not your lies.'

'Charming,' said Hegarty, as the big man prepared to slam the door in their faces. 'And us specially recommended, by Jeremy Kane.'

It was a calculated move, and it worked. Jarman tensed, and his eyes narrowed.

Samson took his cue and followed up instantly. 'Jeremy thought you could do something for us,' he smirked. 'We've got a whole album lined up. We're calling it "Glycotane".'

'You'd better come in.' Joe Jarman's brain was racing. He backed into his hallway, his gaze never shifting from the two agents. He reached behind him and flung open a door that led into a back room, soundproofed and equipped with recording gear far more sophisticated than the outside of the place would have suggested.

Jarman motioned them to take a pair of seats, and moved to a desk set in one corner of the studio. He said: 'You're mates of Jeremy's?'

They nodded, but in that moment, Jarman stepped back, and brought his right hand into view from the top drawer. It was a big hand, and it almost dwarfed the .38 Police Positive revolver, even with the ugly snout of the silencer screwed into the barrel.

Samson and Hegarty sat perfectly still, their expressions unchanged. The gun pointed exactly between them as, one-handed, Jarman flipped the receiver off a telephone and began to dial a number.

'He's going to check with Kane,' said Hegarty.

'He'd be a fool if he didn't.' Samson folded his arms and crossed one leg over the other in apparent unconcern.

'Hullo. Jeremy . . .?' Jarman spoke the moment that the receiver at the far end of the connection was lifted up. The voice of Commander James G Rice came back at him, as smooth as silk. 'Mr Joe Jarman, I presume. From Topnote Sound Studios . . .?' Beside the Commander, teeth bared in a savage snarl of fury, Jeremy Kane struggled helplessly in the grip of a large member of Rice's strong-arm staff . . .

Jarman flung down the telephone, but Samson and Hegarty had galvanised into action! They hurled themselves apart, and a shot from the .38 coughed out to slam destructively into a large and expensive pre-amp.

An ordinary man would have lost his balance, but not Vince Samson. With the liquid grace more suited to a ballet dancer than to an expert in the martial arts, he spun round and back-kicked, his shoe taking Jarman's gun arm at the wrist. The Police Positive spun away and clattered into a corner. The big man's roar of fury sounded strange in the acoustically dead confines of the studio, but the crash of equipment came close to echo as Jarman hurtled backwards, propelled by the bullet red head of Jeff Hegarty, who had launched himself from a kneeling position like a human battering ram.

Samson spun round and back-kicked, his shoe taking Jarman's gun arm at the wrist.

Incredibly, Jarman peeled off and came in for more. One horny foot flashed up and took a strip of skin from Samson's forehead. The huge man landed lithely and grabbed up a massive mixer in his hands. Yet even as he raised it above his head, Hegarty lunged with a stand mike, and the bulbous end of it snapped clean off as it took his adversary in the throat. Choking and gasping, his fingers clutched to his windpipe, Jarman fell, the mixer disintegrating at his feet. Samson, breathing heavily, retrieved the fallen revolver and cocked it. . . 'Okay, Jeff. I'll keep him covered. You give this place the once-over . . .'

They sat in the office of Commander James G Rice . . . Samson lounging in his chair, his long legs spread in front of him, and Hegarty, as usual, perched on the edge of his seat like a feral cat about to spring.

'The case is quite clear,' said Rice. 'We've determined from the tapes you took that Ronan Kellaway's confession was a fake, skilfully edited together from fragments and recorded. We know that in fact, Jeremy Kane was the double agent selling secrets to the other side. Fearing discovery, he decided to get rid of Kellaway and put the blame on him. Both Kane and Jarman are highly-trained operatives of the opposition.' He paused. 'The problem is, we have no definite proof that would stand up in a court of law.'

Samson looked at Hegarty, and both grinned. 'One of these days,' said Samson, 'our boss is going to get very, very stroppy with us.'

'What the devil do you mean?' Rice scowled irritably.

Hegarty took from his pocket a tape cassette and tossed it onto the Commander's desk. 'Conclusive evidence, sir,' he said. 'We thought we'd keep it as a kind of surprise.'

Samson put in quickly, for he thought Rice was about to blow his stack, 'Jarman *recorded* all the arrangements Kane made with him, sir. My guess is that he was ready to keep it for blackmail, if ever he needed it. I know recorded evidence isn't normally admissible in court, but the trial's hardly likely to be public, is it?'

Commander Rice beamed at them. 'Gentlemen, you have done very well. I am pleased with you.'

It was praise indeed, from their stern boss. But as Samson and Hegarty left the room, they glanced at each other wryly. 'Pity poor old Kellaway couldn't have been around to see our flaming success.' But they shrugged. Human feelings were so often something that agents in the so-called Intelligence Service could ill afford . . .

The Worm

John Wagner

NO ONE AT MONDO-WILSON CHEMICALS had ever liked Errol Ross. To put it bluntly, he was a creep. He had an unpleasant, ingratiating manner about him, and a handshake as limp as a wet tissue. As union shop-steward Jack Hodgman put it: 'That one's so slimy, I'd swear he lives under a stone!'

It was Hodgman who'd given Errol Ross his nickname – 'the Worm'. The union man had known him ever since Ross joined Mondo-Wilson straight from university, seventeen years previously.

Ross had been a junior research chemist then, with his sights set on much higher things. Right from the start he'd tried to worm his way into his superiors' good books, sucking up to them in his wheedling, simpering fashion, doing whatever he could to show his rivals for promotion in a bad light.

But his superiors had seen through Ross as easily as Hodgman had – and now, seventeen years later, while all his contemporaries had been promoted, Ross was still a junior chemist.

Once, old Frobisher – the Head of Research – had tried to fire Ross, and much against his will Jack Hodgman, as union shop-steward, had had to defend the Worm. Although routine and uninspired, there was nothing actually *wrong* with Ross's work. The fact that everyone detested him was not sufficient reason for dismissal.

His workmates' dislike for him was not lost on Errol Ross. More than a few of them had made their feelings patently obvious. Often, the workers on the factory floor would hoot and cat-call him: 'Hey, Worm!' and 'Here comes old slimy!' and worse. Now Ross avoided the shop floor whenever he could, and took care to leave work well after the five o'clock crush to avoid further embarrassment.

Even the boy who called with samples from the Lab Annexe, when he had a delivery for Ross, would push open the door and call out: 'Samples for the Worm!'

The baiting wasn't always verbal. The tyres on Ross's car were frequently slashed and his white lab-coat had been smeared with factory muck countless times. But the worst incident – and it still made Ross seethe – was the dead rat in his locker.

Ross had gone to change out of his lab-coat after work one evening, and there it was, lying on the top shelf of his locker. One of Ross's florid bow ties had been fastened carefully round its neck.

Ross saw himself as the innocent victim of a hate campaign. As the years went by and his alienation increased, he became more and more bitter. Until finally he was presented with the opportunity to get his own back on the company and its mocking employees.

A man had approached Ross at a petro-chemical convention held at a top hotel in London. He said his name was Trevor Siddons. He was a sales rep for the giant Eurox Oil Syndicate, a big jovial fellow, always laughing and very popular with the other delegates.

He started by buying Ross a drink, then another. Before long he was taking him to dinner. 'Hang the expense, Errol,' Siddons joked. 'It's all on the company!'

Ross, always the social outcast, was flattered by the other man's hearty camaraderie. He longed for companionship like this all the time, instead of the open hostility of his fellows at Mondo-Wilson. How different things would be with men like Trevor around him!

'Listen, Trev,' Ross said towards the end of the evening, 'what's the chance of me getting a job with Eurox?'

'Could be good, Errol. Eurox are always looking for bright, go-ahead chemists like yourself. Mind you, with the employment situation the way it is . . .' Siddons' voice tailed off and he looked thoughtful. 'Tell you what, though – you'd do your prospects no end of good if you showed the company how much you wanted to work for them.'

'How d'you mean, Trev?'

'I mean, if you didn't come empty-handed.' Siddons leaned closer and said softly, confidentially: 'Like if you could find out Mondo-Wilson's projected production of petrochemicals for next year . . . oh, I'm not suggesting you could get those *particular* figures –'

'Oh, but I could!' Ross blurted. 'It's easy. That's all low-grade information. Why, I could have it for you tomorrow.' He gulped eagerly. 'D'you think I'd get the job then?'

'Hundred per cent sure,' Siddons smiled.

Next day, Ross photocopied the production figures. He felt no qualms about what he was doing. The information was relatively unimportant – and besides, what had anybody at Mondo-Wilson ever done to deserve his loyalty?

He met Trevor that night and handed over the photocopies.

'You've done a good job, Errol,' Siddons congratulated him. 'I'll pass these on to the powers that be. You'll be hearing from us.'

Ross was overjoyed. At last he could see a new future opening up for him. He began to make plans, and even drafted out his letter of resignation to old Frobisher. But he didn't hand it in. Not yet . . .

It was just as well. Ross didn't hear from Siddons for three weeks, and when eventually the Eurox rep did get in touch, the news was not good.

'We've got a bit of a problem, Errol,' the other man told him. 'Eurox loved the figures you provided, but it seems the Sales Director's nephew is after the same job as you are.'

Ross pursed his lips. 'That's bad, Trev. I *need* that job – I've just got to get away from Mondo-Wilson! What can I do?'

'Well. . .' Siddons began, 'with the boss's nephew running against you, it would have to be something really big, something Eurox couldn't do without.' He shrugged. 'Might as well forget it, I suppose. There's nothing Mondo-Wilson has got that's that important.'

Siddons got to his feet and extended his hand. 'Well, Errol, it's been nice knowing you.'

But Ross's mind was racing furiously. 'Wait a minute, Trev – there *is* something.'

Siddons turned as he reached the door of the pub where they were meeting, and Ross hurried on:

'Old Frobisher's got a special team working on a new petrol additive. I don't know the ins and outs of it, but word is it's a real winner. It costs next to nothing to produce and it can reduce an engine's petrol consumption by half.'

Siddons was sitting again. 'Go on, Errol,' he urged.

'Getting the formula wouldn't be easy – but I can do it. I know I can!'

The broad, beaming smile was back on Siddons' face. 'That sounds really interesting, Errol. Tell you what – you get that formula for me and we'll sign your contract on the spot.'

Ross's limp hand was grasped in the other man's firm grip. It was a deal.

Siddons got up to go. 'It's best for us not to be seen together – you understand that?'

Ross nodded and Siddons handed him a slip of paper with a telephone number scrawled on it. 'When you get the information, contact me here.'

On his way to work next morning Errol Ross purchased a small camera with a close-up lens. He'd been awake half the night working on his plan. Now he was ready to put it into action.

The details of the new petrol additive were kept locked in Frobisher's safe, except when in use by the elite team of chemists. Ross was no safebreaker – he knew he'd have to engineer his access to the papers while they were actually in use.

It was industrial espionage, pure and simple. But Ross no longer cared. Now that he'd made up his mind, the fact that Mondo-Wilson's entire future rested on the success of the new additive only increased his determination to steal it. It would pay every last one of them back for the seventeen years of humiliation he had endured. The Worm was turning – and served them right!

It wasn't until after the morning tea break that Ross was able to put his plan into action. Through the plate glass partition that separated Frobisher's team from the rest of the research lab, he could see the chemists working on the confidential documents. Quickly, he left the lab and ran downstairs to the basement storerooms.

As he took hold of the tiny brass-headed mallet attached to the fire alarm, the full enormity of what he was doing struck home. He tried to swallow, but his mouth was too dry. At last he steeled himself, and then with one swift blow he brought the mallet hard against the glass of the alarm – and was rewarded by the shrill, insistent clanging of fire bells throughout the factory.

Already he could hear the pounding of feet as workers ran

from the factory floor. Jack Hodgman's strident voice cut above the din:

'Walk, don't run! No need for panic! We'll all get out alive!'

Errol Ross slipped into the storeroom and punched the button for the goods lift. It was perfect for his purpose. Fire regulations prohibited its use during an alarm, so he was sure no one would be using it. And it led directly into the section of the lab which had been partitioned off for Frobisher's team.

Inside the lift, Ross forced himself to wait two minutes to give the lab above plenty of time to clear. Then he pressed the UP button and the lift jerked into life.

It ascended slowly, then the doors clanked open again. As Ross had expected, the lab was empty. His eyes ran over the desk tops and he breathed a sharp sigh of relief. The petrol additive documents were still where Frobisher's team had left them.

He moved across the floor and checked the door in the partition. It was locked. As he'd thought, Frobisher had considered that sufficient security. The old fool!

He pulled the camera from his lab-coat pocket and switched on the automatic flash. He fiddled with the lens, adjusting it until it focused sharply on the first of the documents. Click! The first photograph was taken.

Working quickly, he photographed each page in turn. Then he froze as he heard Jack Hodgman's voice shouting above the alarm bell: 'Check the upper offices, Mick – the fire might be there. I'll check the labs.'

Of course! Hodgman was fire warden. It was his duty to check every department to see that they had been cleared.

Ross ducked down behind Frobisher's desk – not a moment too soon. The handle of the partition door rattled. Then Ross released his breath as he heard Hodgman's departing footsteps.

Click! The first photograph was taken. Working quickly, he photographed each page in turn.

He leapt to his feet and, working furiously, photographed document after document, page after page of complicated chemical symbols – some of which even he did not understand. Pausing only long enough to ensure that everything was exactly as he'd found it, he made his way back to the lift and descended once more to the basement storeroom.

As he reached the storeroom door he again heard Hodgman, booming to his fellow fire warden: 'I found it, Mick – it's the alarm in the basement!'

Ross opened the door a crack and peered through. Jack Hodgman and Mick Spooner stood by the smashed alarm. 'There's no fire,' Hodgman was saying. 'Some joker must have set this off. I'll switch off the alarm and tell the fire brigade – you get everybody back to work.'

The two men left, but Ross stayed where he was until the workers began to stream back into the factory. Then he sidled through the door and joined them, as if returning himself from the fire drill.

No one had noticed his absence. One of the benefits of being unpopular, Ross thought bitterly. No one cared whether you were there or not.

Still, his plan had worked like a dream!

He spent the rest of the day in a turmoil of needless anxiety. No one had even the faintest suspicion of the real purpose behind the fire alarm.

He phoned Trevor Siddons that night and arranged to meet him in the pub where they'd met before. A tremor of achievement ran through Ross as he handed over the three rolls of film he'd taken.

'Good work, Errol!' Siddons congratulated him. 'I'll pass these on to the powers that be. I should be in touch with you very soon.'

'But what about the contract?' Ross demanded. 'I mean, you promised . . .'

'Yeah, well,' Siddons said evasively. 'Can't sign anything until I've checked these out for authenticity.'

'When then?' Ross spluttered.

'Next week some time. Leave it to me, Errol. I'll be in touch.'

Before Ross could protest further, the Eurox man was gone.

Outside the pub, Siddons paused for a moment, patting the pocket into which he'd dropped the films. What a mug Ross was! He'd played him like a fish, dangling the bait of a job in front of him simply so that he could get his hands on this formula. Rumours of it had been in circulation in the top echelons of Eurox for months. Now they had it – and Siddons would be well-rewarded for his ingenuity.

As for Ross – who cared? A worm like that deserved everything he got!

It was the longest week of Errol Ross's unhappy life, and at the end of it Trevor still hadn't called.

At last Ross gave up waiting and rang the number Trev had given him. There was an electronic whine, nothing more. Ross dialled the number several more times, with the same result. He then tried the operator, who checked the line and informed him: 'Sorry, sir. The number you require has been disconnected.'

Desperate now with the fear that something had gone very wrong, Ross dialled Eurox and asked to be put through to Trevor Siddons.

'I'm sorry, sir,' a bright voice came back at him, 'Mr Siddons is no longer with Eurox UK. He left this morning to take up his position as Assistant Director of our New York office.'

For a long time Ross sat with the dead receiver in his hand, staring numbly at it. He'd been duped, played for a fool! And there was no comeback. A spy couldn't go to the police to complain, not without paying a heavy price himself. All his hopes were dashed. Now before him stretched only the same grim future with Mondo-Wilson . . . and the workers who hated him.

It turned out to be a brief future. Only two months later Eurox announced that they had patented a new petrol additive which would halve any vehicle's petrol consumption.

The news stunned everyone at Mondo-Wilson. There could be no doubt about it – it was *their* additive. But there was nothing they could do – Eurox had beaten them to it.

An emergency board meeting was held the day after the announcement. It lasted three hours and came to a grim conclusion. Mondo-Wilson was ruined.

Next morning the managing director summoned all trades union officials and notified them of the company's forthcoming closure.

'There's no other way, men,' he told them solemnly. 'The company's borrowed heavily to finance the new additive. Now that Eurox have got the patent, we've no hope of recovering our losses.'

'Couldn't you take it to court?' Jack Hodgman suggested.

'No use, Jack,' came the reply. 'There's no way we can prove Eurox stole it from us.'

That afternoon the factory was as cheerful as a morgue. Every worker had been placed on one month's notice. There would be redundancy payments, of course, but it was losing their jobs which most concerned the workers. In the current harsh economic climate, there was little hope of many of them finding alternative employment. More than eight hundred men and women were about to be thrown out of work.

Jack Hodgman took the news hardest. As a staunch union

man, he regarded the workers' betrayal by one of their own to be the worst of all crimes. He was determined to find out one thing – the name of the filthy spy who'd stabbed them all in the back.

He got in immediate touch with his opposite number in the Eurox organisation, Marcus Mellon.

'I want the name of that spy, Marcus,' he told him bluntly.

'That's management business, Jack,' Marcus replied cagily. 'They won't tell me.'

'You can make them. Put a lot of pressure on, Marcus – threaten them with a work-to-rule, an all-out strike – anything! I'm asking you for a little solidarity on this issue, brother.'

There was a long pause. At last Mellon's resigned voice came back: 'All right, Jack. I'll see what I can do.'

Twenty-four hours passed. It was late the following afternoon when Hodgman got the information he wanted.

The name that Marcus Mellon gave him brought the bitter taste of bile into the union man's throat.

The five o'clock hooter sounded. As usual, Errol Ross delayed a little before leaving the lab. He threw his lab-coat into the laundry trolley and slipped on his corduroy jacket.

Perhaps things had worked out for the best, he thought. After seventeen years his redundancy payment would be substantial. He could use it to start a small business of his own. At last, he'd be free of Mondo-Wilson and its hated employees.

He was whistling almost cheerfully as he left the factory gates. As he walked along the street, a harsh voice hissed from the shadows:

'Hey – Worm!'

He turned – and his heart sank. A group of about twenty men were waiting in an alley. Mondo-Wilson men!

Ross made to brush past them, but a burly labourer blocked his way.

'Stick around, Worm – we've got a little matter to talk over with you.'

Strong fingers clamped themselves on Ross's arms. 'Jack Hodgman found out something interesting today. Seems there was a worm working in the research labs – a worm that turned out to be a snake in the grass!'

Then the first fist lashed out, and blows began to rain down on him. And Errol Ross heard no more . . .

Body Snatch

Terry Deary

THE BOY LOOKED AT THE SHABBY GREEN DOOR, then back to the crumpled scrap of newspaper in his hand. He peered at it in the fading light of the October evening.

'Unleash the secret forces of your mind!' said the bold black letters of the advertisement.

Underneath, in smaller print, it went on: 'Improve your memory and amaze your friends! Develop your will power and be a success!! Increase your confidence and impress the people who matter!!! Release your hidden mind power through hypnosis. Consult: Dr Simpson, 37 Market Street, Durham.'

The boy strained his eyes to read the tiny print at the bottom: 'Special rates for scientific subjects.'

He thrust the paper into his pocket, then turned to look again at the green door. He rapped boldly. The swirling wind made him shiver and pull the collar of his school blazer up to his ears. There was no reply. Gently he turned the handle and was surprised when the door swung smoothly open.

The stairway inside was lit by a weak bulb. It showed a worn red carpet leading up to a landing with a single door at the top. The boy climbed the stairs. For a moment he had the urge to turn and run down the stairs, not stopping till he reached home. Instead, he took a deep breath and knocked on the door at the top.

'Enter!' boomed a voice from inside. The boy was surprised by the rich warmth of the scene that met his curious gaze. The room was cheerfully lit by a crackling log fire and a gleaming brass oil lamp on a polished walnut table. Two high-backed chairs covered in dark red velvet stood by the fire.

'Come in. Take a seat by the fire,' came the voice from deep within one of the chairs.

'Dr Simpson?' asked the boy. He could see very little of the man; just a plume of white hair rising from a cloud of amber smoke.

'Come in, come in my friend!' The doctor stood up, carefully marked his book before placing it on the table, and turned to knock his pipe on the hearth. 'Excuse me. Filthy habit. Don't ever start my boy.'

'No . . . I . . . er . . .' the boy stammered. The doctor was not a very tall man but the mane of white hair made his head look large and powerful; his bright black eyes seemed to look right through the boy, making him feel quite small.

'Take a seat, take a seat,' said the old man, stepping forward to grasp the boy's hand in a friendly hand-shake. 'Oh, but you're cold!' he exclaimed with real concern. 'Come along now, take this seat by the fire.'

'Er . . . thank you, Dr Simpson.'

'Ah, so you know my name!' The doctor's fluffy white eyebrows shot up to meet the untidy tangle of hair. 'You have the advantage of me. I don't believe we've met.'

'No . . . we haven't. I'm Ian. Ian Ferris.'

'And why have you come to see me?'

Ian groped in his blazer pocket and pulled out the tattered scrap of newspaper. 'I saw your advert and I thought you might be able to help.'

'Ah, yes,' boomed the doctor. 'I get a lot of enquiries from people your age. You want to increase your hidden mind powers, and you've come to the right man.'

'Well, not exactly. It's about my exams . . .' Ian put in.

'Of course! You want to improve your memory and amaze

your friends. Let me tell you, you've come to the right man. I myself have the most amazing powers of memory, John.'

'Ian.'

'What's that?'

'Ian . . . my name's Ian.'

'Er . . . exactly . . . hmm . . . Ian.' For a moment Dr Simpson seemed to shrink a little like a punctured tyre.

Ian felt a little sorry for the old man. 'It's about increasing my confidence,' he went on.

'Confidence?' the doctor asked vaguely, as if he'd never heard the word.

'Yes. "Increase your confidence and impress the people who matter!"' Ian read from the paper.

Dr Simpson stared at the fire for a long moment so that the only sound in the room was the crackling of logs in the fireplace. At last he said quietly, 'Confidence. Very important. If you're *confident* you can do something, then you *can* do it. A man with confidence can do anything. Anything at all,' he said wistfully, like a man in a dream. He fell silent.

Ian felt uncomfortable. He cleared his throat nervously. 'Can *you* give me confidence, Dr Simpson?' he asked.

The doctor looked up sharply and the sparkle had returned to his eyes. 'Of course, my boy. I am *confident* that I can do it.' He chuckled at his own joke and the boy smiled weakly in return.

'I've saved ten pounds from my Saturday job . . .' Ian said hesitantly.

The doctor waved his hand quickly. 'My normal fee is twenty-five pounds, but I don't take on a case just for the money anyway. I have to be sure my medical services are needed.'

Ian pulled out the newspaper advert once again. 'It says here you have special rates for scientific subjects. I'd be willing to be a scientific subject,' he said.

'You would?' the old man said eagerly.

'As long as it didn't hurt,' Ian said cautiously.

'Oh, no, no, no. It isn't that sort of scientific experiment. It's a study of mind hypnosis. You wouldn't feel a thing. Let me tell you about my experiments. If you still wish to go ahead when you've heard the details, then we shall proceed.'

'Oh, I will,' Ian insisted eagerly.

'Patience, my boy, patience. Let me finish.'

'Sorry,' Ian said, and sat back quietly in the chair while the doctor lit his pipe. 'First . . . you . . . must . . . understand,' he began, between draws at the smouldering pipe, 'that the human body and the human mind together make up the human being. The mind and the body normally work together . . . but, under certain circumstances they can be separated . . . under hypnosis, for example. The body is just a shell – it's like a motor car that carries its passenger, the mind, along a short journey from birth to death. At the end of the journey the car is left to rust . . . but the passenger goes on.'

'So, you believe in life after death?' Ian said slowly.

'Yes. And before birth,' the doctor added.

'So are you suggesting that my mind has been in other bodies, but has forgotten about them?' Ian shuddered at the thought.

'That is correct,' the old man said with an encouraging smile.

'Under hypnosis my mind will remember?'

'That has been my experience in the past,' the doctor said.

Ian chewed his lip nervously, then came to a sudden, bold decision. 'I'll do it. You can hypnotise me . . . and use me as a subject for one of your experiments!'

'And you are certain you want to go ahead with this?' Dr Simpson asked. Ian nodded. The doctor moved his chair so that it faced the boy's and his voice dropped to a soft, deep tone. 'Very well. First we must relax. Forget about the world outside . . . your school, your exams. They are all a long way away – in the past or the future – but a long way from this room, now.'

Somehow Doctor Simpson's saying that they were a long way away made them so. The deep voice was so sure of itself that he could have said Ian was the Mayor of Durham and the boy would have been tempted to believe it. 'Rest your head on the back of the chair . . . that's right, let your hands rest lightly on your knees. Now then, if you look at the centre of the mantelpiece you will see a clock; and it's so quiet in this room that you can hear that clock ticking.'

Ian's breathing was so shallow that he could indeed hear the soft ticking of the handsome brass clock. 'I want you to keep looking at the clock . . . concentrate on what I am saying to you, but keep your gaze fixed on the face of the clock.'

Slowly the room faded from view . . . the glowing lamp and the doctor's white hair blurred and disappeared from the edge of Ian's vision until only the white enamelled face of the clock swam in front of him.

With a great effort he kept his eyes open till the minute hand reached 5.49, then his eyes closed, leaving just the sound of ticking and the gently droning voice of the doctor.

The boy's head fell forward on to his chest. The doctor reached for his pipe and began to fill it. His voice brightened from the dull monotone he had used to hypnotise the boy. 'Well now, Ian, you're feeling better already. All the tensions and the worries of the day are seeping from your body. Now, listen carefully. When you come across a situation where you feel unsure of yourself, I want you to remember just four words. The words are: 'You can do it'. When you say those words to yourself you *will* be able to do it!'

'You can do it,' the boy mumbled to himself.

'That's right, Ian. You will remember nothing of what I've said to you when you wake up, but somewhere, deep in your mind, those words will stay until you need them.'

The boy nodded. Dr Simpson walked over to the walnut table where he slid open a drawer to reveal a tape-recorder. He didn't take the machine from the drawer, only the microphone, which he placed on the centre of the table facing the boy. A push of the red button sent the machine whirring into life.

'Ian?'

'Uh?' The boy moved his head towards the doctor's voice but his eyes remained closed. 'You may remember we talked earlier about exploring the other lives of your mind.'

The boy just nodded.

'We'll start with something simple to see how you respond. Let's go back to the year 1972 – ten years ago. You are six years old. How old are you?'

The boy opened his eyes and his thumb crept shyly to the corner of his mouth where he began to chew it. 'Six,' his voice piped in an odd, high pitch. The doctor showed no surprise; indeed it was as he had expected – the boy was speaking and behaving as he had done at that age.

'Where do you live, Ian?'

'Brandon.' The name sounded more like 'Bwandon' with the childish lisp.

'Do you live with your mum and dad?' the doctor asked in a gentle, encouraging voice.

The doctor was a little surprised to be met with a vigorous shake of the head. 'No mam,' came the reply.

'Oh . . . I thought . . .' For once Dr Simpson was a little confused.

'Mam's gone to live with granny,' the little boy explained.

The doctor thought quickly that he was opening old wounds in the boy's life it would be better to leave closed. 'Never mind,' he muttered hurriedly, 'I'm sure she'll be back soon.'

But the old man only cut deeper into the misery. 'Daddy says he doesn't care if she never comes back,' the boy mumbled then quickly sniffed away the threat of tears. The doctor cursed himself for his clumsiness and hastily said, 'Ian, the year is 1982 and you are sixteen years old.' The boy recovered from his snivelling, turned to stare at the clock once more and slowly drifted back into his sleeping trance.

The doctor sighed, took a large handkerchief from his top pocket and mopped his brow. He sometimes doubted the wisdom of digging into the past, and at times like this felt embarrassed at stumbling upon the unhappy secrets of his patients.

The old man poured himself a large glass of sherry and drank it quickly to steady his nerve. He wanted to wake the boy and send him home with his new-found confidence. Yet, at the same time he wanted to explore the past . . . to prove his theories of life and death, of mind and bodies.

At last the doctor's curiosity triumphed over his conscience and he turned back to the boy.

'Ian.' The boy raised his head slightly. 'The year is 1982 and your name is Ian Ferris. But you haven't always been Ian Ferris. Before Ian Ferris was born in 1966 you had another name . . . didn't you?'

For a long while there was no sound in the room but the ticking of the clock and the harsh breathing of the tense old man. At last the boy in the chair began to slowly nod his head.

'Mah . . . un,' the boy slurred like a drunkard – or like someone struggling with the long forgotten art of using lips and tongue to speak.

'Marne?' said the old doctor. 'Marne? Is that your name?'

The boy's eyes were still closed; his forehead creased into a frown and he shook his head as he fought to control the alien body he found himself in. 'Mah . . .' he repeated, then with great care put his tongue behind his teeth and pushed out the second part of the word. '. . . *tun!*'

'Mah – tun. Martin! Is that your name? Martin?'

The boy relaxed and nodded his head. 'Martin Cross.'

'Well, Martin, you can open your eyes now.' The boy did so and looked at the doctor with a dull curiosity.

'Where . . .?' the boy began.

'Don't worry, Martin. I'll explain everything in time. You are in a rather unusual situation and I wouldn't like to scare you or confuse you by rushing into it. Just answer one or two questions for me first, then I'll answer all yours. Now, the first thing you must tell me is what year are you living in?'

'What year?' the boy repeated stupidly. 'Don't you know?'

'Yes, I know,' the doctor answered with a nervous laugh. 'But I need to know what you think.'

Martin gave a shrug and answered, 'Well, it's 1840 . . . isn't it?'

'Mmmm.' The doctor stood up and warmed his back at the fire. 'You have a strange accent, Martin. You aren't from around these parts, are you?'

Martin nodded vigorously. 'Oh, yes. I've never left the county in my life – I've always lived here.'

'And where is "*here*"?'

The boy looked around him and then uncertainly at the old man.

'This must be Inglewild Hall – though I've never been in the library before – and you must be . . .'

The doctor did nothing to help the boy work out who he was but went on, 'And how did you get here?'

The boy shook his head, agitated, and sighed, 'I don't know. Look . . .' He stopped suddenly, seemed to turn deathly pale then clutched at his chest in a panic. 'I was shot!' he cried. 'His Lordship shot me. Here in the heart . . . I remember . . . the pain . . . the wound.'

Dr Simpson stepped forward quickly and put a comforting hand on the boy's shoulder. 'Don't worry. That happened a long time ago . . .'

'The wound's healed?' the boy asked in disbelief.

Again the doctor evaded the answer. 'Look, Martin, I'll help you and answer all your questions if you'll only relax and tell me just a little about yourself.'

Slowly the character of Martin had been seeping into Ian Ferris's body and had begun to change it. The eyes narrowed from Ian's worried innocence to a more mature look with just a hint of cunning. The arms and legs began to tense like springs, ready to leap from the chair if it became necessary. 'I'm sixteen years old,' he said carefully. 'I work for Lord D'Arlay at Inglewild Hall.'

Dr Simpson returned to his chair and began filling his pipe. 'What do you do at Inglewild? Are you a farm-worker?'

Martin gripped the arms of the chair with a flash of anger and replied tersely, 'I am not. I'm a groom.'

'I'm sorry,' the old man answered, sensing that he had said the wrong thing and not wanting to upset the delicate conversation. He struck a match and noticed that his hand was shaking as he tried to hold it to the bowl of his pipe, for he knew that he was talking to a boy who had died over a hundred and forty years ago. 'Of course a groom is a much more important job than a mere farm labourer,' he said soothingly.

The boy relaxed a little. 'It is,' he answered, proudly. 'Especially as I have charge of the ladies' hunters,' he added with a frown.

'The ladies . . . Lord D'Arlay's wife?'

'Yes.'

'Lord D'Arlay's daughters?'

'Mind your own business!' the boy exploded and jumped to his feet.

The doctor felt he had touched a raw nerve as he cut into Martin Cross's memories. He could withdraw his probing questions now and maybe never find the truth or he could take advantage of the boy's uncertainty and press on. He decided to go ahead. 'Tell me, Martin, why did Lord D'Arlay shoot you?'

'What's it got to do with you?' Martin whirled round till he was facing the doctor and the fireplace.

'I'm a doctor. Dr Simpson. I'm the one who . . . shall we say . . . brought you back to life. I have a right to know how you lost that life.'

'I was with a gang of local lads,' he began sullenly. 'In the churchyard at midnight – digging up a fresh body to sell to the doctors . . .'

'You were a body-snatcher!' Dr Simpson said with a faint tremor in his voice. In the old days criminals used to dig up corpses and sell them to doctors, who used them to study anatomy.

The boy was silent. After a moment the doctor realised that Martin was not looking at him but at the mantelpiece – or, rather, at the mirror above the mantelpiece. 'Sit down, Martin!' the old man said sharply.

It was too late. The boy had seen the reflection and slowly brought his hands to his face to explore the strange features. 'My face . . . what have you done to my face?'

The doctor jumped to his feet and gripped the boy's shoulders. 'Sit down. Sit down and I'll explain.' Weakly, the boy let himself be pushed back into the chair and sat staring blankly into the fire. It was then he began to look at the strange clothes he was wearing; fear twisted his face.

Dr Simpson was pacing the hearthrug and talking quickly. 'Martin, the first thing you must understand is that back in 1840 you were shot by Lord D'Arlay . . . you were shot dead.' The boy shuddered and the doctor cursed himself for the

*The doctor realised that Martin was not looking at him but at the
mirror above the mantelpiece.*

clumsiness with which he had put it. 'What I mean to say is that your body died, but your mind lived on. You became another person. You lived and died as that person with no memory of Martin Cross. Your mind has lived through the hundred and forty years since Martin Cross died – but lived in a series of identities.'

The boy looked up sharply. 'So, what year is it now?'

'1982,' the doctor answered, looking carefully to see how Martin would react. The boy's face remained like a mask.

'And whose body is this?'

'A boy called Ian Ferris.'

'And where is Ian Ferris's mind while I am in his body?'

'Asleep. I put him into a trance and released your mind from his.'

'Released?'

'Yes. I believe that Martin Cross and Ian Ferris are the same person. But, when Ian is awake, he has no memory of Martin.'

'No!' the boy answered with a voice as cold as steel. 'I am Martin Cross. If Ian Ferris is me in a hundred and forty years from now, then why hasn't Ian Ferris any memories of me?'

'He has! But they don't come to the surface till he's under hypnosis.'

'What's that?'

'In a trance.'

'And what will happen to me – to Martin Cross – when Ian Ferris wakes up from this "trance"?'

'Well . . . I suppose . . . I mean . . .' The doctor felt he had walked into a trap and was searching desperately for a way out.

'Martin Cross will cease to exist.' The doctor was silent. 'I will die again. I don't want to die again, doctor. You've given me a second chance of life and I'm going to take it.'

'You can't!' the doctor gasped.

'Why not?'

'Well . . . because . . . because you couldn't adapt to life in 1982. Things have changed so much since you were . . .'

'Alive?'

'No. Since your mind was . . . you are a boy of the nineteenth century. You couldn't learn to live in the twentieth century – things have changed so much.'

'What things?'

The doctor licked his lips nervously as his mind raced to think of reasons why this dead boy could not be allowed to come back to life. 'You probably haven't learnt to read. Well it's essential in 1982 that you know how to read. And . . . and . . .' Suddenly the doctor tried a new tack. 'You must have known lots of people in 1840. Relatives, friends . . . perhaps one special girl . . .'

Martin reacted sharply. 'How do you know?'

The doctor spread his hands. 'There is someone for each of us. What was her name, Martin?'

The boy was silent for a long while before he replied, 'Ellen.'

'Ellen,' the doctor repeated quietly. 'Don't you realise that Ellen has been dead for about a hundred years. If you were to step outside that door into 1982 you would be totally alone in the world. No friends . . . no home . . . no Ellen.'

The boy looked down at the floor, deep in thought. The fire was burning low and its light was so dim that the doctor missed the odd smile of cunning that flickered over Martin's lips. 'I suppose you're right, doctor,' he said carefully.

The doctor leaned back with a relieved sigh. 'Of course I'm right. It's only fair to Ian that you let him live his life to the full.'

'*I* didn't,' said Martin bitterly.

'You lived more in your life than Ian has so far.'

'How do you mean?'

'You've grown to be a man – you've lived . . . you've loved.'

'And Ian?'

'He's still a boy. His life is school, exams, his heartless father; he has a long way to go before he learns about life.'

Martin nodded. 'What do I do?'

'Just sit back and close your eyes.'

Martin clenched his eyes tightly shut and the doctor went into his routine to relax a patient. At last he was sure that the boy was deep in a trance again. 'Now, I want you to return to the year 1982. Tell me, what is your name?'

'Ian Ferris,' the boy mumbled.

'Good. Now then, Ian. I'm going to count to three, then snap my fingers. When you hear the click, you will be awake and will remember nothing of what has happened. Do you understand?'

The boy nodded dreamily.

'One . . . two . . . three . . .' Click!

The boy's eyes flew open. He looked up and smiled at the doctor. 'I'm ready.'

'Ready?'

'To be put in a trance,' the boy said.

'Oh, it's all over,' the doctor said. He seemed strangely troubled and ill at ease. There was something odd about Ian that he couldn't put his finger on.

'Really. Oh, in that case I'll be going,' the boy said and jumped to his feet. For a few moments he looked uncertainly around the room until he chose one of the three doors and walked towards it.

'Ian!' called the doctor. The boy ignored the call and opened the door. 'Ian!' the doctor repeated.

The boy turned round with a look of surprise on his face which he quickly covered. 'Yes? That's me.'

'Ian. Do come back and see me some time to let me know

how you are getting on after the treatment.'

'Of course, doctor,' the boy said with a grin. He walked out on to the landing at the head of the stairs and began to whistle as he walked down them.

'There was something wrong,' the doctor muttered to himself as he twisted his pipe between his thin, white hands. 'Something wrong. His voice . . . that was it! Ian has a Durham accent – Martin has some sort of Midlands or East Anglian accent. Now, that boy who walked out . . .'

The old man sat down shakily in his chair. He ran his hand through the tangled white hair and sighed. 'That was *Ian* who went out,' he muttered uncertainly. 'It *was* Ian. It must have been . . . oh, God, let it have been Ian!'

The boy reached the bottom of the stairs and puzzled for a few moments over the fastening on the door. At last it swung open and he stepped out carefully.

Martin Cross chuckled. It had all been so easy. The foolish old man had believed everything.

What had the doctor said? That Martin couldn't adapt to life in the nineteen eighties? – that too much had changed? He smiled to himself. 'One thing hasn't changed – in 1840 the lads in the village made a handsome living by stealing corpses from the local churchyard . . . and here I am in 1982 snatching a body. The difference is that *this* body is *living* . . . and I'm not going to sell it to some doctor. I'm keeping it!'

And the empty city streets echoed with the laughter of a body-snatcher who had died a hundred and forty-two years before.

Detailed to Die!

Angus Allan

CAPTAIN NIGEL MCKAY was surprised to find that he felt nothing. He had enjoyed twenty-four years of his life, and regretted not one moment. He was not married, though he'd spent many an hour in the company of girls he'd liked. He had managed to escape the awful debacle of Dunkirk, and had been a popular and admired officer in the Sixteenth Battalion of the Gordon Highlanders, much in demand for convivial evenings in the Mess, where he'd sung bothay ballads in a rich, Aberdonian dialect. He had been liked by his men, who had nicknamed him 'Nutty Nigel' because he revelled in telling them jokes that he'd heard in civvy street, where he'd been – of all things – a writer of children's stories.

The Medical Officer of the Sixteenth Gordons repeated what he'd said. 'Nigel. You have an incurable disease. I'm sorry, boy, but the X-rays show it clearly. You have – at the most – one month to live.'

'At least three of my pals have been killed already, in North Africa,' said Nigel. 'They've gone as surely as I will, sir. It really doesn't matter.'

'You can *say* that? Knowing what I've just told you?'

'Life is a fleeting thing, sir.' Nigel McKay shrugged. 'Nobody lives for ever. Is there any cause to weep and moan when you're told of your allotted span?'

'I'm sorry, boy. Really sorry. I say it again.' The Medical Officer, an elderly Lieutenant Colonel of the RAMC, turned away to hide the tears that sprang to his eyes. To him,

Captain Nigel McKay was little more than a youth. 'I shall recommend that you are discharged immediately, to make whatever arrangements are necessary for your parents . . . and so forth.'

'As you say, sir. And please – don't distress yourself. In this war, surely no man's survival is certain . . .?'

It happened that Captain McKay's discharge was not accepted. The report on him filtered, through official channels, to the War Office. A certain Major Wilkinson intercepted it first, and passed it on to a Colonel Graves. Graves was concerned with a highly secret section of the military machine that specialised in counter espionage. And his boss was the formidable, white-haired Brigadier Rowe, a man whose string of university degrees more than matched the line of medal ribbons on his barathea jacket.

'Sit down, McKay,' said Rowe. 'Let me say immediately that I am aware of your – ah – unenviable situation.'

'Yes, sir.'

'We have some documents,' Rowe continued. 'Documents that have been specially drawn up by one of our more, shall we say, clandestine departments. They would be of maximum interest to the enemy, and indeed, we wish them to have them.'

McKay grinned. 'I wasn't a writer for nothing, sir. I think I get your drift. The documents are phoney, correct?'

'Phoney is an absurd American term, McKay. But they *are* – misleading. Point is, the Germans who get them will have to be sure that they are genuine war plans.'

'I see your scheme, sir,' said McKay. 'It's no use leaking the information to the enemy. It has to be captured, fair and square. I take it *I* am to be the chap who gets caught.'

Brigadier Rowe took off his glasses, polished them, and stared at the young captain with undisguised admiration.

'You really *are* a perceptive chap,' he said. 'I admire you. There'll be a posthumous VC in it, of course. Your father and mother . . .'

'They'll be well pleased, sir. If I have a month to live, I'll live it for my country, and relish every moment. Now – give me the full briefing, if you would . . .'

There was a commando raid on the occupied French coast. It was a fiasco. An entire force of Canadians, Londoners from a machine gun regiment, and Lowlanders from the King's Own Scottish Borderers had been wiped out by determined Nazi opposition just north of Brest. It had been secret, and was not recorded in the annals of the Second World War. The combatants had failed to penetrate even ten metres beyond the beach-head.

But one man had got ashore. Deliberately landed some three kilometres south of the main assault zone from a rubber dinghy launched from a submarine. He was Captain Nigel McKay, clad in the uniform that would identify him, when captured, as a member of the attack group.

He knew his task. His first instruction was to slip to the north, without being seen, and he did it magnificently. Not even the sharpest-eyed French farmers of the Breton coast saw the figure who slipped towards the shipyards of Brest, and McKay reached the outskirts unchallenged.

His uniform, deliberately soaked with sea water, hung stained and unsightly about him. His inner pocket held the plastic-wrapped documents he had been entrusted with. In his hands, the sten-gun – that ineffective and mass-produced weapon so irritating to most who carried it. It had a possible range of thirty metres and a diabolical tendency to jam. And jam it did (as in fact it was meant to do) as McKay rose from a ditch and confronted men from the 44th Bavarian Infantry Regiment.

Nigel McKay bared his teeth in a theatrical snarl. He jerked at the cocking handle of his Sten, hurled a mass of broad-Scots invective at the Germans, and then, as they rushed him – grinning (as he thought) like baboons – tugged papers out of his jacket and attempted to set fire to them.

Nigel allowed one of them, a big, burly Feldwebel, to kick his hand away from them. His American-made Zippo lighter spun into the air, to be exultantly caught by a sharper-than-average Gefreiter who yelped, in English, 'Mine, I believe!' Then McKay was jerked to his feet, relieved of his bayonet, and marched towards the low, ragged houses that marked the perimeter of Brest's suburbs . . .

The Wehrmacht Oberleutnant who interrogated Nigel was politeness itself. After all, he was a soldier, too. And not, apparently, a Nazi. Not a member of the savage political party ruling his own country. But he knew his duty. 'You are clearly a member of British Intelligence,' he said. 'The papers we have taken from you prove it. I would suggest, Herr Kapitän, that you make a statement now, otherwise . . .'

'Otherwise,' put in McKay, 'you have to turn me over to the Gestapo, which won't be so good.'

'I fear they have methods of persuasion that are – distasteful. Be sensible, my dear fellow. What we have taken from you is in code. Tell us that code, and you will spend the rest of this war comfortably in a prison camp. Refuse, and you will suffer pain that I, as a German gentleman, would not like to think of.'

'You can take a running jump,' said McKay, evenly. 'And if you happen to bump into Hitler on the way, so much the better.' He knew he was tempting a violent reaction, but with less than a month to live, what did he care?

The Oberleutnant was not to be drawn. Stiffly, he ordered his men to take his prisoner into the town jail, still

Nigel McKay bared his teeth in a theatrical snarl.

staffed by French policemen who were under German orders. And then – albeit reluctantly, for he grudgingly admired McKay's fearless attitude – he rang the political head-quarters. The stronghold of the dreaded *geheime Staatspolizei* – the Gestapo.

They came for him that evening. McKay had been given a meal, of sorts. And the soldiers of his guard could not meet his eyes as he, apparently unworried, was led from the jail into a black car by men in long leather raincoats and trilby hats that made their white faces look somehow evil and sinister. McKay thought: 'They're convinced. They've gone through the documents they took from me. They'll move heaven and earth to get the code, and I'll crack. At the eleventh hour. I'll tell them what they want to know, and then they'll chuck me inside like a useless rag doll. They'll think they've won – but they'll have the wrong information!'

It was hell. More than hell. Gestapo methods began with basic treatment. McKay was flung into a cell and deprived of sleep for three days. Lights glared down at him incessantly, and every fifteen minutes, a guard would pound the door with the butt of a rifle. He came to long for sleep . . .

Then it was the soft approach. Red-eyed, he took visits from a smooth-talking, friendly man who chatted about pre-war days in London.

'Do you remember that nice little bar, just along Pic-cadilly, Nigel? What was it called? The Captain's Cabin? Ah, what pleasant times I had there when I was on the staff of the German Embassy. Do you recall Johnny, who used to mix such good cocktails . . .?'

And then there were the beatings. Big, hulking guards would burst in without warning, and belabour McKay with rubber truncheons unmercifully, until he screamed for them to stop . . .

Yet still his spirit hung together, and he held his tongue.

What had he got to lose? He formed a picture of the man he had never seen, Obersturmbannführer Karl Leittner, boss of this filthy prison into which he had so willingly come . . . McKay thought of him as a fat, obscene, drooling sadist, a pig of a man riddled with the disease of insanity . . .

Leittner, a mild, small-statured fellow with thinning hair and the calm, rather care-worn face of a university don, sat behind his desk and tapped his right hand – the only sign of neurosis was that his nails were bitten to the quick – on his blotter. McKay, his head held fast in the grip of a steel-helmeted guard, was forced to stare at him. Another guard had just hit him sickeningly in the kidneys with the butt of his rifle. 'Now, Captain,' said Leittner, equably. 'You have been here four weeks. It is not – um – like the Savoy Hotel, is it?'

'I always preferred the Ritz,' whispered Nigel, his eyes betraying nothing of his pain.

'Highly amusing. We Germans have a sense of humour, no matter what you *verdammte* English care to say.'

'I'm a Scotsman, you despicable Hun,' snarled McKay. 'There's a difference.'

'A dead man is a dead man,' sighed Leittner. 'Let us have an end to this nonsense. May I tell you that we have a couple of dozen other prisoners here? Some Belgians, some French, some Dutch. I propose to execute them – for they are of little importance. You shall watch.' He steepled his fingers and fixed the British officer with his dark, evil eyes.

McKay knew it was time to crack. And he did so, with commendable artistry. He flung the hands of his guard from him, leaped to his feet, and shrieked like a madman. He pounded his head on the wall, ran this way and that, called Leittner countless unprintable names – in German – and eventually subsided into a flood of abject tears . . .

Leittner sat back, folded his arms, and sighed, happily.

'And now, Herr Kapitän, you are going to give us the code to those documents . . .?'

'You start with a simple transposition,' began McKay, his voice thick and helpless . . .

Taken back to his cell, McKay knew he'd won. His act had been superb. Neither Leittner nor his superiors in the German government could possibly doubt that the information he'd given them was genuine. They would act on it, and Britain would have a chance of striking at them where they were least prepared. And what would they do to him now? Kill him? What did it matter? By his reckoning – by what the Medical Officer had told him – he was dead anyway. With scarcely a fortnight to live.

At the door of his prison, McKay saw his jailer turn, look away from him and fumble for the key that hung from a chain at his waist. Afterwards, McKay could never have told *why* he did it, but in that moment, he swung round and hit the man with every ounce of his remaining strength. His clenched fists took the German in the midriff, and doubled him up like the covers of a book. Nigel McKay's right hand drew back, and whipped like a piston to jack-knife the soldier against the wall, and the Schmeisser machine pistol, falling from his nerveless hands, fell into the Highlander's grasp cocked and ready for action!

Like a maniac, Nigel McKay shot his way out of the Gestapo headquarters in Brest. His lips were bared back from his teeth, and he knew later that they were sore from strain. He had vague impressions of the hateful, coal-scuttle helmets rolling wildly in the street as he shot down the opposition. Snarled with glee as a motor-cycle combination, speeding round to head him off, crashed headlong into a telegraph pole, snapped it, overturned and burst into flames. This was war. This was what it was all about!

His last conscious impression was leaping from the concrete wall of Brest harbour into the launch where the startled,
drop-jawed faces of two German sailors gaped up at him. The
butt of his gun sent them both spinning into the sea, and then
he was revving the engine that took him north-westwards,
and away from occupied France . . .

Captain Nigel McKay was picked up by a British destroyer
on Channel patrol. He had passed out. According to the
officer of the watch who had spotted his launch, which was
out of fuel and drifting, he was a possible enemy agent . . .

But Nigel managed to establish his bona-fides with the
destroyer captain, and the next stage of his adventure was
being put ashore at Plymouth, with no less a person to greet
him than Brigadier Rowe. They met in hospital, for that was
where McKay, suffering from his injuries at the hands of the
Gestapo, had been taken.

'You did remarkably well, my boy,' said Rowe, when
McKay had given him the full story. 'And I have something
to tell you. Something that will perhaps make you want to
take me by the throat and throttle me for a scheming, crazy
old fool.'

'Not that, sir,' murmured McKay. 'I've done what I
wanted to do, and it's enough. I don't know what made me
make such a desperate rush home, but maybe it was the awful
thought of – dying in that – Nazi place . . .'

'You're not going to die at all,' said Rowe. 'You'll find this
hard to believe, but there was a mistake. Your medical X-
rays were mixed up, and far from having an incurable
disease, you're as healthy as – as *I* am.'

McKay sank back on his pillow and laughed out loud.
Every move he'd made had been with the belief that his life
was, anyway, forfeit. Now he'd come through, and only to find
that he had a possibly long, long future.

'Don't send me back to the Sixteenth Gordons,' he said to Brigadier Rowe. 'Put me into Intelligence, permanently. I'd like to go back and do my bit against those diabolical fiends who call themselves the Gestapo . . .'

Brigadier Rowe nodded, and patted the Captain's arm. He approved; but then he couldn't have known that Nigel McKay, VC, was to be put to death in a concentration camp, on August 10th, 1944 . . .

In the Line of Duty . . .

Kelvin Gosnell

THE MORNING WAS BRIGHT AND CLEAR as only a November morning can be. It was the year 1894 and the trees in Hyde Park glittered in the glaring sun just after dawn.

The park was empty but for two figures, one of whom was a royal servant from Buckingham Palace. He walked briskly along the side of the lake, struggling with a disobedient spaniel on a lead. The other figure lurched unsteadily from one clump of bushes to another. Then he spotted the dog-walker and stopped to watch . . .

Ten minutes later the dog walker, a singularly mournful chap at the best of times, by the name of Wylie, staggered into one of the Palace kitchens breathless and bloody. 'Send for the guard,' he gasped. 'Th–the dog! He stole her majesty's dog. Tried to fight him but – but too strong for me.' With that he collapsed on to the large kitchen table.

The dog that Wylie had been walking – the spaniel called Winslow – was one of the Queen's most favoured pets, and Mary, the cook who had witnessed Wylie's astonishing performance, had served her Queen long enough to know that instant action was called for. She sent for the guard immediately and a search was started straightaway. But there was no sign of the dog or dog stealer. Until either of them, or hopefully both, was found, life around the Palace would be very, very unbearable. Mary prayed silently that the forces of law and order would be swift and efficient in their duty and find the dog without delay.

By the following morning most of the capital knew of the theft. *The Times* ran it as their lead story, for it was indeed important news: anything which affected the health or well-being of the Queen was a matter for concern to the Victorian public. Victoria had ruled her country for nearly sixty years – longer than most of her subjects had been alive – and she was much loved by them. That someone should want to harm her, especially in so malicious a manner, was shocking, distasteful.

The man called Albert Gaunt read the news item in *The Times* quite calmly. If he was shocked then he did a good job of hiding the fact. Mind you, it was many years since that hawk-like face with its hooded green eyes had showed any emotion stronger than mild surprise. Gaunt was taking his breakfast in a Long Acre inn on his way to work: a quart of warm ale with two freshly pickled herrings – standard working man's fare.

Gaunt had a strip of herring half way to his mouth when he read the item about the Queen's dog. The herring stopped in mid air as his eyebrow raised a fraction in an outburst of suspicion. His eyes lifted from the newspaper and seemed to focus on something far away from the dark, smoky room. The odd gaze lasted about two seconds. 'Strange,' he murmured to himself and allowed the herring to resume its upwards journey to be washed down a little later with a draught of the warm ale.

Gaunt's interest was purely professional. He knew a great deal about thieves and thieving and all sorts of other criminals for that matter – in his job as a sergeant in London's police you had to. Mind you, from the neat cut of his dark brown suit and matching derby bowler hat, you would be forgiven for thinking him anything but a policeman – Gaunt was a member of the recently formed (and much hated) plainclothes branch.

'Coppers in disguise' was what villains called Gaunt and

his colleagues. And they weren't far wrong in applying that phrase to the man in the brown suit. He had an uncanny knack of blending in with almost any background or crowd of people.

The man looking for the detective was only too well aware of this disappearing knack – he had been told he could find Gaunt at the inn, but try as he might he could not distinguish his man from the rest of the bodies in there. Since he had come armed with a full description of Gaunt, he had not imagined having trouble in finding his man, especially since he assumed all policemen stood out wherever they were.

Gaunt had watched the man from the moment he entered. He was tall, obviously very well-off, and wearing a frock coat and topper. There were only two possible motives for a man like that to enter such a grubby drinker: he was either looking for a villain to do some dirty work, or looking for a copper to clean up some dirty work which had already been done. Gaunt would have bet his money on the latter and he would have won. He was not at all surprised when the man asked at the bar for, 'a chappie name o' Gaunt, said to be here?'

Old Joe behind the bar had an understanding with Gaunt. He stalled the toff at first, just long enough to fire an inquiring glance at Gaunt to check whether he should tell the truth. Gaunt nodded his head perceptibly and soon the stranger was settled alongside him.

It was immediately obvious that the stranger was more than your common-or-garden toff – there was that little extra touch of arrogance about his manner, the disdainful way in which he brushed the dust from his topper. Above all though, there was the opening insult which a man in Gaunt's position had come to expect from one bearing high office.

'So you're Gaunt, eh?' the man sneered. 'Thought a so-called overworked policeman ought to be at work by now, not sitting in some low drinking house, reading.'

'Ah, but I am at work, sir,' Gaunt replied charmingly. He beckoned the man closer with a conspiringly crooked finger. 'See that cove over there,' he whispered, indicating a great gross barrel of a man seated on the opposite side of the room, who was apparently trying to ram a whole plate of oysters down his throat at once *and* continue talking. 'Well he's the prime suspect in the Wapping Murders case . . . some do say as he did 'em *all* himself! Tore all six victims limb from limb with his bare hands. I'm ordered to watch him and report any suspicious moves.'

'Ah, yes. I see, Gaunt.' 'Topper' was suitably brought down to size by Gaunt's words. He continued his introductions in a less haughty manner. 'I'm going to have to order you to come off this, er, Wapping case for the time being. Something a trifle more urgent has come up – at the Palace, you understand. I've already spoken to your superiors at the Yard and they told me everything would be in order . . .'

'At the palace, sir?' Gaunt answered, pretending not to understand. 'Then surely a visit to Penge village constabulary would be in order – Crystal Palace is under their jurisdiction.'

'No! Buckingham Palace, Gaunt – *Buckingham* Palace – where your sovereign resides.' The old haughty arrogance was back in full. Gaunt laughed inwardly – they were all alike these upper crust toffs, all mouth and very little brains. Didn't even know when they were having the rise taken out of them.

Gaunt allowed a dim look of understanding to smear itself over his face as Topper continued and introduced himself as Major Jackson of the Queen's household. Gaunt then smiled innocently as he dropped his bombshell on the Major's lap. 'Come about the dog then, have you, Major?'

Stunned astonishment gripped Jackson and Gaunt thought for a moment that he was going to choke to death on the spot. 'Oh, please don't look so shocked, sir,' Gaunt continued, 'it was a simple deduction to make. I've read the story about the man Wylie being beaten up and the dog taken. Since you are from the Palace, I can easily guess that Her Majesty wants her dog back swiftly and with the minimum of fuss. Since neither your own men nor the uniformed branch of my own service have the necessary knowledge of the villainous coves likely to make off with the royal pooch, and since I do have that knowledge, then it is now a case of "send Gaunt to catch the mutt". Am I right, Major?'

'P-perfectly,' the major stammered.

'It shall be done, then,' Gaunt said jauntily as he rose and popped his brown derby on the back of his head. 'Do me a favour though, sir, would you?' he asked as he jerked a thumb at the fat man (now on third plate of oysters). 'Keep an eye on me suspect over there till I can relieve you. Don't want to lose him after all this time.' With that he strode quickly out of the room, scarcely able to hide a smile at the thought of a Major of the royal household sitting all day watching a totally innocent Covent Garden porter consuming his customary monumental breakfast.

The taking of dogs from their rich owners in order to give them back to said rich owners after a suitable 'finder's fee' had been paid was a well-practised piece of villainy in early Victorian London. In fact, up until the 1870s it had not actually been illegal to make off with someone's dog, since dogs were not classified as normal property and therefore could not be stolen. If you caught the culprit, then you usually had to nick him for stealing the mutt's collar and not the mutt itself. Thankfully all that had changed with the passing of a new law and 'dog finding' had become a rare crime.

What the villains were up to now was nicking very expensive pedigree dogs and selling them to unscrupulous breeders both in Britain and France. But to steal Queen Victoria's very own animal, one which would be so easily recognisable! That was a very dodgy prospect for a careful villain. There were other things about the case which did not ring true to Gaunt. They nagged at him like a bad tooth. He headed eastwards . . .

Benny Capstick knew Gaunt very well – he'd been arrested by him several times and that was why he was running now! For once, Gaunt's ability to melt into a crowd had not worked – nothing like that would work with Benny, he almost had the second sight when it came to rozzers; he used to swear he could *smell* 'em coming round corners. When you were a working villain like Benny, you had to have some warning system!

Benny had been carrying on the legitimate side of his business on his Dad's stall down Petticoat Lane when he'd spotted Gaunt approaching through the crowd.

He didn't know whether Gaunt was after him or not, but he wasn't taking any chances. He handed the stall over to his assistant and was away in a matter of seconds. The narrow winding alleys that infested the warehouses around the Lane were home ground to Benny. He shot along their reeking flagstones like a rat through a sewer. He was making towards Aldgate where he could disappear properly and just as he was rounding the slippery bend in one corridor, the ground seemed to disappear from under him! He landed face first in the slime and slithered to a halt against a pitted wall. Looking painfully up, he saw a familiar face, high above the familiar foot that had tripped him . . .

'Careful, Benny-boy,' Gaunt said. 'Could do yourself a shocking mischief running along these alleys without looking where you're going.'

Benny couldn't believe his bad luck, but decided to try and bluff. 'Oh, Mr Gaunt. Haven't seen you for ages . . .'

Looking painfully up, Benny saw a familiar face, high above a familiar foot that had tripped him . . .

'That's a lie, Benny. You saw me a couple of minutes ago back in the Lane, and decided to leg it.' Gaunt smiled mirthlessly as he helped Benny back to his feet. 'Benny,' he said, 'you are not only a terrible villain. You are a terrible liar. However, I do not want to talk to you about something you have done. I want to talk about something you *know* about. Now come on, let's get away from this stinking alley into the fresh air where we can talk.'

Soon they were down on the river embankment in front of the Tower of London. Leaning on the railings overlooking the Thames they watched an army of navvies working on a great structure that rose up from the water: Tower Bridge was due to open officially very soon, a feat of engineering daring to be admired all over the globe.

Benny looked at it proudly. 'Amazing, innit, Mr Gaunt? We'll be sending men to the moon next, you see if I ain't right . . .'

'Oh, I believe you, Benny. It'd make a great penal colony up there, be a bit like Australia only better since it's further away – *and* there'd be no chance of villains like you escaping . . .' Gaunt's hint to Benny that he wanted to return the conversation to the subject of dogs was quickly taken.

'Er, yeah, like I said – there ain't been a lot of dog finding going on these days. Getting to be a mighty dodgy business it is, and most of the lads have taken to exporting their stuff. But I tell you there ain't no-one would have the Queen's dog away. I mean, that's gotta be treason, innit? They chop your bonce off for that! Besides, every punter knows what that mutt looks like and there ain't none of 'em would buy the animal.

'No, Mr Gaunt, it's got to be a nutter that's done it – none of the professionals in the trade would knock that Wylie geezer over the head, they ain't the violent type. They use special baits and creams and ointments and all sorts of things I don't care to think about to *lure* the mutts away. Chelsea George knows all about them things . . .'

'Chelsea George?' Gaunt asked. It was a new name to him.

'Yeah,' Benny answered. 'Chelsea George was the best dog finder as there ever was. He retired ages ago though, well before you joined the force, Mr Gaunt. He must be at least seventy by now. Lives in a garret over in Bermondsey. He might know something more, Mr Gaunt. I can't tell you any more. Honest . . .'

Gaunt's green eyes levelled at Benny. The villain squirmed on the spot – it felt like they were burning holes into his brain. They flicked away, back to the bridge. 'Very well, Benny. Give me the man's address and I'll leave you in peace – for now.'

The tiny room in which Chelsea George existed was easy to find and George was at home when Gaunt arrived. But he wasn't going to be any help at all to the detective: Chelsea George, greatest dog stealer of the century, had purloined his last pooch – he was very dead indeed. The room showed signs of a violent struggle, which had ended with George being viciously stabbed many times.

Gaunt was no stranger to murders, for he had seen many in his profession – but this ranked as one of the nastiest. George had been an old man, one strong blow would have done the job. The repeated frenzied stabbing had to be the work of either a man in blind panic or a sadistic lunatic.

Gaunt moved over to the body. It was still warm, very warm! The killing had probably been done only a few moments before he arrived. Gaunt re-ran his memory of people and events just before he entered the building . . . there had been a flower-seller, a beggar slumped against the wall, the well-dressed chap carrying a bag, an old woman pushing a market barrow . . . which one was most likely?

As he thought, something caught his eye in the room's pathetic fireplace. The fire had not been lit that morning, but something had been burned recently . . . a small piece of paper. He snatched it from the grate and read those words which remained on the singed note, 'SEEN WHAT YOU DONE. KEEP QUIET MONEY GOT THE DOG'. All written in a semi-illiterate scrawl of capitals, such as might come from the hand of George.

Gaunt's mind speeded up. The twisted logic that a police officer gets used to using in his dealings with criminals spilled out a vast number of possibilities, but only one made sense – and it called for immediate action!

When he reached the outside of the building again, the well-dressed figure was almost out of sight. He was heading west along Tooley Street and had just reached the junction with the new road which led to Tower Bridge. By sheer good fortune he was just passing the police station on the corner. Gaunt was running hard now, he had to catch his man before he hailed a cab and was lost completely. He drew his police whistle and blew hard!

The sharp penetrating shrill of the whistle made the man whirl in Gaunt's direction. For a moment he became like a rabbit rooted to the spot in front of a fox. Then the spell broke and he ran – up the road towards the new bridge, he still held on grimly to the bag.

He had hardly disappeared round the corner when the Tooley Street police station seemed to explode with blue serge. Ten uniformed officers sprang down the steps outside the building. Gaunt shouted to them to pursue the villain up the bridge road and then he himself ducked into a side turning. He would skirt round the back of the brewery behind the station and try to head his man off before he reached the bridge.

When he emerged breathless at the foot of the bridge, he allowed himself a smile. The villain was already past the spot where he stood but there was no way he could escape across the great elevating roadways of the bridge – they stood vertically upwards! The engineers had chosen exactly the right moment to test the engines of the great structure.

The uniformed officers were coming up fast and the chase seemed over but the smile vanished from Gaunt's face as he followed the gaze of his quarry – upwards – to the catwalks. The new bridge had been designed with two pedestrian catwalks high above its road surfaces so that people on foot were not delayed when the bridge was raised.

Things started to happen very quickly. The man with the bag looked back to Gaunt and the officers in panic, he dropped the bag over the bridge into the Thames and ran into the stairway which would take him up to the catwalks. Gaunt knew he had only seconds to act. 'You!' he barked at one constable. 'Get into the river and get that bag before it sinks.'

'What the flaming 'ell . . .?' was all that the constable could stammer in reply. Gaunt flashed his warrant card at him. 'Gaunt, plainclothes,' he said. 'The bag contains Her Majesty's dog. Now get in the drink, man, before the pooch drowns.' The man obeyed.

With the remainder of the men at his heels, Gaunt raced to the first great tower of the bridge. There he split his party into two groups. The first was to follow the fleeing man up the stairs, the second was to contact the bridge engineers and get the roadways lowered at double time – they might then stand a chance of cutting him off before he reached the other side.

Gaunt headed the group chasing up the stairs. It was an exhausting climb and all the men were breathing harsh and heavy by the time they reached the top.

As soon as he emerged on the walkway, he knew that he

had won. The walkways were constructed from great iron plates rivetted together and what could not be seen from the ground was that this walkway was incomplete. There was a section missing from the floor in the centre. It was too wide for a man to jump and the man that stood on the edge of that wind-torn gap did not look like the type to risk climbing along the bottomless side of the walkway, not with that deadly drop below . . .

Gaunt relaxed slightly. The end was in sight now, but it still needed careful handling. He motioned the uniformed officers to move back – what he wanted to do had to be done alone. He stepped slowly out on to the iron floor high above the chilling Thames.

'Come on, Wylie,' he called. 'The game's over. Nowhere to run any more.' The grim-faced royal servant spun round to face Gaunt. 'H-how did you know . . .?' he asked, confused. Gaunt slowed his pace. So his crazy guess had been right, the twisted logic had worked again.

'You should have burned the note properly, Wylie,' Gaunt replied. 'As soon as I read it, I realised that it had to be you. The only thing that still puzzles me is why . . . what happened in the park?'

Wylie's face seemed to collapse in a mess of grey flesh. He spoke very despondently. 'I – I tried to drown the stupid thing. I really, really hated that dog. It was always biting me, going for me at the least excuse. God! I loathed that thing but it was always me had to take it for its drag. I couldn't stand it any longer so I tied a brick round its neck and dropped it in the lake. I added some cuts to the dog bites I'd already got and staggered back to the palace. I'd have got away with it too, if it wasn't for that meddling old man. He'd seen what I'd done and fished the mutt out after I'd gone. He took it back to that slum of his and, when he found out whose dog it was, he tried to blackmail me.

'I – I didn't mean to kill him. He was threatening me with what he was going to do to me, bleed me dry, he said, and I just lost control.'

'Well, we'll let the judge make up his mind about that, Wylie,' said Gaunt calmly as he came closer to the man. He stopped as he saw the look of uncontrollable panic rising in Wylie's face. 'Hold it, old son,' Gaunt said softly, trying to calm the man down.

'They'll t-top me, won't they?' Wylie stammered. 'I don't want no rope round my neck, copper. You ain't caught me yet – no! I'll take me chance with the river – got a better chance in the water than I have in front of a judge.'

Without glancing down, Wylie leapt backwards through the gaping hole in the walkway. Gaunt took a dive forward to try and stop him. 'No, Wylie!' he shouted. But it was too late. With the wind whipping at them on the walkway, it had been impossible to hear the great roadways being lowered beneath them: at the instant that Wylie had stepped off the walkway, he thought he would be dropping to the water of the Thames – in fact he dropped smack in the centre of the two roadways just before their vast bulks met and closed. His scream was cut short by two thousand tons of massive metal and masonry.

Gaunt looked down sadly, then he raised his glance to the foreshore downstream. He could see a very muddy copper emerging from the river – there was the tiny shape of a dog walking unsteadily at his side. At least some good had come out of this awful business. He started the long climb back down again.

An hour later, Gaunt re-entered the inn at which he had had breakfast. He was playing very long odds but – yes! The Major was still there, obediently watching the fat man, the latter now being fast asleep and snoring after countless quarts of ale. Gaunt had forgotten that it was payday for the porters and Fatty habitually drank away half his week's wages as soon as he got them.

He walked over to the major and dumped the cleaned-up spaniel on to his lap. 'There you are, major,' he said. 'One royal dog returned with the compliments of the Metropolitan Police Force.'

The major was beside himself with a mixture of joy and disbelief. 'But how?' he gasped. 'You've only been gone a few hours.'

'I didn't have time to hang about, sir,' Gaunt replied with a smile. 'Wanted to get back and keep an eye on me suspect over there.' Still astonished, the Major rose to leave, thanking Gaunt profusely. Just as he walked through the door, Gaunt called after him, 'Oh, by the way, sir. Her Majesty will need to recruit another servant to replace Mr Wylie. He won't be returning to her employment, I'm afraid. He had a rather, er, *pressing engagement.*'

Race Against the Gun

Allen Sadler

THERE WAS A BUBBLING UNDERCURRENT of excitement all around the stadium. The crowd knew they were going to see something special. All the seats had been filled. The new stand was packed and standing space could not be found. It was an evening meeting in September, at the end of the athletic season. All through the summer the two giants of the track, Gomez (Brazil) and Kimber (United States) had battled it out, clipping the world record for the 5,000 metres at every race. The score stood at three wins each, but Kimber still had the record at 13 minutes 10.24 seconds, the fastest the world had ever seen. Tonight's race gave Gomez his chance to improve on the record and gain a final victory over Kimber. Kimber was there to be shot at. The man who holds the record is always in danger.

The British runner, Pete Morgan, had been improving lately, although he always came a bad third behind the powerhouse champions of North and South America. The race had also drawn the national champions from France, Turkey, Bulgaria, Eire, Finland, Denmark and Norway. The runners, all champions and record holders, knew that they would not be in the hunt when either Kimber or Gomez turned on their final burst, but in the race of races, everybody wanted to compete.

It had rained most of the day. The red track glistened and the grass oval sparkled in the early evening sun. It would be dark before the race started. The floodlit stadium would increase the drama of the scene, the spotlight picking out the leading runners as the race drew to a climax over the last three laps. But that moment was still three hours away, and before it could happen Ben Brown had to find and eliminate the threat hanging over Pancho Gomez.

IF GOMEZ RUNS TONIGHT HE IS A DEAD MAN.

The note was made up from newspaper clippings, stuck on in a crazy jumble. It looks silly, childish even, but it was something to be taken seriously. An upset could threaten further meetings and other sports events.

'Some nut,' said Pancho Gomez, but Ben could see that the big man was worried. The organisers of the meeting were worried. The police were worried. Twelve thousand people were spread out in tiers in a circle nearly a kilometre around. Any one out there could have a gun. There were any number of ideal spots for a marksman on the roofs of the stands. Beyond the limits of the stadium there were blocks of flats where lucky people got a free view of the events, through hundreds of windows that would give a gunman with a telescopic rifle lens a very easy sight on his target. No wonder the police had asked Ben, a private investigator with a reputation for finding needles in haystacks, to help them find the assassin before he got to work.

The police had another problem. Any public announce-ment of danger might cause a panic. A mad rush for the exits could cause injury and damage. The police had asked Gomez to consider standing down, to pretend an injury, a pulled calf muscle, anything. But Gomez would have none of that.

'These people have paid their money to see me run. I came here to run, and that's exactly what I'm going to do.'

The threat had only arrived an hour before the meeting opened. Nobody seemed to know how the alarming note had got on to the desk in the manager's office. The office door was not locked, but it must have happened before the public were admitted to the stadium.

On the face of it someone on the staff could have been responsible, but there was hardly time to question all the attendants, now distributed all around the stadium.

Ben knew that the police were looking for a gun, for a long range marksman who could strike and be far enough away to make good an escape, but there were many other ways of making sure Gomez did not run. Ben decided to stick close to Pancho and leave the police to do the long-range scouting.

In the changing room with its peculiar smell of sweat and strange ointments, most of the runners were doing limbering up exercises, warming up for the extreme exertion to come. But Pancho Gomez had spread his large frame along the bench.

Ben sat down beside the enormous athlete.

'Have you any idea who might want to stop you from running? What about Bill Kimber, for a start?'

Pancho grinned.

'Bill wants to beat me,' he said. 'He can't do that if I don't run. Off the tracks Kimber and me get on great. It's only in a race we get mad at each other; it don't mean nothing after it's over.'

'What about this threat? Is it going to affect your performance?'

'Sure,' said Pancho. 'I'm going to be faster than ever. I want to get it over with before anything happens.'

It seemed ridiculous that a man of Pancho's size and strength should need a bodyguard. Pancho was a man in the peak of physical condition. He glowed with good health. He made Ben feel tired, just looking at him. A man like Pancho could run up the side of a house.

Bill Kimber came in and started to change into his kit.

'Hey Pancho, what's this I hear about you ducking out?'

Pancho gave his rival a lazy smile.

'No chance,' he said. 'You'll have to fight me. All the way.'

The contrast between the two men was startling. Bill Kimber was short and squat. The power was in his shoulders as much as his legs. Kimber's style was hunched, leaning forward, his heavy shoulders and trunk forcing his legs forward by tipping the point of balance. He only came up to Pancho's shoulder, and yet the pair were well matched. When Pancho flew over the ground as though his feet were hardly touching the track, Kimber charged. Pancho was capable of turning on electrifying spurts; Kimber on the other hand wound up more slowly, but always kept going, increasing speed and sustaining it to the tape. The styles of running were entirely different, but each worked just as well when it came to a race.

Pancho lifted his long legs into the air and pedalled briefly.

'You want to know what this is all about?' he said.

'Sure,' Ben said. 'Give us a clue.'

Kimber looked up from lacing his training shoes, paying attention.

'Well,' said Pancho. 'I think there's a lot of heavy money on Bill to win.'

'Betting?' Ben said.

'Yeah. Athletics is a clean sport mostly. No bets, no bribes, no large prizes; nothing like that. But that doesn't stop people outside from running books.'

'That's true,' said Bill Kimber, nodding his head. 'I was offered five thousand dollars once, to throw a race.'

'Just think,' said Pancho, 'how much money was at stake with that kind of money on offer.'

The two runners picked up their bags and made their way to the nearby warming-up track. Ben followed, puffing.

The meeting had started. Field events were in progress and the sprinters waiting for the early eliminating rounds were limbering up. The crowd were appreciative and cheered every effort, but they were reserving their biggest cheer for the 5,000 metres.

All through the warm-up period Ben kept Pancho in sight. He couldn't keep up with him, but he stuck as close as he could. With half an hour to go the runners were called over to the track and Ben still had no idea what he could do to protect Pancho from his would-be killer.

When they got on to the green oval Ben looked around at the blur of faces, and shook his head. The threatening note had not said that Pancho would be prevented from running, but only promised punishment if he did. It was Pancho who was taking the risk. He might win the race and then be cut down as he was leaving the stadium. On the other hand, if Pancho's betting theory was right, the object would be to stop him winning, which meant that the strike would come any time between now and the end of the race.

When the runners were being introduced to the crowd Ben realised that Pancho's life could be down to minutes, and that it was mad to think that he could do anything about it.

There was a good deal of good natured kidding between Pancho and Bill Kimber as they lined up for the start. But Pete Morgan was pale and silent, presenting a picture of quiet determination.

There was the usual jostling for position after the starter's pistol. There were twelve runners. They all wanted to get in their favourite places in the file. Kimber soon led, with Pete Morgan lapping on Kimber's heels, then the rest of the field, with Pancho loping along at the rear. There were shouts and whistles as the first lap went by in 60 seconds dead. The second lap went out to 64. Kimber charged down the back straight, trying to shake off the persistent Pete Morgan. The crowd stood up, the atmosphere was electric. The race was on from the bell. There was no dawdling from Kimber, who had set out to break the field and smash his own record.

As the file began to string out Pancho slipped a couple of places. Not really turning on any speed, but just keeping in touch. The crowd sensed that Pancho was winding up slowly and cheered as he passed through into sixth place. Pancho kept to the outside of the other runners, determined not to get blocked or boxed in when the time came for the final sprint.

Kimber was employing his well-known tactics of running a slow bend and turning it on for the straights. Pete Morgan, keeping up with these fits and starts, was already looking strained. Pancho, still lying handy but not yet in a position to challenge, was running even laps. With runners of this class, evenly matched, it was tactics that counted, as much as physical fitness. This race had to be thought out.

Although Ben's eyes were drawn to the titanic struggle he realised that it would be fatal to give the race his full attention. Somewhere in the stadium was a killer who was calculating that all eyes would be on the travelling drama on the track. In this situation it was possible to get away with murder in full view of thousands of people. On the green oval, athletes and officials were all watching the race, turning slowly as the runners wound around them. All except one man. He was laying on the grass, face down. The autumn air was balmy but not all that warm and Ben could not help wondering why he was not wearing a jacket. He was a small man, lying very still, wearing just a shirt and trousers. As the race entered the fourth lap, with around eight minutes to go, Ben sprang into action.

When Ben turned the small man over he could see the blood on his shirt front. Clenched in his hand was a pistol. It was not a weapon for killing, it was a starter's pistol. All eyes are on the starter at the beginning of a race, but as soon as he

When Ben turned the small man over he could see the blood on his
shirt front. Clenched in his hand was a pistol.

has fired the signal nobody watches him anymore. Now Ben had that prickling sensation at the back of his neck that told him he was on the right track. If this man was the starter, where was his red jacket and his red cap? It was obvious. The only man who could walk about an athletic stadium with a pistol was the starter. With a red jacket and a red cap anyone could be a starter. The starting pistol would not kill anyone, but this could easily be substituted for the real thing.

Ben looked around for the bogus starter. Although it was a brilliantly clever idea, once you had noticed the switch-over it was easy to spot the criminal, in a red jacket and cap. Ben heaved a sigh of relief. There was a chance of saving Pancho after all.

Meanwhile the race was hotting up. Pancho had moved up into fourth place. Pete Morgan looked as though he had died three laps back, but was still hanging on grimly to the sudden spurts and equally sudden cuts in speed of Bill Kimber. Then Kimber surprised Morgan. Pete was expecting another cut in speed around the bend but Kimber kept going. You could see the look of shocked surprise in Morgan's face as he realised he was losing ground. He hadn't expected Kimber to strike out with nearly 2,000 metres to go. It was early. It was suicidal, but Kimber, heavy shoulders bent forward and legs going like pistons, didn't seem to be suffering.

Kimber's tricky move not only left Morgan struggling, but Pancho Gomez, seeing the danger, suddenly notched up to pass the Turk he had been following and edge up to Pete Morgan's shoulder. Pete, fearful of losing his second place, shot off like a startled rabbit after Kimber. The three leading runners were well detached from the rest of the field in a private battle of will, strength and tactics.

At this point all the 12,000 people sitting in the stands stood up as though they had been given an order. Ben could hear the television commentator screaming with excitement.

Now the heat was on. Pancho was at least twelve metres behind, a long distance to make up in a race of this class.

Bill Kimber put in a lap of 58 seconds. Pancho passed Morgan, but Kimber was eating up the ground, going further and further in front. The stadium light went down and the spotlight came on. It was Kimber in his full glory; another spotlight picked up Pancho, maybe fifteen yards back.

Ben, trying to span the whole track area, blinked as the lights went down. Was that a speck of red he had picked out just before the lights went down? It was in the area of the finishing line. Ben ran across the grass, trying to remember the exact spot.

As Ben got to the finishing line Kimber scorched by with two laps to go. Then Pancho, beginning to close, but not yet within reach. The next lap was the bell. The time was ridiculous, averaging four minutes for 1,500 metres. At this rate Kimber would put the record beyond reach for years to come. He was like a man running for his life.

While Ben was staring around wildly for a man in a starter's jacket, a figure came out of the tunnel that led from the changing rooms to the centre of the track. It was too gloomy for Ben to make out the colour of his jacket, but the cap with the long peak was a sure means of identification. The man, emerging briskly from the tunnel, walked purpose-fully to the edge of the track, holding a pistol, low down. Ben ran, bending low, dodging behind the backs of track officials, flinging himself down behind the man with the gun.

By this time the noise in the stadium was deafening. Pancho was inching his way up to Kimber, trying to get within striking distance before the bell for the last lap. Kimber, who had run the finish out of Pete Morgan and everyone else, obviously thought that hanging on would be enough. But, at the bell, Pancho suddenly found another gear. He stopped clawing at the distance that separated him from Kimber and leapt forward as though he had been fired from a cannon. He was more like a sprinter at the start than a long distance runner at the end of a gruelling race. Suddenly it looked obvious that Pancho was going to win. He had held something in reserve, timed his burst perfectly. He was tapping on Kimber's heels, now up to his shoulder. The final bend would see the ultimate revelation of Pancho's strategy.

But Ben Brown, dimly aware from the crowd noises that something stupendous was going to take place, was carefully watching the man dressed as a starter who had raised his pistol and was tracking the arc of Pancho's progress, waiting for the big man to pass. Ben hurtled from the ground and flung himself at the bogus starter, rolling with him clear across the track, just clearing the first two lanes as Pancho and Kimber came thundering by.

Ben clamped an iron grip on the man's wrists until he released the gun. Pancho unwound his final spurt around the final bend, but Kimber was not done. He held on, coming again down the final straight. Now it was Pancho who was holding on, with Kimber gritting his teeth. It was hard to separate them as they hurled themselves across the line. Pancho got the verdîct by a whisker.

Ben, dragging a struggling gunman into the arms of a pair of policemen, was hardly noticed in the uproar. But Pancho had seen him rolling across the track and rushed over to see if Ben was all right.

'I'm OK,' said Ben. 'But there's a badly injured starter laying around somewhere who needs an ambulance.'

The assassination attempt had been well planned. The real starter was shot as he fired the pistol to start the race. The sound of the real shot was lost behind the accepted explosion of the starting gun. The man, working for a betting syndicate, had been hired for the job.

Pancho's last burst had brought the world record down by

a full 5 seconds. The triumph was celebrated all around the stadium. One thing puzzled the crowd. When Pancho set off on his lap of honour he took Ben Brown with him.

Fall Back on Plan 'B'

Alan A Grant

NIGHT. THE SOFT DRONE of a light Bristol bomber was almost stifled by the dense, humid mist that hung above the Burmese jungle.

As it crossed the wide sweep of the Irrawaddy River, flowing south to distant Rangoon, the bomb-bays opened and a white parachute billowed out. The plane banked and sped quickly west, towards the Allied landing strip at Imphal.

The parachute drifted down towards the treetops below, and in its harness Captain James Sparks grinned ruefully. He was going to miss the clearing. Pity.

Then he was crashing feet first into the upper branches of a tall tree. They whipped and stung him, breaking beneath his weight. The 'chute snagged, and Sparks was almost winded as his body was jerked violently against the hard trunk.

'Ah well, I suppose getting there's half the fun,' he muttered to himself as he checked for damage. No broken bones. He unslung his thick-bladed machete from where it was strapped across his back and severed the 'chute cords one by one.

When he was free, Sparks shinned carefully down the trunk to the ground. The 'chute would have to stay where it was, entwined in the branches above.

Take me all night to untangle it, Sparks thought. I'll just have to leave it for the Japs to find. Meanwhile, I'd better put some distance between it and me!

Not a trace of moonlight penetrated the thick curtain of foliage which formed a canopy ten metres above the moist ground. Sparks took his torch from his backpack and switched it on. The beam cut a swathe through the inky darkness.

If I remember my maps, Sparks thought, there's a jungle trail not too far from here. Better start cutting . . .

He swung the machete's heavy blade in a swift arc, hacking at the dense undergrowth. It was slow work; the foliage gave way reluctantly, even though Sparks was cutting a passage wide enough for only himself.

He was sweating profusely and his clothes stuck to his body when at last he reached the trail. He sat down for a minute or two, swallowed three salt pills to combat dehydration, then checked the compass from his pack and struck out quickly along the trail, moving as fast as torchlight would allow.

It was over an hour later when Sparks considered it safe to stop again. He selected a tree a little back from the path, and climbed up into its lower branches. There, he wrapped himself in his ground-sheet; he tied a rope firmly round his waist and fastened it securely to the tree-trunk. Tomorrow was going to be a busy day; Sparks would need every moment of sleep he could snatch.

James Sparks' mission in Burma had come at short notice. Two days earlier, he'd been summoned to an inconspicuous building in a Calcutta backstreet; this unprepossessing front concealed an operations centre for SOE, the British intelligence network.

There, he was shown into the office of the Controller.

'Got a real stinker for you this time, Jimmy boy.' The Controller's words were light, but his face was grim. 'Seems one of our American friends has got himself into a spot of bother – it's up to us to get him out.'

'As usual,' Sparks grinned. 'Who is it this time?'

'"Fireball" Sherman, no less.'

Sparks whistled. General Herman Sherman's foolhardy exploits had earned him the ironic nickname 'Fireball'. His latest escapade had been a personal surveillance flight over Japanese-occupied Burma. He'd been shot down.

'Our local agent reported that the general is still alive . . . and in Jap hands,' the Controller went on. 'He's being taken south under heavy guard in three days, for interrogation in Rangoon. Obviously, he has information which under no circumstances must fall into enemy hands.'

He paused and eyed the younger man thoughtfully. 'That's your job, Jimmy boy – bring him back.'

The Controller had every confidence in Sparks. Though only twenty-three, he'd had a distinguished service record with the Coldstream Guards before being seconded to SOE duties. His spare frame and boyish blond hair belied the tough, battle-hardened veteran that Sparks was. A schoolboy gymnast, he had added expertise in unarmed combat and an almost computer-like knowledge of small arms weaponry to his repertoire.

Since joining SOE, he'd completed five missions – every one of them successfully – and was now scheduled for an overdue rest. But Sparks had not requested any leave, and the Controller was happy to ignore it in his case. Sparks showed no sign of the cracked nerves and general fatigue that affected other agents; his natural good humour wouldn't allow it.

If anyone could bring Fireball Sherman back, it was young Jim.

'Might be a bit tricky, sir,' Sparks mused. 'Sherman's a big fish. The Japs will be taking no chances with him. What if I can't get him through?'

The Controller held his gaze steadily. 'In that case, you will fall back on Plan "B".'

'Righto, sir.' Sparks got to his feet. 'That's all I wanted to know.'

Dawn. Even as the sun's first rays struggled to penetrate the forest canopy, James Sparks was rolling up his ground-sheet. He was covered in mosquito bites, so he added quinine to his drinking water. He breakfasted briefly from a ration tin, then set off along the trail.

It wound south and curved sharply westward towards the banks of the Irrawaddy, and Sparks' senses were alert as he loped along at a steady pace, pausing every so often to listen intently. But there was no sign of enemy patrols.

The sun was high in the sky by the time he reached the narrow, rutted road that ran parallel to the river. The heat and humidity were oppressive, almost overwhelming, but Sparks was used to these conditions. He moved carefully along the road, his keen eyes searching for the perfect spot. Suddenly, he froze . . . then melted back into the thick bushes that flanked the road.

Soundlessly he crouched there as a Japanese troop-truck rumbled by, packed with singing soldiers. It was a full minute before Sparks moved again and returned to his quest.

About a hundred yards on, he found it: a place where the road looped round a large rocky outcrop. Deftly, Sparks scaled the jutting rock.

From the top he had a clear view of the road on both sides. Behind him he could see that the undergrowth thinned as it ran down towards the flood basin of the river: a handy escape route. Plenty of cover, but not enough to hamper his progress. He only hoped Fireball Sherman hadn't been injured in the crash; carrying him would be out of the question.

On the rock's flattish top Sparks neatly laid out the tools of his trade: one Thompson M1 sub-machine gun with magazine, capable of firing off 700 rounds per minute. One 1.38

Webley standard issue British Army revolver. One machete, somewhat blunted from his assault on the jungle – but still an effective killing tool. Six hand-grenades on specially-shortened 4-second fuses.

From his bulky pack Sparks pulled out the last item in his arsenal: a dough-like lump of plastic explosive, two kilos in all.

He made his way back down to the road, backtracked round the bend, and continued almost twenty metres down a short straight section of the road still visible from the rock. Moulding the explosive into a long, thick sausage shape, he jammed it down into a deep rut. Then he planted two detonators in it. One should be enough, but it was always better to have a safety margin – a Plan 'B'.

Using the machete, he gouged a narrow channel from the rut back across the road and into the undergrowth. He connected up the wires to the detonators and trailed them along the channel into the jungle. Swiftly, he covered explosive and wire over with dry earth, hiding them from view. Trailing the wire behind him, Sparks climbed back up the overhang and linked them to the detonator box.

He surveyed his handiwork, and thought wryly: At least I'll have a lot less to carry back!

There was no saying when he'd be able to eat again, so he wolfed down two tins of the unappetising rations. All he could do now was wait.

Two hours later, he heard the approaching rumble of several vehicles. Others had passed while he waited, but only single troop-transports, and Sparks had let them go.

The convoy came on slowly, making heavy going on the rough track. Then from a bend in the trail some 50 metres ahead, the dull metal tracks of a Chi Ha tank butted into view, followed by the stubby barrel of its 57 mm gun. The

Japs certainly *were* taking no chances!

Immediately behind the tank came a hardtop truck. A Japanese soldier armed with a sub-machine gun sat on the cab roof—looking very edgy, Sparks observed. That had to be the one they were ferrying Fireball in.

The rear of the truck partially shielded the third vehicle, a staff-car with a Japanese captain sitting beside the driver; a gunner in the rear manned the vicious-looking machine gun mounted there. Behind that, Sparks could just make out the dark shape of a troop-transport lorry, two ranks of well-armed soldiers in the back.

But the tank was grinding on beneath him round the rock, and there was no more time for observation. Sparks turned his attention to the tank; it had almost reached the rut in the road which concealed the explosive.

'Just a bit further, my friend,' Sparks muttered. 'Come on . . . come on!'

Then his hand slammed hard on the detonator box – and below him the road erupted. The tank lurched over at a crazy angle, then exploded in a blinding red fireflash.

Already Sparks was on his feet, his Thompson chattering. Immediately beneath him the soldier on the roof of the prison-lorry screamed once as he was ripped apart by the deadly hail.

Sparks sprayed a burst through the cab roof and was rewarded with fresh cries. That took care of the driver! Then the machine gun on the staff car opened up, and Sparks hit the rock as jagged stone splinters filled the air.

His hand clasped a grenade and he pulled the pin. Here's hoping, he thought grimly as he tossed it, unsighted. It fell in a looping arc, bounced off the staff car bonnet and came to rest in the startled officer's lap. Then exploded.

Three more grenades followed, almost simultaneously. Sparks lobbed them further this time, and caught the first of the soldiers as they streamed up from the fourth vehicle in the convoy.

Before the blast of the third explosion had died away, Sparks' Thompson was stuttering again, mowing down the surviving troops.

So far, the whole fight had lasted less than a minute.

Sparks satisfied himself that there was no more opposition coming from behind; then, clutching a grenade, he leapt for the roof of the prison-truck.

Leaning out over the edge of the roof, Sparks brought the unprimed grenade swinging down – to smash through the glass in the small barred window of the truck's rear door. As it bounced on the floor inside, there was a shriek of horrified realisation – then the door burst open. Four Jap guards leapt out and hit the road.

'Up here, boys,' Sparks called. The four men whirled and stared open-mouthed at the slim figure on the truck's roof. Then the Thompson spoke again.

Sparks leapt nimbly to the ground. He stood slightly to the side, his gun covering the open door. 'Come out with your hands up,' he yelled – once in English, once in Japanese.

The large beetroot-coloured face of 'Fireball' Sherman peered out. 'It's okay, boy – don't shoot! I'm on your side!'

Sparks motioned the general out and quickly checked the truck's interior. It was clear.

The general was staring at the scene of destruction all around him. 'Hot damn, boy!' he exclaimed. 'You and your squad sure polished them Nips off. Where are the rest of your men?'

'There's only me, General Sherman,' Sparks replied.

'You did this all on your own?' Sherman said in astonishment. 'Goddamn it, boy, I don't believe you!' He paused for a moment, then: 'Hey – you know who I am!'

Sparks quickly filled the general in, and pointed beyond

The large beetroot-coloured face of 'Fireball' Sherman peered out.
'It's okay, boy – I'm on your side!'

the overhanging rock. 'We've got to make it to the river and head downstream to my pick-up point. Are you fit for travel, sir?'

'You bet your little cotton socks I am, boy!' Sherman's bluff voice boomed. He was a barrel of a man, standing a full head above Captain Sparks. He'd lost a little weight during his brief captivity – but then, he had a lot to lose! ' "Fireball Sherman" can run the hind legs off a jack rabbit!'

Sparks doubted it, but he held his tongue. While he climbed the rock and retrieved his weapons, General Sherman helped himself to a rifle from a fallen Jap. Both men clipped fresh magazines into their weapons, then they moved off through the thinning vegetation.

Sherman was puffing and panting by the time they reached the river. 'Boy, I thought *I* could run,' he gasped, 'but you ain't even breathing heavy!'

'Forget the running, General,' Sparks replied. 'How's your swimming?'

'Passable, boy. Why'd you ask?'

'Because from here on in, we go by river.'

A large dead treetrunk was floating by in the swollen, muddy river. Sparks plunged into the water and struck out with powerful strokes.

'Come on in, General,' he called back over his shoulder. 'The water's just fine!'

Behind him, the older man grasped the idea and struck out after his rescuer.

Soon, they were both clinging to the gnarled sides of the trunk, hidden from prying eyes beneath its broken branches.

They drifted downstream awhile, passing a small village where fishermen were casting their nets. Then, round a bend in the wide, meandering river, a Japanese motor vessel veered close by. Sparks and the general ducked-under the water, and passed unseen.

Minutes later there was a drone overhead and the two men ducked again as a Jap spotter plane swooped downstream. They passed three more patrol boats in as many kilometres.

'They sure are keen on getting you back, General,' Sparks remarked.

'Ain't surprised, boy.' Sherman kept his booming voice low. 'I could tell them slanteyes a lot of things they'd like to know.' He glanced sideways at Sparks. 'What happens if we *are* spotted?'

'We fall back on Plan "B", General.'

Then the conversation ended as they ducked beneath the water again . . .

It was almost dusk when they reached the wide basin which Sparks recognised as the pick-up point. They left the log to continue its downstream journey, and hauled themselves up into the long reeds on the muddy bank. When they were well-concealed, Sparks pulled a small box of matches sealed in oilskin from his belt. He slipped out of his wet clothes, draped them up on the reeds to dry.

He pointed to the small, slimy black objects dotted here and there over his flesh. 'Leeches, General. You'd better strip off, too!

The general complied, and Sparks struck a match. He held its flaming tip close to one of the bloodsuckers for a moment, making it curl so he could easily pull it off. The general shuddered.

By the time they'd finished the long and painful task, the warm evening breeze had dried their clothes. 'Make yourself comfortable, General – we have a long night ahead of us.'

They remained there all night. Several times they were wakened from their fitful sleep by the throaty throb of a patrol boat engine.

And then it was dawn, and Sparks was shaking the general awake. 'Here's our transport home,' he breathed. 'And bang on time, too.'

The general could hear the growing whine of an aircraft engine. Then it lumbered into sight, coming in low over the trees and splashing down in the calm water of the basin, a small grey cargo plane fitted with water-skis.

Sparks was already in the water, forging out into midstream. He had abandoned his weapons and boots. The general did the same.

The pilot kept his engines running as the two figures ploughed through the water towards him. Sparks hauled himself up on to the metal strut of the ski and reached back to help the general.

Then they were both scrambling inside and the plane was turning for its take-off run. Suddenly, one of the Japanese patrol boats was roaring downstream, its machine guns beating out a staccato rhythm of death. Its murderous stream of lead perforated the plane's cockpit, killing the pilot instantly.

As Sparks came into the cockpit, the pilot slumped to the floor. Sparks heaved the body aside and slid into the seat, running his gaze over the bank of controls. He gunned the engine and the plane shot forward amid another barrage from the patrol boat. Then they were gaining speed, faster, faster . . . and Sparks' hands pulled back on the joystick.

They rose into the air, and skirted the treetops. As they climbed, Fireball pulled himself into the cabin.

'Damn it, boy – you've done it again!' he thundered, slapping Sparks jovially on the back. He bent to examine the pilot, but Sparks said curtly:

'Forget him – he's dead. Strap yourself in, sir. Things might get a little hairy.'

Sparks levelled out at 1,500 metres and gave her full

throttle, heading west towards the British lines. Below them, the endless expanse of jungle streamed by, and Sherman could hardly contain a whoop of delight.

'Yee-haaa, boy! We've done it! We'll sure be celebrating in your NAAFI tonight!'

'Don't speak too soon, General.' Sparks' voice was calm. 'We've got trouble.'

Behind and above them, streaking down in the clear morning air, were three Zero fighter planes. They swooped past the lumbering cargo plane, each one firing a burst across its prow. Then they banked and circled back, waggling their wings.

'Looks like they want us to land, General.'

'What do we do, boy? Do we fight them – or do we set down?'

Sparks' quick brain had summed up the options open to them. Flight was useless – they'd be blown out of the air. To land and surrender would mean that, once again, Sherman would be in enemy hands. That left only one choice.

Sparks' voice remained calm. 'I'm afraid we're going to have to fall back on Plan "B", General.'

'Just what *is* this mysterious Plan "B" of yours, boy?'

Sparks pushed forward on the joystick, and the plane's nose tilted downwards. 'It's a code name we have in SOE, sir. It's a nice way of saying that when all else has failed, you do what you have to do.'

Now the plane was diving steeply, and the lush green jungle rushed up to meet it. In the cockpit, Sparks smiled for the last time.

'You're too valuable to lose to the Japs, General. I'm afraid it's my unpleasant duty to ensure you do no talking at all!'

Realisation dawned on the general's bluff countenance. Beside him, the young British captain's good-natured smile never faltered.

'Sorry, General – but as you Yanks would say, that's the way the cookie crumbles.'

A split-second later the plane ripped through the treetops and burst like a fireball on the jungle floor. Plan 'B' had been a complete success.

Rockfist's Last Case

Alan A Grant

REPORT BY DETECTION AGENT NEO-933 TO
AUTHORITIES, PLANET EFNEB, SYSTEM Y-R/WW.

SUBJECT: WANTED CRIMINAL KRYPTO-101.

OFFENCES: MULTIPLE BREACH ALL SECTIONS
GALACTIC CRIME CODE.

PLANET EARTH, TIME-QUAD *1.

My search for criminal krypto-101 has led me to the
planet Earth. My instruments have traced his ship here.

As is stipulated in the Galactic Policing Code, I took care to
avoid detection on planetary entry. At all times, my presence
here must remain unknown to the inhabitant races. My ship
came in well-disguised amid a meteor shower, and I set it down
to land in the densely-wooded area where my tracers had
located my quarry's vessel.

It was there all right.

In accordance with standard procedure, I used my ship's
destructors to render it useless. As my own craft is geared to
admit only my own gaseous form, Krypto-101 could no
longer escape from this planet.

I drilled my ship into the soil beneath the roots of a large
tree. It would be safe there.

I opened the hatch and drifted out. The wind caught me

and I allowed myself to be carried along by it. I had no way of knowing where it would take me, but that was relatively unimportant. Once I acquired a body, I would soon get my bearings. According to my data, the dominant species on this planet is a bipedal humanoid (known locally as 'people'). Though they are low in intelligence, their bodies make perfect hosts for a gaseous epiphytic being such as myself.

I soon encountered a potential host. My nebulous tendrils brushed by him, but I could not achieve the necessary grip to remain with him. Then I sensed many people around, and as the wind whipped me against one I clung on.

I located the part of the body housing the brain (it is called the 'head') and proceeded to enter. As is stipulated by the Galactic Policing Code, I would cause no lasting harm.

The person I now inhabited was approximately 1.3 *eegs* high, well-built for his kind, with short-cropped *thangg* (here it is called 'hair'). His costume consisted of a striped scarf made of wool, a jacket covered in badges, torn leg coverings and heavy footwear.

He was with a group of about fifty similarly attired people, all engaged in the task of striking each other with severe blows, often employing the aforementioned footwear.

Swiftly, I scanned my host's mind. He was a member of a cult called 'football fans', and they were engaged in a ritual battle.

Through my host's auditory sensors (or 'ears') I heard a wailing siren. Vehicles arrived suddenly and shrieked to a halt on all sides of the warring cult members.

The newcomers wore mainly blue, and quaint domed helmets. Many carried punishment batons with which to strike the cultists. This they proceeded to do.

I learned from my host's mind that these were the forces of Law and Order – though anything less like a Detection Agent I can hardly imagine.

My host launched himself at a policeman, bringing his head into sharp contact with the nasal protuberance (or 'nose') of this person.

I did not interfere. Instead, I took the opportunity to evacuate my first host's mind and move into the mind of the policeman. Winds are so severe and unpredictable on this planet that the only sure way of host transfer is by actual physical contact.

The policeman's mind was whirling, confused by the blow he'd been dealt. I gazed out through his visual receptors (or 'eyes'). He was sitting down amid the turmoil, blood streaming from the aforementioned nose. Two of his blue-clad colleagues had moved in to restrain the cultist.

Elsewhere, the confrontation had almost ceased. The majority of the cultists had fled, although a significant number had been apprehended.

My host was taken in a vehicle with other wounded policemen to receive medical attention. His name, I discovered, was Reg Cooney, PC 459. As he recovered his wits, I scanned them. PC Cooney's mind was an acceptable base from which to begin my search for Krypto-101.

There are billions of the species known as people, and Krypto-101 could be hiding in the mind of any one of them, controlling his carrier for his own evil ends, as he has done so often before on other worlds. My task would be difficult, though not impossible.

I required immediate access to the police data-banks. Unfortunately my host was a low-grade officer with only limited powers. I scanned his mind and learned that the head of his department was a respected individual called Chief Inspector Rex Reagan, known to his subordinates as 'Rock-fist' (apparently a reference to his method of dealing with criminals).

As soon as my host had received his treatment, I began to

exert my control over him – as permitted by the Galactic Policing Code, Regulation 1. I directed him to return to his base, known as New Scotland Yard, where I had ascertained that Rockfist would be available.

His work-compartment (or 'office') was on the fifth floor. PC Cooney had strong reservations about approaching his superior without going through the 'proper channels', but I over-rode him and made him walk straight in.

Rockfist was seated behind a desk. He was a large specimen, with jutting aggressive jaw and thick hair above his lip (this is a 'moustache', which many of these creatures affect). His hands were larger than my ship.

'Were you never taught to knock, Constable?' he barked.

'S-sorry, sir. I . . . I . . .' Cooney started, but I stopped him and took complete control. I made him walk straight up to Rockfist, lean down and place his forehead against that of the other man.

As their heads touched, I transferred to the mind of my new host, leaving Cooney open-mouthed and confused. He had known nothing of my presence and hadn't the slightest idea of why he was here or what he was going to do now that he was.

'What the devil are you doing?' Rockfist's voice thundered, and then I exerted control. 'Go on – get out of here. Get back to your beat and don't waste my time!'

Cooney left and I sat there inside Rockfist, pondering my next move. If Krypto-101 ran true to form, he would have sought out a host in a position of power through which to operate. This would give him a firm base for his eventual intention: planetary domination. The first thing to do was check on any individuals whose fortunes had suddenly and inexplicably increased since Krypto-101's arrival, approximately twelve Time-quads ago.

I had Rockfist pick up his telephonic communicator and

speak to his secretary. 'Cancel all my cases until further notice. Something big's come up.'

'But sir,' she protested, 'what about the "bodies-in-the-bath" murders? The Commissioner himself was asking —'

'The Commissioner will have to wait!'

We went down to the Computer Room, where I had Rockfist use his privileged status to extract the relevant information from the data-banks. The operatives complained that his action was out of order, so I had Rockfist place them on a disciplinary charge. Interference at this stage had to be minimised.

There were no names showing the sudden miraculous increase in wealth that I'd expected. However, there were a dozen possibilities of people in the area where I now was (a small nation-state known as 'United Kingdom') whose fortunes had taken a substantial turn for the better. There were six politicians, two stockbrokers, three businessmen and one person of shady character whom I took to be a criminal.

I checked him out first.

TIME-QUAD *2

It is unfortunate that the range of my perception is so limited. Within 10 *eegs*, I could detect the presence of Krypto-101 without fail; beyond that distance, his host would seem as any other person to me. It meant a lot of leg-work for Rockfist.

The gangster lead proved negative – as did another seven names which I managed to visit in person.

Rockfist needed a rest-period, so I suspended operations for the remainder of the Time-quad.

TIME-QUAD *3

I had Rockfist commandeer a noisy flying vehicle (known as a 'helicopter') from the police aerial unit, who demanded an explanation.

'Top secret,' Rockfist said. 'Hush-hush stuff. Can't tell you a word about it.'

213

I was a little anxious that my actions would cause problems for my host later, but I had no choice. The apprehension of Krypto-101 took precedence over the well-being of any single individual.

Using the helicopter, I checked the other four names, all of whom lived in outlying areas. It occupied the entire Time-quad, but I met with no success.

TIME-QUAD *4

I did some deep thinking as I allowed Rockfist to take in his morning sustenance (or 'breakfast'). He spooned large globs of nutrients into his mouth with obvious enjoyment. His noisy chewing and slurping caused so much disruption to my thought processes that I had to give him a sharp pain in his abdominal area to make him stop.

Krypto-101 *hadn't* run true to form. I tried to put myself in his place. He knew I was after him, knew I was bound to track him to Earth. His only chance would be to avoid detection until pressure of work demanded I forsake the search.

So perhaps he didn't go for the obvious host-type. No, Krypto-101 was a clever gas. He'd choose an inconspicuous carrier, a nobody, a person without fixed records, a person other persons would avoid.

I checked through Rockfist's mind. The lowest of the low on this planet were called 'down-and-outs' or 'tramps'.

Of course – that was it! It hit me with the sudden clarity of a supernova bursting in my vapours. That was Krypto-101's kind of move; it would appeal to his sense of humour.

I had Rockfist drive at top speed through the morning vehicular crush, his warning siren blaring. At New Scotland Yard, his secretary was waiting.

'Sir – the Commissioner wants to see you about the 'bodies-in-the-bath case'. He's also had a complaint from Inspector Davison in the Computer Room, and another from Aerial Division.'

'Rot the Commissioner!' Rockfist boomed. He had a forceful way about him that I was able to employ to good use. 'Tell all Divisional Section Commanders to report to my office – now!'

Shortly, Rockfist's ten immediate subordinates stood before his desk. I looked them over. An unlikely bunch, but they would have to do.

I let Rockfist give them their orders in his own no-nonsense style: 'I want every – and I mean every – officer in the division pulled off whatever they're doing. Take every van, every car – every pushbike, damn it! – and get them out there on the streets.

'The purpose of their mission – to round up every down-and-out, every tramp, every person of no fixed abode, every layabout and wastrel in the city . . . and *bring them in!*'

The subordinates looked at each other blankly. Then – 'B-but *why*, sir?' one asked.

'That's top secret, Inspector Cartwright. Yours is not to reason why – yours is just to get out there and carry out my orders!'

'But, sir – you're talking about a hundred thousand people at least! Wh-what are we going to do with them all?'

I searched in Rockfist's mind and came up with a suitable venue. 'Clear Hyde Park. Take them there!'

TIME-QUAD *5

It took longer than I would have liked. During the day Rockfist had to fend off several angry calls from the Police Commissioner, outraged citizens and latterly the Prime Minister. I allowed him to do it in his usual forthright manner, and I am afraid I may have got him into more difficulties.

But it was worth it. The end of my chase was in sight.

At last my suspects were impounded in Hyde Park, surrounded by a thin blue line of Rockfist's men, plus a horde of off-duty constables, to each and every one of whom Rockfist had promised immediate promotion.

The helicopter Rockfist had commandeered overflew the massive gathering in the park. Over 157,000 people, according to one officer's calculations. A massive operation!

Word of it had, of course, got around, and photographic crews from the nation's media were there in numbers. We came in low over the park, dangling from the end of a rope ladder beneath the helicopter, the better to inspect the assembled suspects.

Rockfist, never shy of publicity, ordered the pilot to fly right past the cameras. Although I am sure he cut a dashing figure on the nation's video screens, I fear it will cause him only more trouble in the future. But the urge in him to do it was strong, so I let him have his way.

Then we were skimming over the long lines of tramps and deadbeats that blackened the park. My entire attention was concentrated on the tell-tale tinge that would warn me of Krypto-101's presence.

Face after face passed below us in a blur, a teeming multitude of suspects – one of them probably the most dangerous creature on this planet.

Then I had him! The tingle coursed through my nebulous fibres, and I had Rockfist shout an order to the pilot:

'Repeat that last sweep, and hover!'

The helicopter circled and came in again. Krypto-101 was no fool. He realised at once that he was flushed (or 'sussed').

A tall powerful tramp in a ragged overcoat broke and ran, pushing his way through the assembled crowd.

We leapt from the ladder after him into the crowd. Rockfist landed heavily, twisting his ankle. I forced him to ignore the pain, however, and we limped quickly after our quarry.

'Stop that tramp!' he yelled, and up ahead a police officer

The helicopter Rockfist had commandeered overflew the massive gathering in the park.

moved in to grapple with the fleeing figure.

Their foreheads brushed together, and I knew that Krypto-101 had made the transfer.

'Stop that constable!' Rockfist roared, as his puzzled men piled on to the tramp.

The first constable was pushing his way through the unkempt throng towards the cordon that blocked off the exit to the Bayswater Road. Rockfist was gasping as I forced him to increase his pace.

'Stop that constable!' he called again, and a cordon sergeant barred the fleeing man's way.

'Hold it, lad! You heard the Chief Inspector—'

The constable lunged, there was a brief struggle. Then the sergeant was on his feet and running out of the park into the road.

'Stop that sergeant!' Rockfist bellowed.

Then Rockfist himself was through the gate and pounding along at the head of a large number of no-doubt confused constables.

Up ahead, the sergeant had hailed a taxi. As the driver skidded to a halt, the sergeant leaned into the cab and gave the driver's forehead a sharp tap with his own.

The taxi sped off like a rocket.

'Stop that taxi!' Rockfist screamed, as enthusiastic constables brought the deserted sergeant to his knees.

I couldn't believe it. That Krypto-101 was one slippery ball of gas!

Already I had Rockfist running into the road, raising his hand, forcing a passing motorcyclist to an emergency stop.

'Off the bike, son,' he ordered.

'You what?'

'Police business!' Rockfist sent him crashing to the pavement before I could stop him. Then we were astride the bike and careering through the traffic after the cab.

We soon caught up with the speeding taxi, and Krypto-101 veered dangerously across the road, forcing the motorbike to swerve into the gutter. As it crashed, Rockfist leapt.

His fingers grabbed onto the cab's roofrack and clung there. Krypto-101 glanced back, saw us and tried to scrape us off against the side of a lamppost.

But I already had Rockfist scrabbling up and across the roof. He swung down viciously with his heel, and the windscreen shattered. Krypto-101's host driver couldn't see a thing, and his foot automatically hit the brake.

The cab hit a traffic bollard at a speed of approximately 2 *xox* (about '25 kph' on this planet).

Rockfist was thrown bodily into the path of the oncoming traffic, which most fortunately screeched to a halt. He was winded by his impact with the hard road, and as he struggled for breath Krypto-101's host staggered from his wrecked cab and stumbled away. He slipped and fell, and lay by the roadside, his leg obviously injured.

He stretched out a hand, beckoned to a passing nomadic quadruped (or 'stray dog').

'Here, boy,' he said enticingly.

I forced Rockfist to one last valiant effort. We got to his feet and hobbled towards Krypto-101. The dog had come up and was licking the cab driver's face.

The dog turned, started to run. Rockfist lunged at full stretch—

—and caught it by the tail! The dog yelped and turned to bite, but Rockfist's powerful hand was round its throat, forcing it down. Then Rockfist was kneeling on its struggling form, and crying:

'I know you're in there, Krypto-101! I'm coming in after you!'

As I made Rockfist bend his head towards the dog's, the first of the video cameras arrived to record the final moments of the chase. They were just in time to see Rockfist butt the dog sharply on the muzzle.

I transferred.

The brain was tiny, cramped. Krypto-101 was waiting for me. This was the showdown.

We struggled in gaseous silence for a moment. But the outcome was never in doubt. Krypto-101 is not the physical type of gas.

I slapped the psycho-cuffs on him, and he hissed at me: 'You've caught me at last, Neo-933. But I had a good run, eh?'

'It's all over now,' I told him. 'I'm taking you in.'

I had the dog trot away from the scene, and directed it on the long journey back to the ship. As we went, we passed Rockfist sitting on the kerb, gasping, gibbering, staring at the cameras and wondering why they were there.

Poor Rockfist. I'm sure he would feel happier about his ruined career if he could only know that his endeavours had helped to save his world.

Would that I could tell him.

Regulations, alas.

Escape to the West

Brian Burrell

JOE GILLIS BREATHED HIS USUAL SIGH OF RELIEF as he approached West Berlin from the Eastern Sector. The American only had to get through the Russian security point and then it was just a matter of yards to Checkpoint Charley in the Western Zone – and safety.

Gillis edged his car forward in the long line of vehicles. He could see the massive wall which the Soviets had built in 1961, three years before. It looked bigger, more formidable than ever. He couldn't remember how many East Berliners had died or been captured as they had desperately tried to scale it or dig beneath those cold, heavy, grey bricks.

Anyway, as a small-time courier for US Intelligence it really wasn't his concern. Gillis was thankful he did not belong to the big-time spy league. He was just a businessman whose routine work took him to the East every now and then and, because of this, he had agreed back in '62 to deliver the odd message to help out his side, 'the good guys', in the Cold War.

Gillis' thoughts were quickly jolted back to the present. The Mercedes in front had pulled up in the long line of cars and Joe had to stamp hard on the brake pedal to avoid colliding with it. He recognised the car as one he had seen entering the Western Sector several times before.

Its owner, like the vehicle, looked big and expensive. But to Joe Gillis there was also something unsavoury about the guy. He had the look of a profiteer, and there were plenty of them in Berlin since World War Two. They were men who grew rich supplying this and that at inflated prices to keep themselves in cigars and champagne. Even the guy's number plate, HK 1, had the ring of a man who never dealt in anything less than twenty dollar bills.

Gillis was getting edgy and he knew it was because he still had to get past Brodski before he was home and dry.

Brodski was the man in charge of the Soviet check-point . . . the man who took great pleasure in practically pulling every British or American vehicle to pieces to see if it concealed any would-be escapers.

As the Mercedes pulled up in front of the security building, Joe spotted the big Russian who, as usual, looked as though he hadn't shaved for two days and had slept in his uniform all night.

A big handful of cigars ensured the fat guy had no trouble from Brodski. The Soviet simply looked quickly in the boot and the back seat of HK 1 then, with a big greasy grin, waved the vehicle off towards the US checkpoint.

Brodski wasn't so courteous when it came to Joe's turn.

The Russian did the sort of demolition job on his car that a breaker's yard would have been proud of and then he examined and re-examined his papers three times before letting him through.

No, Gillis didn't like Brodski. But he knew he had to smile and put up with it or find himself detained indefinitely on a technicality. Still, he didn't care now that the safety of Checkpoint Charley was waiting to greet him.

If the American felt secure, Erickson didn't!

At that moment the good-natured, jovial Berliner was waiting alone in his car in a deserted street in the Eastern Sector. It was dusk, nearly curfew hour, and Steiner was late for the rendezvous.

Erickson touched the 9 mm automatic in his jacket pocket. The cold, hard feel gave him some comfort, but if forced to use it against the heavy artillery of the KGB or the East German Police, he realised it would be about as useful as a water pistol.

Where in the hell was Steiner . . .?

Erickson had chosen this lonely, cobbled street to pick the man up because he could see clearly for almost 500 metres in either direction. He also knew the numerous side-roads leading off it like the back of his hand. If he waited too long, however, a local might get suspicious and make a phone call to the wrong people.

When the gunshots came, Erickson jumped. From experience he knew the gunfire came from small Soviet automatics. But his mind reeled for a second as he tried to sort out from which direction. It was the street over there, to his left, and as he gunned the engine of the car he heard the running footsteps as well.

He prayed it would be Steiner!

A figure lurched around the corner, half running, half stumbling. He knew it was Steiner although they had never met. The grey hair, the rimless glasses, the frightened look . . . yes, it was Steiner all right.

Erickson gunned the car forward and flung open the passenger door.

'Steiner?' he said, as the breathless figure humped itself inside.

'*Ja*, I'm Steiner. Hurry, please . . . the KGB . . . they are on to me!' The tyres screamed as Erickson thumped the accelerator and the car leapt forward.

Erickson's brain was now working computer-fast as it told him to take the nearest side street, head east and then double back to the 'safe house' on the other side of the Eastern Sector. As he was about to turn he glanced anxiously into his mirror and saw two men carrying Kalashnikov rifles running out of the street Steiner had just left.

'Get down, man,' screamed Erickson as he grabbed the old man by the neck, thrusting him forward as he did so.

A row of shots stitched themselves high across the back window and made their exit through the windscreen just above Erickson's head as he made his turn. He snatched a look at the shaking Steiner. The man was scared, shaking uncontrollably.

'That was close,' said Erickson as their car turned into the side street and mercifully out of line of the rifle fire.

Steiner forced a smile. 'I will be safe in West Berlin soon, *nicht wahr?*'

'I hope so. I'm going back as well, so let's hope our luck holds out.'

What Erickson did not bother to tell the old man was that the Eastern Sector was now as hot as a beehive in June. The Soviets had discovered 'the tunnel' earlier that same day and now all hell would be let loose in an attempt to stem the increasing tide of defectors.

'The tunnel' was the most successful escape route to the West ever devised since the Berlin Wall was first built. The tunnel ran from the bathroom of an apartment block in the East to the cellar of a bakery in the West. Once in the tunnel, it took a refugee exactly eleven minutes to scamper along it to freedom. Fifty-seven people had made the trip safely, but today something had gone wrong. Erickson had heard rumours. Evidently a comrade, Dorfmann, who operated the tunnel from the West, had gone into it to guide some people back to the bakery but found the bathroom full of East German guards. Luckily Dorfmann was armed. He shot two of the guards then bolted back to the West. It was a lucky escape for the guards had tried to flush him out with tear gas and small arms' fire.

Joe Gillis had no idea of the tunnel's existence, let alone its discovery, as he pulled away from Checkpoint Charley. Besides, Gillis had other things on his mind. There had been a message at the checkpoint to say Wasnick wanted to see him urgently and Joe was to go straight to his office.

Wasnick was one of the top men in American Intelligence and was rarely seen by any of the couriers. Gillis had met him once or twice when there was a really tough job on, but usually he got his instructions from a junior in the organisation.

Joe fretted as he juggled his car through the city's early evening traffic. His mind recalled Wasnick's attempt to talk him into joining US Intelligence on a full-time basis. But Joe hadn't been interested. True, he had worked with the OSS (Office of Strategic Services) in Europe during World War Two. His record was fine and it was only natural that when his business interests took him to Berlin in 1960 the hush-hush boys would ask him to join them. True, Joe was as patriotic as the next man. But although he didn't mind helping them out on occasions, in no way was he a James Bond!

'We're in trouble, Joe! You've got to help us out!' Wasnick was uttering the words before Gillis could even take a seat in his office. Gillis was about to protest that he had just returned from a trip to the East, but Wasnick ignored him and carried on.

'The Reds have discovered one of our biggest tunnels under the wall and they are running tight security on anybody trying to get in or out of the East. Have you heard of Franz Steiner?'

Joe dug back into his memory for a second. 'Isn't he one of the top guys in chemical warfare, or something?'

'Right,' Wasnick said. 'He's defecting to the West and we were supposed to get him through the tunnel tomorrow. But now, of course, we can't.'

'Oh, no,' said Gillis, anticipating what was coming next. 'I'm not into that heavy stuff. You've got better, more experienced men who can handle it.'

But, secretly, Gillis could see Wasnick wasn't in the mood to take no for an answer. 'All of our best operators will have to lie low for a while. Our only hope is for *you* to get him out for us. Besides, Erickson is coming through with him.'

Wasnick knew he had hit a nerve!

Gillis and Erickson were friends . . . they had been since early '62 when the jovial Berliner was made Joe's main contact in the East. They shared an avid interest in American football, playing chess and enjoying good food. Yes, Erickson was a good pal and Joe couldn't let him down.

'Okay,' said Joe after a short pause. 'I'll do it, but in my own way. I'll go back in tomorrow. Here . . .' he went on as he scrawled something down on to a piece of paper and handed it to Wasnick, 'get me all the information you can on this. I'll collect it before I leave.' Gillis didn't wait for the Intelligence chief to thank him. As he left the office he knew he had a few short hours to formulate his plan. A plan, which if it failed, would mean him spending the rest of his life in a Soviet Work Camp. It was no wonder he was sweating a little . . .

9am the following day found Joe Gillis parked in a turning facing Checkpoint Charley.

He was busy absorbing the two typewritten sheets of information he had asked Wasnick for. It took him about five minutes to commit it all to memory, especially the addresses.

Then he burned the papers in the ash tray and tipped the ashes into the street. Finally, before moving off, he checked to see the syringe was still firmly strapped to his ankle.

He had surmised the Checkpoint on the East side would be busy and it was. There were more officers as well as guards bustling about, but they were giving most of their attention to the traffic trying to leave the zone. Gillis did not have too much trouble getting through and while he was making a mental note of the height of the hinged barrier on the outgoing vehicles side, he saw Brodski. The Russian looked smarter than usual this morning, no doubt because of all the top brass around, Joe mused, seeing the way the man rushed about to show his superiors how efficient he was.

Once Gillis had left the Checkpoint he drove around East Berlin for five minutes, doubling back on his tracks every so often to make certain he wasn't being followed.

As soon as he felt safe he quickly made his way to Erickson's home on the outskirts of the city. The man looked elated when he saw that Joe was the contact who would get him and Steiner back to theWest.

'How is the old boy?' asked Joe, fearful that the man might be too exhausted for the rough trip they had ahead of them.

'He's asleep in the back room,' Erickson grinned. 'But don't worry, Joseph, he's as tough as a goat. He'll make it.'

'Good. He can continue to rest until tomorrow morning when we make the break-out. In the meantime I want you to get a low, very low, fast sports car. Can you do it?'

Erickson said it would be no problem, as he fixed Joe a drink.

The American didn't explain the reason for his request. Instead, he slumped into an easy chair to ponder the many other things that had to be done before they made the break.

Brodsky yawned and stretched. It had been a tiring but rewarding day. He had personally been involved in the arrest of six refugees trying to sneak through his Checkpoint. The fools! Surely they knew that once 'the tunnel' had been discovered, all security in the city would be increased. He handed over to his relief and strolled down into the damp, dark street. It was only a ten-minute walk to the seedy apartment where his wife would have his supper waiting. Then he could get some well-earned rest.

As he turned off the main road and into a deserted side street, Brodski was only half aware of the figure strolling towards him. An hour later and he would have challenged him, but it wasn't curfew time yet.

'Have you a light for my cigarette, comrade?' The figure was in front of him now and as Brodski fumbled in his tunic for some matches, he was aware that the man's voice and appearance were vaguely familiar.

There was little time to ponder anything else as Brodski suddenly felt the breath being driven from his body by a blow to the stomach then, as he doubled over, the sharp, agonising sensation of two rabbit punches to the nape of his neck.

Brodski thought he was about to die!

Through a haze of pain the big Soviet felt his hands and legs being tied, then he was dragged a few yards before being tossed into the back of a car. He fought to recover consciousness, but it was like somebody had switched off the light. He plunged into a deep, black well that muffled everything.

Had the Russian been conscious, he would have sensed his assailant was driving him into the wealthier part of East Berlin and was having a little trouble finding the location he was seeking. But Brodski was oblivious of what the man had in store for him.

'More coffee?' asked Erickson as he watched Gillis and Steiner gulp down the last of their breakfast.

'There's no time,' replied Joe. 'Are you ready, Steiner?'

'*Ja*,' said the old man.

In the garage next to the house Gillis looked at the sports car. It was a convertible, just what he had wanted. Erickson had done a good job.

He opened the boot and spread out some blankets.

'You understand you might be in there for hours, Steiner, and there won't be much air?'

The German did not answer. He just gave the thumbs-up sign and climbed in. Erickson gently closed the boot.

'Here, Joe,' he said grimly as he handed the American a .38 revolver.

Gillis slipped it in his pocket and grunted. 'Let's hope I don't need it, eh?'

They had been parked in a side road just off the main highway eight kilometres from the East Checkpoint for over an hour. Gillis, who was driving the sports car, looked at his watch for the umpteenth time. It was 10.50am.

'How much longer do we wait?' enquired Erickson.

'For as long as it takes,' was the sharp reply, which he regretted immediately. 'Sorry, pal,' he grinned, then slapped the Berliner on the shoulder. 'I guess I'm not used to this part of the game. It's been a long time since I played cloak and dagger in the OSS.'

He knew he should have explained the plan in detail to his friend, but maybe it was better not to. Then his orders could be followed without question.

Erickson understood.

At last Joe said, 'Here it comes,' as he suddenly saw the Mercedes approaching in the traffic heading east. Gillis gunned the engine and slipped in behind the big car.

He could see the heavy man in the driving seat chewing on a five-dollar cigar.

'With luck,' he said, pointing ahead at the Mercedes, 'that man is going to make sure we get through the East German Checkpoint.'

'If we do,' replied Erickson nervously, 'tonight I will buy you a bottle of the finest wine and the biggest steak in Berlin.'

Joe only half heard the remark, he was thinking about Steiner huddled up in his boot. If the old boy suffocated all this effort would be for nothing. Gillis would have liked more time in getting them out. Used a safer plan, maybe. But Steiner had to be got out now and this was the best way he could think of.

His hand tightened on the wheel. The cars ahead of him were beginning to slow down for the Checkpoint. Joe sensed Erickson take the automatic from his pocket and slip it into the waistband of his trousers, ready for instant use.

The American prayed there wouldn't be a shoot out. In the tiny sports car they were sitting ducks.

Soon it was the Mercedes' turn at the Checkpoint. Gillis thought there were more guards than ever as he kept his eye on the East German Police captain approaching the car in front. The fat man, smiling confidently, got out of the car, and while the captain looked in the backseat, he unlocked, then began to open, the trunk.

'That's funny,' said Erickson. 'I don't see our friend Brodski anywhere.'

Joe's eyes were glued on the Mercedes as the fat man slowly opened the boot.

'You won't,' he said to the puzzled Berliner. '*He's in there!*'

Gillis paused for an instant to watch the horrified look on the faces of the Mercedes-driver and the captain as the bound and gagged figure of Brodski, only half-conscious, sat up in the Mercedes boot like a corpse rising from a tomb. The captain drew his pistol to cover the fat guy whose mouth had gaped open so that the cigar dropped from it, scattering ash over his expensive but flashy suit and shoes. Guards moved in from all directions on the Mercedes.

Then Joe made his move!

He hit the gas pedal, swung the sports car around the Mercedes and headed for the low barrier which was in the

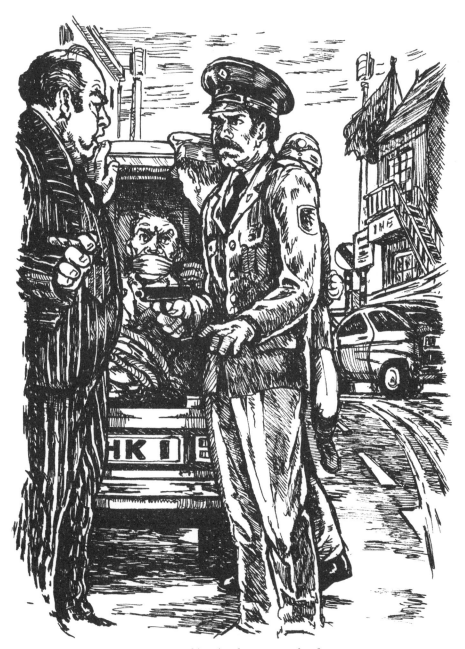

The captain drew his pistol to cover the fat guy.

down position only a few yards in front of him.

For a moment he thought the car was too high to go beneath it. The two men automatically ducked their heads as the car screamed under the heavy wooden strut, which tore through the windscreen showering metal and glass everywhere.

'We made it, damn it, we made it!' cried Erickson as they approached the US guards on Checkpoint Charley.

Gillis shot a glance over his shoulder. He smiled as he saw the East German Police dashing forward, fumbling with their weapons. They were shouting, but he could sense rather than hear what they were saying.

'Those men back there don't know what's hit them. Brodski and the Mercedes-driver will have a lot of explaining to do.'

Not long after, Gillis and Erickson were driving through West Berlin towards Wasnick's office. The security people at Checkpoint Charley were taking care of Steiner.

'You were right, pal,' mused Joe. 'The old boy is as tough as nails. All he kept saying when I said goodbye was "*Ja, Ja*" and giving me the thumbs up sign.'

As they neared Wasnick's office Gillis thought it right to give Erickson some explanation about the escape. The man hadn't asked for one, but the ordeal had been a tough one for him and he had a right to know.

'Before I started the mission,' began Gillis, 'I gave Wasnick a note. On it was the registration of the Mercedes, HK 1 – I'd seen the car many times before. I also put Brodski's name on the paper and Wasnick gave me information about him and the car owner, including their movements and their addresses in East Berlin.

'The man with the Mercedes is Hans Kröger. He's a shady businessman who travels into the Western Sector three times a week. I needed fall guys to distract the men on the East checkpoint so I chose him and Brodski. Last night, when Brodski was on his way home, I knocked him out, took him to Kröger's house, and secretly dumped him in the boot of the Mercedes. I'd also smuggled a syringe full of TN4, the knockout drug, in with me, and that stopped Brodski from waking up.'

'But supposing Kröger hadn't made the trip this morning, Joe . . . what then?'

Gillis smiled. 'That was a chance I had to take . . .'

Shortly after, the two men were relaxing in Wasnick's office. The Intelligence chief was pleased.

'You did a good job, Joe. There's a tail piece to this mission that you and Erickson might find interesting. Steiner was on our side all the time. For years he's been feeding the Soviets false info on chemical warfare. Through our channels we're going to convince them we pressured Steiner to join the West against his will. Hence his defection. The scientists in Moscow will pull out all the stops to develop the worthless formulas he left behind. It will take them years to find out they're no good.'

'Our intelligence will get good propaganda value through the press in the West because of Steiner's defection as well,' added Erickson after some thought.

'Correct,' smiled Wasnick, 'But the East German press will play it all down the way they usually do and report it on their back pages as a small incident at Checkpoint Charley.'

'Say,' said Gillis, 'didn't you mention something about a bottle of wine and a steak, Herr Erickson?'

Wasnick interrupted. 'The meal, gentlemen, is on me!'

Perhaps, thought Wasnick as they got up to go, he might still be able to convince Gillis to join the organisation full time. A sharp Intelligence chief never lets a good man like that off the hook if he can help it.

All Aboard for Oblivion!

Angus Allan

THEY CAME IN DROVES. Those who had saved up all their lives for the 'holiday of their dreams'. Those who had won the pools. Those who had bought 'Ernie' bonds and had scored. Those who were rich, anyway, and had fancied a trip to the sun.

In floral shirts and jazzy skirts, with ridiculous yachting caps, parasols and Panama hats worn over expensive tropical suits bought from the most exclusive of London tailors, they filed up the gangways of the cruise-ship *Queen Caroline*. Each of them was intent upon enjoying a voyage from Tilbury through the Bay of Biscay ('We'll all be sick,' they chuckled), to Madeira and then across the Atlantic to the scattered islands of the Caribbean. Trinidad and Tobago. Barbados. Antigua. Sint Maarten and Curaçao.

They were separated, even so. Those who had been able to afford it travelled first class, and boarded the shining white vessel via the for'ard entry. Passengers like Sir Ronald Germayne-Mortensen, who ignored the hand of Third Officer Clive Johnson and said: 'Didn't go to sea as a mishipman in the *Royal* Navy to be helped on to this floating hotel by a jumped-up commissionaire.' And like Maisie, one-time film starlet, who gushed: 'I just *love* men in uniform, sweetie.'

Aft, there were the more down-to-earth. Hubert Huggett, one-time grocer. Like the others of the second class, he had to make do with Martin Forsythe, apprentice. 'By gum, lad,' said Huggett, 'You'll have to grow a bit before you fill that uniform of yours! I can see I'll have to put you on to Percy's Perfect Pies. That's me, lad. Percy Huggett, see?'

Martin smiled dutifully. It was his job. 'I'll bear it in mind, sir. My mum always said I was a hungry boy, and needed feeding.' He directed Huggett towards the cabin shown on his ticket.

Immediately behind Huggett came a tall, sun-bronzed man with a lean, saturnine face. Martin Forsythe instantly summed him up as a loner. 'Your ticket, sir?'

'Number forty. B-deck.'

'Ah, yes. Mr Dunblane?'

'The very same. Point me in the right direction.'

The apprentice risked holding up the queue for just a moment. 'Curious surname you've got, sir,' he said. 'Name of a town in Scotland. And as a matter of fact, it's where I come from.'

'You don't say, said Dunblane. 'Canadian, myself.'

Archie Dunblane went the way he'd been told, and found his berth. He was pleased to see, when he opened the door, that his luggage had already been stowed within. He sat down on the bunk, shrugged off his shoes, and lay back, his head on his hands. He looked up at the cream-painted steel above him and let his mind drift back over the events of the previous three months. A hectic chase through central Europe in pursuit of a man who had tried to abscond with military secrets to the other side. He'd had a bad time in Berlin. A worse time in Vienna, and an even tougher run in Budapest.

He flexed the fingers of his right hand and looked at his index. There was a corny callous between the first and second joints that hinted – no, declared – the proficiency of it with the trigger of a gun. Dunblane smiled and closed his eyes. That was all over. He was on leave. He was set for three weeks of trouble-free cruising, and Sir Humphrey Kellingham, his boss, could go to hell . . .

For'ard, Third Officer Clive Johnson handed in a squat, rather rough-hewn individual in an over-heavy suit. Hardly the thing for a sunshine trip, he thought. But he knew the man was Vassily Orensky, a senior official of the permanent trade delegation of the USSR to London. He said: 'dobar dan', which was a reasonable version of the Russian for good morning.

Orensky grunted some reply, smiled thinly, and passed on his way.

At the same time, right in the bows, a short-bodied man in denims, one of the dock workers, it would have seemed, appeared from a hatchway, rubbed his hands together as if to rid them of some unseen dirt, and sidled off the ship by the crew's companion-way. He was Michael Seviroff – a man with a deadly secret. He had gone aboard with a small package, and he had left it behind him. He had left it ticking. It was in a place that, he was sure, nobody would ever find it. And even if they did, tampering with it would only make things worse.

Seviroff, on the quay, ducked behind a stack of crates and peeled off his denims. Beneath them, he wore faded slacks and a T-shirt. He slipped along and blended easily with the crowd of well-wishers gathered to see their friends, relatives and associates off on their cruise, and as the *Queen Caroline* cast off and slid gently out of harbour, he waved dutifully at nobody in particular, and with a forged pass, walked quietly back through the terminal.

He had not gone fifty metres before a man stepped out of the shadows of a warehouse and accosted him. Michael Seviroff beamed, and raised his hand in greeting. 'Ah Georg! I didn't expect to see you here!'

Georg grinned thinly. 'Of course you didn't, my friend,' he

said, and pulled a short but effectively silenced small-calibre automatic from his pocket. It made no more than a plop of sound, but Seviroff was dead before he hit the ground. His killer, without emotion, stuffed his body into a crate marked for a far-off South American destination, before even the whiff of cordite had dispersed . . .

The *Queen Caroline* had passed through Biscay. Practically everyone had been sick. That part of the in-shore Atlantic had well and truly lived up to its stormy reputation. Many were those who complained. Huggett of the pies fame (he couldn't bear to think of his pies, of course) had demanded to see the Captain. Sir Ronald Germayne-Mortensen had insisted that, had *he* had command of the vessel, he would have made the passage of the Bay less fraught. Even Maisie the ex-starlet had been upset that her stack of creams and cosmetics had been virtually destroyed.

The Captain, Digby Nelson, had lived well and truly up to the stern reputation of his famous seafaring namesake. He dealt with Huggett briefly. 'My dear sir, by the time we reach Madeira, you will be capering like a ten-year-old. You are a man of meat – no, I'm sorry, I shouldn't have said that. It clearly makes you feel ill. You are a man of strength. Why not forget your worries and organise some deck games? Perhaps "pig in the middle" . . .?'

Maisie had been almost too easy. 'My dear lady,' Nelson had said, turning on the maximum charm. 'Ill? Why, my dear – you look sensational. A vision of loveliness . . .'

The ex-Royal Naval chap was a little more tricky. But – 'be assured, Sir Ronald, you're welcome on my bridge at any time, *if* you can show good reason to over-ride a Captain of the Merchant Service.'

'Blast them all,' said Digby Nelson to his Third Officer, Clive Johnson, who was at that time on watch. 'Sometimes I despair of passengers.'

Johnson said: 'I'm afraid it's not over yet, sir,' and inclined his head to where Archie Dunblane was pushing his way through the door from the starboard wing.

'*Now* what!'

Dunblane said: 'Cable, captain. From my boss. It's coded, so your radio man wouldn't know. But I've pencilled in the message underneath.'

Nelson's eyes widened. His breath came slowly and more slowly as he read. 'There – is – a bomb. Aboard your ship. Motive – timing – origin – unknown . . .'

Dunblane shrugged. 'I'm as wise as you are. I work for – let's say – an organisation used to these things. Personally, all I wanted was a bit of peace and quiet.'

While the captain gaped at him, Dunblane went on: 'I took the liberty of asking your purser for the passenger list. There's Vassily Orensky aboard. A prime target for Eastern European dissidents. There are many who would want him dead at any price. Even if it means sinking this vessel and all the innocent people in her.'

'Innocent people!' spluttered Nelson.

'Yes. Including me,' said Dunblane. 'I'd suggest, sir, that you did nothing to alarm the passengers.' He produced his credentials, which would have convinced an Admiral of the Fleet. 'I'm trained, I'm skilled. I can try and find the bomb, and attempt to disarm it. But I'm also tired. Let's say, exhausted, from a spell of duty elsewhere. I'll do my best, if you'll give me permission.'

'What the hell else can I do?' raved Digby Nelson. 'Get started, man!' The captain turned to Third Officer Johnson. 'Go with him. Make sure that everyone – but every single man of the crew, gives him complete co-operation!'

'Yessir! But – but what do I tell them . . .?'

'Tell them anything but the truth!'

A cruise ship is not a small boat. From bows to stern, from the depths of the hull to the deck, there are countless departments, each with their own bosses. Galley – kitchens – bakery – laundry. Bank and storage, games and recreations, never mind engine-room, communications area, passenger cabins. Archie Dunblane, with the young apprentice Martin Forsythe, whom Clive Johnson had detailed to be his assistant, began at the stern and worked his way painstakingly for'ard, deck by deck, searching for the bomb. The ship by this time was well out into the Atlantic, and an explosion would send it irrevocably to the bottom.

They were hindered time and again by the very presence of those aboard. The captain had announced the possibility of seeing and photographing flying fish, and though many had left their cabins with their cameras, there were those who hadn't.

'What d'you want here?' mumbled Huggett, in his bunk with another bout of sea-sickness. 'Sorry to disturb you, sir,' said Forsythe. 'Just a routine check.'

From end to end of the *Queen Caroline*, the two men took everything apart. To no avail. Archie Dunblane had to admit that he had found nothing. 'A hoax?' Martin Forsythe stared at him hopefully.

'No. My guv'nor wouldn't have been wrong, blast him,' said Dunblane. 'There *is* a bomb here. And we've missed it.'

'So what do we do?'

'We start again. And hope we get it. In time.'

Dunblane cursed fate. Why had this happened to him, when he was supposed to be enjoying himself? He found himself hating the *Queen Caroline*, the Captain, and all who sailed with him. Even the white-faced apprentice who hung on his coat-tails, gibbering and (as Dunblane put it) whining like an idiot.

Then the 'idiot' came up with a tentative suggestion.

'There's the tunnel,' he said.

'The what?'

'It's a crawl-way, alongside the propeller shaft. You're not supposed to go into it unless the ship's in dock.'

'So *show* me, kiddo. Don't just stand there like a dummy!'

In the deepest part of the engine room, Martin Forsythe pulled up the curved cover of a hatchway. Inside, both he and Dunblane could see the whirling mass of the central drive of the ship. They crawled in, flinching away from the spinning metal, the smell of hot steel strong in their nostrils. The inspection tunnel itself stretched away into the darkness beyond. Forsythe handed the agent a torch that he'd been smart enough to bring with him.

Unaware of what was going on far beneath them, some of the passengers were becoming annoyed at what they considered the neurotic behaviour of Captain Digby Nelson. Sir Ronald Germayne-Mortensen had made it clear that he thought the course for Madeira was wrong. 'I know these seas,' he had said, pounding the table in the First Class Bar. Even Vassily Orensky, himself an ex-naval man, had expressed doubts about the handling of the vessel.

But below, Archie Dunblane found what he was looking for. A tarpaulin-wrapped package taped against the main drive, and right above the thinnest part of the *Queen Caroline*'s hull.

'My oath! That youngster was right,' he said. But then he turned, and looked straight in the face of that youngster himself. Martin Forsythe!

'What in thunder are you doing here? You should be back at the hatch! Suppose someone closes it on us, you young nitwit!'

Nobody did, but the boy scrambled back just to make sure. Leaving Dunblane to cautiously unwrap the bomb and begin to search for the means of defusing it. He bared a clock

Archie Dunblane found what he was looking for. A tarpaulin-wrapped package . . .

mechanism, that was still ticking solidly away, and he saw that a creeping red hand was rapidly approaching the upright position that would detonate the explosive and blow them out with the bottom of the liner.

There was something else. A piece of equipment that even he, Dunblane, hadn't seen before. It was a dreadful chance, but he took it, and wrenched it free of the main charge. Then, using his teeth, he nipped off the thin wires that connected the bomb to its timer . . .

White faced, apprentice Martin Forsythe was waiting to help Dunblane out of the shaft-tunnel and escort him up to the bridge, where Captain Digby Nelson was actually sitting on the swivel seat normally reserved for the relief quartermaster, the man detailed to steer the ship.

'You've done it?' Nelson mopped the sweat off his brow.

'Yes. There's no more need to worry,' said Dunblane. 'I don't know who set all this up, Captain, but it needn't concern you. You may be told by your superiors in due course, or you may not. That's the way these things work.'

The cruise continued. Vassily Orensky left the *Queen Caroline* at Barbados, having enjoyed himself thoroughly. Many others, including Maisie the ex-film starlet, quit in the Bahamas, with nothing but kind words for Digby Nelson and his crew. Germayne-Mortensen stayed aboard until the return to Tilbury, claiming to the last that he could have commanded the vessel with much more panache than a mere merchant skipper. Huggett got off feeling just as sick as when he'd joined. Not one of them would ever know how Archie Dunblane had saved them from a sudden and violent end.

Dunblane? He'd been due to leave the ship at Tobago, to take a well-earned rest. But he'd gone the whole trip, philosophically. 'Once you're in this job, you're in this job for ever,' he told a wide-eyed apprentice Forsythe. 'It seems to chase you around, see?'

'It's funny,' said the apprentice, as he watched Dunblane shamble off down the quayside. 'He didn't look like any kind of special agent.'

Third officer Johnson patted the boy on the shoulder. 'He wouldn't exactly have it tattooed on his arm, would he . . .?'

Later, in an office just off Whitehall, Archie Dunblane reported to his boss, Admiral Sir Humphrey Kellingham, KG, OBE and a lot more besides. He said: '*Now* could I go on holiday, sir? Just for a real rest?'

The admiral picked up a folder, opened it, and began to read. 'We've picked up some chappies who murdered the bod who tried to bomb the *Queen Caroline*,' he said. 'The trail leads to Patagonia, of all places. Fancy going . . .?'

'Why should I?' said Dunblane, scarcely concealing his irritation.

'Well,' said Kellingham, 'that bomb you dealt with had a neat little booby-trap on it. From your report, it seems you tore it off. And it was a thousand-to-one chance it didn't go off. It didn't . . .'

'No,' said Dunblane thoughtfully. 'It didn't.' He looked down at his hands and saw that they were suddenly shaking. 'If you don't mind, send someone else. I feel like spending a fortnight somewhere safe. You couldn't get me a suite in the Tower of London, could you . . .?'

One Jump Ahead

Kelvin Gosnell

THE MGB ROADSTER bored through the pitch black tunnel of forest in East Germany. From behind the wheel the English-man, Steele, could only just make out the monotonous trunks of pine trees as they flashed past at 150 kph. It was a tribute to Steele's driving skill that the frail old man who was his passenger was able to doze fitfully in the seat alongside.

Steele saw the lights of the van in his mirror while it was still half a mile behind. The one advantage of these shocking roads was the fact that they were straight. There was a five-to-one chance that the van was full of guards and that they were after Steele. Steele didn't bet short odds . . .

He smoothly pressed the accelerator towards the floor of the car. The characteristic hollow drumming of the engine changed slightly in pitch, then the turbo unit cut in and laid a metallic whine over the top of all other noises. Steele watched the speed indicator move steadily upwards: 175, 190, 200 – the gauge stopped there, but Steele knew that the specially uprated car was now singing along at 210 kph, well above the car's official maximum speed.

He guessed that he was some five minutes away from the East-West border crossing. He could easily leave the van behind, but he was sure the guards at the crossing would be ready for him – there was bound to be a radio in the van.

He held the car at 210 kph for as long as he dared, then he let her drop back to 110. Soon he picked out the floodlit crossing two kilometres ahead. He killed the powerful headlights and let her slow still further until she was whispering along at a barely-audible 50 kph. As he came closer to the crossing he could see that it was swarming with guards. He had guessed right again and he allowed himself a smile of satisfaction – his uncanny talent of being one jump ahead had served him well again. It was this talent that had kept him alive for the past ten years as a serving 'front-line' British agent.

He glanced at the sleeping old man and wondered whether to wake him for the forthcoming fireworks. He decided not to – he would stand a better chance of survival if he were relaxed in sleep.

He crept down to only a hundred metres from the crossing before they spotted him. The instant that Steele saw the guard raising the alarm, he flicked the car's lights back on to blinding full beam, slammed her into second gear and floored the pedal.

The effect was spectacular. The turbo unit howled like a dying banshee and slammed both Steele and his passenger back into their seats with fierce acceleration. The sudden light and unexpected noise had stunned the guards for a few moments, just long enough to prevent them bringing their guns to bear until it was too late. The snarling monster of a motor car was among them and they were diving wildly to save their skins.

The sudden shock had also stirred the old man. '*Was ist los . . .?*' he spluttered sleepily. Steele barked an order back at him, 'Keep down. Going through!'

Time seemed to slow down for Steele, as the car hurtled forward towards the big old-fashioned wooden barrier of the crossing. He flinched involuntarily as he saw that the MGB was not going to fit under the heavy pole. It struck the top of the windscreen rail and smashed it back, showering Steele and the old man with a thousand pieces of tiny shattered screen. But the car kept moving – they were going to make it!

As soon as they were clear of the barrier, Steele wrenched the wheel over and plunged the car into the deep pools of shadow under the trees. The guards had recovered now and a hail of automatic weapon fire was pouring at the car from behind. Swerving all the time to minimise the chance of being hit, he kept to the trees until the road bent away from the crossing and he judged it safe to emerge again.

A kilometre further down he made the rendezvous with Simon Hardy, the British agent who would be escorting the old man for the remainder of his journey to Britain. Hardy was waiting for him at the roadside and was pleased to see Steele's battered craggy face – they'd worked together on many jobs before and even though Hardy disliked the way Steele tended to make his own rules, he liked the man. You could trust Steele.

'Problems?' Hardy asked.

'Nothing I couldn't handle,' was the curt reply as Steele eased himself from the tiny cockpit of the sports car. Looking back to the old man, he saw that his head still lay on his chest in the same position he'd been in for all of their journey, asleep. 'Some people'll kip through anything,' he said but the smile went out of his voice when he noticed Hardy's horrified look. Hardy had seen the dark patch spreading from the old man's neck. It glistened wetly in the car headlights. 'Damnation,' Steele growled and Hardy bent to examine the man.

'Must have died instantly,' he said. 'One of the guards got lucky. Bad show, Steele – but, that's how it is, you win some, you lose some.'

Steele's face had turned blacker than the night – to have come this far and have everything turn sour in the last fraction of a second! It was unbearable. 'This is the first one I've lost.' He spat the words bitterly and turned away. 'Let's go home.'

Home for Steele, Hardy and the other shadowy figures who formed the elite of the British secret service was a striking mirror-windowed office block near Lambeth North tube station in London. Two days later, Hardy and Steele stood in front of their section head who debriefed them about the failed mission. The boss had worked in the field himself once and was understanding towards Steele. 'Don't worry about it, man. It's happened to all of us at one time or another – you'll get over it. Look at it from the positive side. It'll sharpen up your wits no end – make sure it never happens again . . .'

Steele had heard the argument before and it sickened him. 'I know it's not going to happen again, sir,' he said, 'because I am resigning from the service, as of now, no matter what anyone else says or does. There is no room for mistakes in this business – you either get it right all the time, first time or you're dead. I survived one mistake, I won't chance my life *or* anyone else's on another.'

A sad look came over the boss's face and Steele was surprised when his resignation was accepted so easily, with so few conditions. 'Very well, Steele. If that's the way you want it. But you must realise that you cannot just walk away from us on the spur of the moment like this.'

'I know that, sir,' Steele replied grimly.

'Obviously, we will do everything possible to process your resignation as quickly as possible,' his boss continued, shuffling a heap of papers on his desk and pulling out a thin manila folder. 'And there's a nice simple job you could handle for us while I'm sorting things out. Straightforward nursemaid job. Pick up a chap from his house and deliver him to a safe house number four. I'm sure you won't mind . . .'

So they were going to get their last ounce of work out of him before letting him go, were they? Well, where was the harm in doing one last job? Steele took the file. 'Of course, sir,

I'll get on to it straight away.' He turned to leave and Hardy moved along with him, but the boss called him back, 'Oh, Simon, could you stay here for a moment, please? There's some query over your expense account records which needs to be cleared up.'

Steele smiled to himself: so old Hardy had been fiddling his expenses, eh? Salaries in the department weren't particularly good and, well, you had to make it up somewhere. Steele hoped that Hardy could bluff his way out of it.

The trouble with some 'customers' who have to be taken into protective custody in a safe house, is that they don't want to come. Jimmy Field was just such a customer. From the moment Steele knocked on Field's door in the middle of that pitch black and rainy night, Steele knew the customer was going to give trouble. Steele heard the bolts being pulled on the back door on the South London terraced house only seconds after he had rung at the front.

Field was certainly quick off the mark, both with his feet and his mouth: he was halfway across the back garden before Steele caught up with him. There was no question of Field putting up a fight – Steele towered over him and once the little man had seen the size of the Magnum revolver that Steele carried, he ceased putting up any resistance except a verbal one: he insisted all at once that he didn't want to go into protective custody, that he didn't know anything about anything, that he wanted to call his solicitor and that he was merely an innocent used-car salesman.

Steele had come across enough small time villains in his career to recognise Field for one. He had dealt with enough of them too, to know how to shut them up – the ride across London in the Granada was quite peaceful after Steele had given Field a graphic account of just what would happen if he didn't shut up.

In the back room of a private drinking club not far from where Field lived, the man with the scar on his cheek picked up the phone. 'Yeah?' he grunted into the grubby receiver.

'Don't talk. Listen,' said the voice. 'Old Bill have snatched Jimmy Field. At this moment he is being taken to an address in North London. He is going to talk and talk about your organisation. This is the address . . .' the voice gave an address in Sumatra Road in Hampstead, and the line went dead.

The man in the club replaced the receiver and ran a perfectly manicured finger thoughtfully down the vivid white scar. He picked up the phone again and dialled a number.

Steele spotted the three cars parked outside the safe house as soon as he entered the road. He had taken the long way round as a safety precaution in case he was followed but somehow the bad guys, whoever they were, had known where he was going.

He decided to abort his arrival at the house and cruised past slowly instead – he should have moved faster. One of the men waiting in the cars spotted Field in the Granada and the squeal of the Cortina's tyres told Steele that the chase was on.

Rule number one in high-speed combat driving is 'do the unexpected' so, rather than speed up, Steele slowed down. By the time he reached the junction at the end of Sumatra Road he was barely moving. The road was narrow and the Cortina could not pass him – instead it sat menacingly on his tail, centimetres from the Granada's rear bumper.

He slowed to a standstill for the junction but instead of turning right as he was signalling, he slammed the big Ford into reverse and kicked it back into the Cortina.

There was a sickeningly satisfying scream of metal as the two cars slammed together. Damage to the rear end of the

Granada would be heavy but it wouldn't stop the vehicle moving. There was super-heated steam gushing from the Cortina's radiator and even if the driver had been in a fit state to drive, he would only have covered a couple of kilometres before the engine overheated. Steele pointed the Granada south and went hard and fast, lights blazing, down the Finchley Road towards the centre of London.

He was breaking every speed limit and traffic regulation in the book and if any speed cops came after him he'd have to bluff very carefully indeed – his branch of the service never carried identity cards – it was far too dangerous in case of capture!

Right now he had far more worrying problems on his mind: if the service's safe house in Sumatra Road was blown, then he dare not use any of the other refuges in case he betrayed them as well. He was totally on his own, searching for his own bolt hole in which to hide.

He'd just decided on his destination when he saw the lights of a Jag coming up fast from behind – it was one of the cars that had been outside the safe house. Whoever these bad guys were, they were one jump ahead of him all the time.

It was time for him to turn the tables again. Back to rule one – the unexpected: he scrapped the plans he had made and turned the Granada towards Battersea. For the past ten minutes Field had sat in the plush rear seat too frightened to speak. Now he chanced his arm; 'W-why don't you give up, sunshine? That's big Lenny Russell in the Jag – he's gonna get me free whether you like it or not. Why not let me go and make it easy on yerself, eh?'

Steele felt only contempt for Field. Screaming between one set of red lights and another, he snarled back to him, 'Your friend Russell is armed with a sawn-off shotgun, Field. I saw it as we passed him – do you think he'd use it only on *me*? Those things destroy everything within a five metre cone in front of them – and in this car that would include *you*! If I let you go all I'd be doing is making it easy for you to be removed from the face of the Earth. So shut your face or I *will* let you out!'

Field didn't talk very much after that. He just rolled himself into a ball on the back seat. He'd read somewhere that was the best way to survive an accident and from the way Steele was driving, he guessed it was only a matter of time before they had one.

In fact they reached Battersea with only a few minor scrapes on the Granada. They'd lost one of the trailing cars when it had had an argument with a traffic island and lost. But the driver of the Jag was an expert – he was still only seconds behind them.

They were screaming past the entrance to the Battersea Heliport when Steele snatched the handbrake on, cut the engine and gave the big car full right lock. It shuddered to a halt in the middle of the road in a stench of burning rubber. Before it was quite stationary, Steele dived from the car and dropped to one knee. The big Magnum was in his hand and it spoke once . . . twice . . . The Jag's screen disappeared and the car mounted the pavement. It rolled incredibly slowly on to its roof, dragging a trail of sparks behind it as bare metal scraped along sharp pavement. One tiny spark flickered into a drop of petrol from one of the large capacity petrol tanks, and it blossomed into a small rose of flame. The rose only bloomed for a fraction of a second, but it was the same fraction of a second in which the tank ruptured. The Jaguar disappeared in a fierce sphere of fire.

Shielding his eyes from the blaze, Steele dragged Field out of the Granada. 'You – out!' he ordered. Field took one look at the blaze Steele had caused, another at the still-smoking revolver in his hand and obeyed. Steele grabbed him roughly by the collar and dragged him into the entrance to the

Heliport.

Using the Magnum and the fierce blaze as an excuse, Steele bluffed and threatened their way out on to the actual pad overlooking the river. There was a company Jet Ranger helicopter warming up for take off. Steele yanked the chopper's door open and motioned the pilot to get out. Even without words to help, the pilot understood – anyone would with a pistol rammed in their face. Before he knew what was happening, Field found himself in a passenger seat – he fastened the belt more by instinct than anything else.

Steele was in the pilot's position doing something to the levers that seemed to sprout out of the floor and console bewilderingly. Field hoped that the big man knew what he was doing. The thought just had time to form in his frightened mind when the small aircraft gave a mighty lurch and staggered into the air. Field's eyes did their best to come out of his head in terror as it started to plunge back towards the river again. When it seemed certain they were going to hit, the blades bit into the air and the chopper levelled off. Field became convinced that the big man definitely did *not* know what he was doing. He rolled himself into a ball again and tried to remember a prayer from his childhood.

To a certain extent, Field's distrust of Steele's piloting skills was well-founded although Steele had flown light aircraft before and he'd been flown in countless helicopters. The next few minutes were an absolute nightmare as Steele struggled to drag from his memory the right control sequence to keep the Jet Ranger straight and level *and* avoid the bridges on the river. The fact that he was skimming the dark cold surface at only fifteen metres didn't help him in his task.

At last, they had jumped over the final bridge and headed downstream towards Greenwich. By this time, Steele had mastered the controls sufficiently for the ride to feel fairly safe and under control. The fuel tanks were full and that meant that he could take his choice of destinations within a 300 kilometre radius. Where would they expect him to go . . .? As far away as possible, surely – that would be safest: so, back to rule one – do the unexpected.

He picked the largest, flattest barge moored in the river below him and guided the chopper in for a bouncy but safe landing on top of it.

The motor was still running as he motioned Field to get out. He didn't need any persuading – he bolted from the chopper like a frightened rabbit. Steele got out and stood by the side of the open cockpit door. Reaching inside, he preset the controls of the aircraft and rammed the throttle fully open. As he dived clear, the craft groaned into the sky, tail first. As it cleared the barge the tail went on lifting until the nose pointed straight down at the water. Gravity eventually overcame lift and the machine disappeared under the surface with only a few bubbles and shards of broken blades to show for its passing.

Field was scared witless and had bolted down into the gloomy safety of the barge's interior – he would be safe there for a while and too tired to try and escape. Steele slumped on to the iron deck and leaned against one of the towing bollards.

He kept a cold vigil for the rest of the night – keeping watch for any waterborne threat until daylight. At dawn he went below.

The hold of the barge was pitch black. He couldn't make out where Field was cowering. 'Field!' he shouted, 'show yourself, man. Come on!' There was a muffled noise from the far end and Steele advanced slowly in that direction. 'Come on, toad,' he called. 'I've got to get some kip and that means you've got to be tied up.'

Halfway to the end of the vessel he sensed something was wrong. He spun round just in time to see the shape of Field scurrying up through the hatch on to the deck. His own exhaustion had got to him: the little weasel had suckered him, slipped past and was even now heading out of his reach.

He sprinted back to the hatch and as he emerged on to the deck he heard the splash of Field hitting the water. By the time he reached the edge of the barge, Field was only five metres away, swimming for all he was worth towards the nearest shore. Steele drew the big Magnum and took careful aim over the top of Field's head.

He squeezed the trigger three times and saw three splashes kick up the dirty water above the man's head. 'Forget it, son,' Steele called. 'You haven't got a dog's chance. Back on the barge – *now!*' The look of desperation in Field's face was clear to see. He looked back, unable to make up his mind whether to chance it. Steele decided to give him another nudge from the gun and squeezed the trigger again, saw the bullet strike the water harmlessly above the man's head and then, astonishingly, he watched Field's face contort in agony and slump face down into the water. He didn't move again.

Steele's tired and numb brain was still struggling to understand what was happening when he heard the voice from the loudhailer. 'Stay exactly where you are. Drop the pistol. You are covered by a police marksman who will shoot you if you do not do exactly as you are told. *Drop the gun!*' Glancing upstream, he saw the black and white high-speed police launch bearing down on him. The officer with the loudhailer leaned from the wheelhouse and he could see a man with a rifle standing behind him.

Suddenly he understood – they weren't going to let him leave the service after all. All this 'just one last job' business had been just a smokescreen to get him into this situation: the dead man floating towards the police launch had been telling the truth – he had no dealings whatsoever with the security services, he was just a minor villain picked at random from

Steele squeezed the trigger three times, and saw three splashes kick up the dirty water above the man's head.

the police files – he was expendable.

Steele looked up towards the disused docks across the river. Somewhere in there would be another marksman with a high powered rifle and a hand-held radio. He would have arranged for the police to be alerted the moment he saw Field appear on deck, and then just waited for his chance to put a slug through him. Steele wondered where the tracer-bug was hidden: it must be in his clothes somewhere. The whole thing was a set-up – he was utterly trapped now.

If he didn't agree to work for the service again, they'd deny all knowledge of him and he'd spend the next twenty years inside for murder. He would *have* to agree to work for them again, but they would always have this hanging over him.

Sadly he dropped the Magnum on to the deck.

Half an hour later, a kilometre away across the river, Simon Hardy climbed down from the rusty old crane and packed away the high velocity rifle. He had tried to refuse the assignment when the boss had called him back on the pretext of querying expenses. He loathed the very thought of betraying a man who had saved his life several times. But the section head considered, quite correctly, that Steele was too good a man to lose. If he wouldn't stay of his own free will then they had to make him stay against his will: Hardy knew him best, therefore Hardy had to do the job – and if Hardy didn't like it, well, they had their 'special' file on him as well . . .